HIS BROTHER'S EYES

BY

ANN TRAVERS

Chapter 1

He climbed the stairs slowly, lowering each foot softly. His mother was busy, but he knew he shouldn't be in this part of the house. The attic. The only floor he hadn't explored. He hadn't been allowed in the attic of their old house either. All the doors up there were locked anyway. This was an old house too, with three stories and a basement. Today was their first day in this house, and his mother was supervising the moving men as they brought in their furniture. He was supposed to be in his bedroom, which already had his bed, dresser, his toys and books. He didn't want to stay in his bedroom again. He wanted to see what his parents locked up in the attic.

The stairs were carpeted down the middle, so he walked there. He could still reach the railings on both sides, so he held onto them as he stepped oh so carefully on each step. If the wood creaked, he paused and waited, listening for his mother's voice. But only two steps made that old wood noise, and it was not very loud either time. Finally he reached the landing. He saw three doors along the hallway. He walked slowly and quietly to the furthest door. He gripped the knob and turned. To his amazement, the door opened. He took one step into the dark room, reaching up for a light switch. He couldn't find one, but as he stood there, he could distinguish boxes piled upon boxes. Faint daylight from a small window in the far wall revealed boxes filling the narrow space. He found a string attached to a light over his head, but he couldn't even reach the string. He knew he didn't have time to open any of the boxes, so he backed out of the room and gently shut the door.

He walked back down the hall to the middle door. He stood outside for a full minute, listening. He could barely hear any noises downstairs. His mother's voice was very faint. His small hand touched the doorknob, squeezed and turned it. It opened, slowly, with no noise. The room was filled with soft daylight. There was a window to his left and three more in the wall that was on the front of the house. The windows were covered with sheer curtains and translucent flowered curtains pulled back to the sides. He stood in an entryway that opened into a much larger space, running almost the length of the house. He could see ahead of him more boxes, a folded ironing board, his old wooden rocking horse, an old-fashioned trunk and a floor lamp. Then he heard breathing. He froze. The breathing was stuffy and not regular, like when someone had a cold, but still soft. He wanted to run and he wanted to see what was breathing. Maybe it was an animal, somehow trapped in the attic. A bat? He was afraid of bats. He'd seen them on TV with their ugly, smushed-in faces. Maybe that made them breath funny. He did not want it to be a bat, but somehow that thought was allowing him to move again, toward the sound. It was ahead, around the corner the entryway made when the wall reached the big part of the room. He walked slowly, quietly, like on the stairs. He reached the corner and turned to the right. He saw a white baby crib, but the end facing him was solid, painted with a cute lamb, so he couldn't see inside. He moved out into the room and faced the side of the crib. Something was in it, breathing, but he couldn't tell what it was, so he stepped closer.

Through the white bars, he saw a little boy, bigger than a baby, but much smaller than he was. He moved closer, right up to the bars, and looked over the edge. It was a child with a large head, long, dark hair and big, shining brown eyes. He was dressed in light blue, just a shirt and diapers and blue socks. Suddenly, his eyes turned toward the boy outside the crib. His head didn't turn, only his eyes, but he looked steadily at the boy and blinked.

Chapter 2

Mac watched Zeke lope across the field, dark brown muscles gleaming in the sunlight. Her pencil paused above the page. She stared, trying to memorize the lines of his movement. Then he stopped. His big head went down to graze and Mac resumed her sketch.

When Mackenzie Field had a commission, she did dozens of drawings and sometimes a few watercolors before she began the final painting. Partly the sketches were to help her learn the horse. She often felt they held more life than the painting. Frequently her patrons liked them too and would buy one or more.

Today she was sitting under a large, old tree, watching and drawing Cat on Fire, a black bay three-year-old Thoroughbred colt, who was running his way into racing history. His barn name was Zeke and he was well loved in that barn. He was getting some turnout mainly so that Mac could draw him in motion.

Mac's pencil flew over the page, the lines not only indicating muscle or mane, but motion. She was working on showing Zeke at a gallop. As if on cue, she heard his pounding hooves before the crack of a rifle. Looking up, Mac saw Zeke tearing toward her, straight at the pasture fence. She dropped her pad and pencil and ran to the gate. He looked like he would explode through the black wood, but he did a perfect sliding stop and stood wild-eyed and snorting at the gate. Mac grabbed his halter and climbed the gate to put it on. Ordinarily, Zeke's groom or one of the stable hands would lead the big colt in or out of the pasture. All Mac could think of was getting him away from whatever idiot was shooting a rifle. She stroked his neck, feeling his body tremble, and talked to him softly as she opened the gate. He snorted again, but put his big head down next to her and walked quietly out. As he moved beside her, she glanced back along his body and saw a long wound on his hip. Blood dripped down his flank. Mac teared up, furious. Someone had shot Zeke. Thank God, she thought, they weren't far from the barn.

"What is wrong, Miss Mackenzie?" called Miguel, Zeke's groom, as he ran toward them.

He slowed as he drew near, and walked on the other side of Zeke, not trying to take the halter from her. His dark eyes moved swiftly over the horse's body and legs.

"He's been shot," answered Mac, "Just a scratch, I think. On his left hip."

Miguel waited until they were inside the barn to move around Zeke and look at the wound. It had stopped bleeding. Gently touching the skin near the four-inch scratch, he looked closely, and shook his head.

"Why would anyone do this?" he muttered.

He walked up to the horse's head, took the lead from Mac's hand and led Zeke to the wash bay.

"What can I do?" asked Mac.

"Just talk to him, while I call Mr. Blake and Doc Flynn."

The big colt stood quietly in the wash bay, looked around, then pushed his dark head against Mackenzie's chest. She leaned into him, her cheek against his forehead, and hummed softly. Her right hand rubbed under his jaw line, which he always liked. When Miguel came in sight Zeke's big head popped up, pushing Mac back a step.

"Easy, boy. Don't knock me over," she said.

"Doc says to flush the wound with cold water. He and Mr. Blake are both on their way," said Miguel.

He pulled a green hose away from the wall, where it was rigged to an overhead support that swung in a 180-degree arc well above Zeke's head. Miguel turned on the cold water and adjusted it to a smooth flow before running it over the long scratch. Zeke flexed his neck to look, but otherwise remained still.

Fifteen minutes later, they heard tires on the gravel outside, and a very tall, very thin, light-haired man strode into the barn, carrying a vet case. At first glance he looked to be in his thirties with his youthful walk, but he aged into his late forties as he came up to them. He put his bag down and immediately looked at the scratch on Zeke's hip. Miguel turned off the water and moved the hose out of the vet's way. Dr. Flynn rubbed Zeke's neck, then touched the outside of the wound, leaning in to look closely.

"Hello, Miguel. It could be a bullet wound. What makes you think it is?"

"Because I heard the shot and saw him tearing across the pasture to get away," answered Mac.

Dr. Flynn looked at her, "And you are?"

Miguel broke in, "This is Miss Mackenzie Field. She is doing a painting of Zeke for Mr. Blake. She brought Zeke into the barn. I heard the shot, but didn't realize what it was at first."

"Sounds like a good thing you were her, Miss Mackenzie," the vet smiled for the first time, looking younger, "I've heard of you. Pleased to meet you."

Mac smiled back at him. Dr. Flynn turned to Miguel and Zeke, "He'll be fine. It's just a flesh wound. I'll clean it out and give him a shot of antibiotic. His tetanus is up-to-date. I checked already. In a few months, there won't even be a scar."

The noisy approach of another vehicle interrupted them. A man in a dark grey suit ran into the barn. His thin face was perspiring and his brown eyes were wide.

His voice was soft when he asked, "Is he OK?"

He leaned in to look at the wound.

"He's fine, John," Dr. Flynn answered, "I would keep him on his training regimen, just a little light for a couple of days. This will heal quickly. As long as he doesn't run a fever, he should be back to full speed next week. Maybe no more turnout, until the sheriff finds who did this."

John Blake stroked Zeke's neck and asked, "Miguel, what happened?"

Miguel said, "Miss Mackenzie should tell you, Mr. Blake."

Again Mac explained what she'd seen and heard. The man gripped her shoulder and said, "Thank you."

Blake shook his head slowly back and forth, "Maybe we should postpone the painting for now."

"Whatever you think best," said Mac, "but I can draw him anywhere: in his stall, when he exercises. I almost have enough sketches and photos anyway. If you don't mind me hanging around for another week or so, I'll finish up and be ready to paint at home."

Blake looked at her steadily, then said, "Alright. Zeke trusted you today, so I will too. Plus, it will be good to have another pair of eyes on him."

Dr. Flynn had finished cleaning the wound and was giving Zeke a shot.

"Flush and clean this every day, until you can tell it's healing from the inside out," he told Miguel, "You know what to do."

Miguel untied Zeke's lead and walked him out of the wash bay toward hi stall. Dr. Flynn and Blake were shaking hands.

"Thanks, Doc," said Blake.

Hope you won't need me for anything like this again, John," responded Flynn, "He's a fine animal. Best of luck."

Mackenzie turned to get back to her sketchbook and bumped into a tall, dark-haired deputy sheriff. Mac felt like she'd hit a wall.

"Whoa, ma'am," he laughed, catching her by the arms, "Excuse me."

Mackenzie looked up at bright blue eyes and thought, "Ma'am? Really?" but said, "Sorry. I didn't hear you come up."

She backed up a few steps, while the deputy turned to John Blake.

"Are you Mr. Blake? You reported one of you horses being shot?" asked the Deputy Sheriff, "I'm Sam Kincaid from the Sheriff's office."

The two men shook hands, as Blake replied, "Yes, I called. We got lucky. It's only a flesh wound, but I'd sure like the shooter caught and locked up before he can do some serious damage. Would you like to see the horse?"

"Yes, sir, and where it happened. I'd like to talk with any witnesses."

"There's only one. Mackenzie Field here. She was sketching Zeke out in the pasture when it happened."

Sam Kincaid looked at Mackenzie again and she held out her hand. He hesitated, then took it. Mac gave a short, firm shake, which the deputy returned, adding a little smile. Mac didn't smile back.

"Ms. Field, why don't you come with us to see the horse, then you can tell me what happened and show me where you were."

When they reached Zeke's stall, Miguel was grooming the dark bay with a soft brush and talking to him quietly in Spanish. Blake introduced Miguel as the stable manager and Zeke's groom. Then he began to talk about his horse.

"This is Cat on Fire, or Zeke, as we call him most of the time. He's the first horse I've owned and the best horse I've worked with. He could be one of the best ever."

"Is there a reason someone would shoot him? Is there anyone you suspect?" asked Kincaid.

Blake glared at the deputy and growled, "Only every damn owner and trainer getting a horse ready for this season! Only every crazy bigot who'd like to take down the first black trainer and owner in racing history!"

Chapter 3

Blake, Mackenzie and Deputy Kincaid walked out of the barn toward the large oak tree under which Mac had been working. Mac stopped where her canvas chair had been knocked over; her sketchpad and pencils lay scattered in the grass. She didn't try to pick up anything, just told her story again. Then another sheriff's vehicle pulled up the drive. It stopped near them and a female deputy got out. She was about Mac's height: five feet, six or seven inches, and solidly built, all muscle, no fat. She looked about 35 years old with long blond hair pulled back in a braid at the base of her neck. She walked toward them and called out, "Hey, Sam. Need any help?"

"It wouldn't hurt, Mary," Kincaid answered, then he introduced Deputy Mary Preston to Blake and Mackenzie. He asked Mac to tell them what happened again from the beginning. The deputies took notes, glancing at Mac now and then.

"There's nowhere for a sniper to hide out here," stated Kincaid, "That old barn is the biggest structure in sight. Is that yours, Mr. Blake?"

"No, " replied the trainer, "That's Whitecross Farms. Owned by Knute Trahern. He breeds Standardbreds. We're not competitors, just neighbors. He's an honest man, as far as I know."

"Well, I'll have to talk with him and check out that barn. The only other options are the walk-in sheds and a few big trees. Too bad someone wasn't out here to watch the shooter leave," said Kincaid.

"I was a little busy getting Zeke to the barn, " Mackenzie retorted, "and if anyone else had been out here, they'd have been looking at the horse too."

"Not criticizing, " said the big deputy, as he smiled at her, "I'm sure you had your hands full. Could we look at your drawings?"

Mac picked up her sketchpad and handed it to the Deputy. He, Preston and Blake looked at her drawings at the same time, studying each page thoroughly. Mac watched them closely.

Deputy Sam Kincaid wore the tan and black Woodford County Sheriff's uniform, minus the hat, so she could see his black, tousled hair drifting over his forehead, but well trimmed at the ears and back of his neck. He was about six feet tall, thin and looked as solid as he'd felt when she bumped into him. He seemed to be studying her drawings carefully, turning the pages slowly, often a little smile turning up the corner of his mouth. Mac wasn't sure what the smile meant and she wasn't sure she liked it.

Deputy Mary Preston was an attractive blond. She spoke with a soft drawl that sounded deeper South than Kentucky. Her brown eyes were friendly and direct. She made several appreciative comments as she looked at Mac's drawings: "Oh, my!" "That's lovely." "Beautiful." "You are certainly talented, Mrs. Field."

Mac's employer John Blake usually wore jeans, Western boots and shirts. Today he was in a dark grey suit tailored perfectly to his trim frame and black Oxfords. He was about 5' 8" with black hair going gray. His face was angular and lined with worry, frown and laugh lines. His nose had a small bump and bend as though it had been broken, and his mouth was wide. What he had said about being an owner and trainer was true. He wasn't the first black trainer by a long shot, but he was the first black American to own and train one of his own horses. At the moment his dark brown eyes were intently searching every line of her drawings. When Kincaid reached the last drawing, Blake asked if he could take the book. He turned back a few pages.

"Mackenzie, " he said, " I like this one a lot. The feeling of movement is so strong. It's what makes Zeke special, even when he's standing still. I'd like to see everything before you start the final painting."

"Thank you, Mr. Blake. I'll let you know when I've finished all the studies. Some will be in watercolor."

Kincaid and Preston had moved a few feet away and were talking near her squad car. He pointed toward the barn. She nodded, and reached into the car, coming out with a camera. She took a few photographs of the area where Mackenzie had been working, the pasture and the old barn in the distance. Then she turned and walked into Blake's barn.

Kincaid had walked over to the oak tree where Mac had been sitting. He was looking at the trunk carefully. He pulled a camera out of a pocket, took two or three photos, and then spoke to John Blake.

"Do you have any objection to me cutting into this tree?"

"Why?"

"I think the bullet's in here."

Blake looked at the splintered hole in the trunk about four feet above the roots.

"Go ahead."

Kincaid pulled out a pocketknife and evidence bag from two different pockets and dug into the hole with his knife, holding the plastic bag in his left hand underneath the splintered hole. Suddenly a lump of metal popped into his hand. Kincaid wrapped the evidence bag around the bullet, then held it up for Blake and Mackenzie to see.

"Damn, " said Blake.

"It looks like a .308 Winchester from a rifle," answered Kincaid, "You're a lucky girl, Ms. Field."

"It's Mrs. Field, Deputy, and I guess I am a lucky woman," she added with a little emphasis on the final word, "It's a good thing for me and Zeke the shooter has lousy aim. Is it OK if I head out?"

"Sure, but I may need to talk with you again," Kincaid handed her his notebook, "Could you write down your address and phone number please?"

As Mackenzie wrote the information down, she asked John Blake if he would let her know when it was a good time to come back and work.

"Come anytime, Mackenzie. If you can work in the barn while he's in his stall, that would be fine. You can come to the early exercise gallops, as well. I won't have him take more than a day off, as long as he's feeling good."

Mac found the rest of her pencils, folded her canvas chair under one arm and the sketchpad under the other, and walked down the gravel driveway to her Jeep Cherokee.

Chapter 4

Mac drove slowly down Blake's gravel driveway, glancing in her side mirror at the Sheriff's vehicles still parked by the barn. Why had Deputy Kincaid rubbed her the wrong way? "Ma'am" and "girl". Ugh. He and the female deputy seemed to get along. She hadn't sensed any antagonism there, she had to admit. He was good looking. Blue eyes. Big. Strong. Mac sighed. It had been a long time since she'd thought about any man that way. Years. Since Bud died, other men were relegated to whatever role they played in her life: teachers, farmhands, horsemen, shopkeepers, husbands of friends, friends of her dad and brother. Nothing more.

Mac followed county roads through other horse farms for ten minutes. Soon she was following the bypass around Lexington, still thinking of Bud. What a sweet, funny man. They had been friends almost their whole lives, meeting in her second year at Belleriver Elementary School. He was in third grade, one year older, but he came to her rescue when snotty Jed Parker knocked her down. She had beaten Jed in a race and he was a poor loser.

"Still is," Mac thought with a little smile.

Bud (Jackson) Field was the tallest boy in third grade and the toughest. He had yanked Jed away by his arm and helped Mac up. She had glared at Jed, told Bud she could have handled it herself, but thanks, and that was that. She didn't know it then, but that was the day she and Bud became fast friends.

Bud was a townie, but worked on his grandfather's farm a lot. Mac's family had a cattle and horse ranch outside of town. Mac's mother, Meg Quinn, was one of two town librarians; she couldn't pick Mac up until after the library closed at 5:00, so Mac went to her Aunt Tina's house after school. (Aunt Tina was a fireman's widow with no children, and her mother's sister.) First Connor would walk her there, but when he went to high school (Mac was in fourth grade), Bud began walking Mac to her aunt's house.

Images floated through Mac's mind. Her catching Bud's pass in the "end zone", earning grudging respect from the boys they were playing. Bud sitting at one end of the porch swing and her at the other, reading. Once she tried to draw him sitting there. He loved the portrait, but she thought her sketch of Aunt Tina's cat was better. Working on homework together. Bud's memory was amazing in history and science, and Mac thought he explained some things better than her teachers. She would explain English grammar to him, but otherwise he liked to figure things out on his own. They had the 4-H Fair every summer: Bud winning the Grand Prize in 8th grade with his grandpa's sow, which Bud raised from a piglet; Mac winning blue ribbons every year in Drawing and Painting and several times winning first or second with her quarter horse Sprint.

One summer was different. Her twelfth: the summer her mother died of cancer. Her father was at the hospital most of the time; Connor took care of the ranch with distracted directions from their dad. Mac was sent to stay with Aunt Tina. Bud tried to help, but wasn't sure what to do or say. If he came over, Mac didn't want to do anything. Sometimes they would silently weed Aunt Tina's garden, or do other chores. Most of the time, Mac would draw or stare into space, and Bud wouldn't stay long. One afternoon they were sitting on the porch swing, Mac trying to focus on drawing Muffin, Aunt Tina's cat, and Bud was pushing the swing gently with his shoe. Suddenly, he stopped the swing, took her hand and said, "I'm sorry, Mackenzie. I hope your mother will be home soon." Then he let go of her hand and left. Mac had a lump in her throat and couldn't call after him. She didn't see him for two weeks. He came to the visitation with his parents, giving her a quick hug and saying, "I'm sorry." He was at the funeral too. He was looking at her every time she looked up, and she tried to give him a smile. He told her years later that it broke his heart.

When school began they went back to walking to Aunt Tina's after school or sports' practices when they could. Often, they would get to Aunt Tina's just as Connor arrived to pick up Mac. She thought Bud would go his own way. He was an eighth grader, after all. In mid-October, Bud called her one evening.

"Would you want to go to the Halloween Dance with me?" he asked quietly.

Mac remembered their costumes: the farmer and his wife from the Grant Wood painting, both of them with sprayed white hair. "Going out" meant they were a couple. Sometimes Connor or her dad or one of Bud's parents would drive them to a movie or a party. Mostly they liked hanging out at each other's houses. They preferred her place or his grandpa's farm, even if it meant doing chores. Then they could go horseback riding or play basketball or whatever struck their fancy.

High school was a blur. Mac knew Bud checked for her in the stands while he played every football and baseball game. She watched for him at her basketball games. He was easy to spot: blond hair, steady gray eyes and the biggest guy in his class. She could still see his grin when his Jeep pulled up in front of her house the day he got his license. They went for a little more than a spin that evening. Mac smiled to herself again. Really everything was easy with Bud, especially sex. They took it slowly. They explored and had fun and avoided pregnancy. She remembered dancing at Homecomings and Proms. Bud would fast dance energetically, looking a little ridiculous, and laughing with her and anyone else who teased him. Thinking of the slow dances, Mac remembered his hand on her back, leading in the old-fashioned way, confident and graceful. He said his mother taught him.

Even Bud's graduation didn't mean separation. He won a small scholarship as the Roker Senior Athlete, but he still needed to work for a year before attending the University of Kentucky. He and Mac could begin together when she finished high school.

Except they didn't. On Christmas Day of her senior year, she and Bud were having dinner with his family after opening gifts. They would go to her house for supper and more gifts. She remembered Bud's excited face when he announced, "I've got some news. I enlisted in the Army two days ago and I leave for basic in a week."

There was dead silence for twenty seconds, then his parents jumped up, his mother hugging him and crying, "Oh, Bud, that's wonderful!". His dad pumped his hand and said how proud he was of Bud. His little sister Laurie was jumping up and down just because her parents were so excited, and toddler Jimmy was banging his spoon on his high chair. Mackenzie just sat in stunned silence; she glanced at him and tried to smile. She didn't remember how she got through the rest of the meal.

On the drive to her house, Bud pulled the jeep over.

"Sorry to spring it on you like that, " he said, "but I thought you'd be proud of me."

" I am proud of you, Bud. We just never talked about the military. Why?" Mac began to cry, "You don't even like to hunt!"

"I haven't been able to figure out what I want to do, Mac. It's been driving me crazy. Somehow majoring in history at Kentucky just didn't feel right. I don't want to teach and I don't know what I'd do with that degree. One day at lunch, I drove by a recruiting office, and I knew it was what I should do. I'm happy to serve my country. It will give me time to decide what I really want to do."

Those were the most words Mac had ever heard Bud say at one time. She looked at his serious, shining eyes and knew she had to let him go. She hugged him tightly, choking back her tears. By the time they reached her home, she was back in control, and ready to handle the excitement her dad and Connor expressed. But that night in bed, she couldn't sleep for hours; her heart was filled with dread and tears ran down her cheeks.

Abruptly, Mac found herself on her road, turning in the long lane to the ranch. She thought about Bud every day, but not like this. She felt very tired and not up for telling Dad and Connor about her day yet. It would be light long enough for her to take Sprint out for a ride.

Chapter 5

After Mackenzie Field left, Sam surprised Thomas Blake by asking where he had been at the time of the shooting. Blake answered that he had been at a luncheon with owners of two of his horses and he readily gave the deputy their names and numbers.

"I don't know why I was surprised that you'd ask," Blake said afterward, shaking his head slowly, "This can be a dirty business."

"No disrespect, sir. Standard procedure," said Sam, shaking Blake's hand.

Sam and Mary followed a long, tree-lined driveway and parked their vehicles in front of a white brick colonial style home with a veranda around two sides. One minute after Mary rang the doorbell, a young brunette woman in a light blue summer suit opened the door. The deputies introduced themselves.

"Could we please speak with Mr. Trahern?" asked Mary.

"He isn't here. None of the family is here, " answered the young woman.

"When will he be home?" Mary continued.

"Not for four or five days," said the woman, starting to close the door.

"This is official business," interjected Sam, leaning on the door to prevent it from closing, "Could you please tell us where he is and how we can contact him?"

"Mr. Trahern and his family are at a horse show," she answered, looking evenly from Mary to Sam with calm blue eyes, "They left yesterday morning. Only I am here, and Jose is in the stable. I can give you Mr. Trahern's cell number."

"And you are?" asked Mary.

"I'm Lynn Richmond, Mr. Trahern's executive assistant. I often stay at the house when they go to shows. May I help you in any way?"

"We need to ask you some questions, " said Mary, " and also talk to Jose. Could we come in, please?"

"How about I go to the stable?" interjected Sam, "And you can talk to Ms. Richmond."

Mary nodded. Lynn Richmond opened the door wider for Mary, and Sam walked down the steps and around the house toward a large white stable with dark green trim. It was at least fifty yards from the house and was about 120 feet long with a short extension on its right end. That looked like an office, so Sam headed there. He passed twelve stall doors, each split in half, but with only two top halves open. He could see horses inside, heads down, munching on hay. Sam walked into a small office with a large wooden desk and two three-drawer filing cabinets behind it. Framed photographs of Saddlebreds performing in many different riding disciplines filled the walls, plus a window that faced the back of the big house. No one was there, so Sam opened a door that led to a large, wood-paneled tack room. He saw at least twenty saddles, mostly English or dressage, two Western saddles with a lot of silver, as well as matching bridles and saddle pads, all in pristine condition. He walked through that room and into the main aisle of the stable. Toward the opposite end, he noticed a small man pushing a wheelbarrow full of grain.

"Hello," called Sam, " Are you Jose?"

The man put down the wheelbarrow and walked toward Sam. He was short, and dark-skinned with black hair that lay on his forehead under a baseball cap. As he drew closer, Sam saw that he was an older man in his fifties with a lined face.

"Yes, " he said with a Hispanic accent, "Can I help you?"

"I'm Deputy Sam Kincaid investigating a shooting at your neighbor's, Mr. John Blake. His horse Cat on Fire was wounded. I'd like to take a look at the old barn and ask you a few questions."

Jose looked stunned.

"Is the horse OK?" he asked, " He is a wonderful horse. Miguel and Mr. Blake have high hopes for him."

When Sam answered that Cat on Fire was fine, Jose said, "I will take you to the barn. We only use it for hay and equipment now."

The two men walked to a central aisle that led to another aisle and a row of ten more stalls that had both inside and outside doors, like the front aisle. Straight ahead was a tall, sixteen-foot door that led to an indoor arena the length of the barn and at least fifty feet deep. As they walked across the soft bed of the arena, Sam saw that the stall doors opened into the arena. The top halves of five doors were open and Sam could see large brown rears and long black tails of horses eating their hay.

"Sorry I interrupted feeding time," he said.

"That's OK, " answered Jose, "They don't care as long as they have hay."

They passed through another large door and out into a grass area with dirt and gravel paths leading around the barn and stable. As they walked to the older barn, Sam could see more pasture past it, a road, then pasture from the Blake Farm, the smaller pasture where Cat on Fire had been grazing and Blake's barn beyond that. Soon they were inside the big wooden structure, walking past tractors, a Gator and a 4 wheeler. Smaller equipment and tools were in the stalls that lined the walls with their doors and front walls removed. The tractors and large attachments were neatly arranged in a central area that was open to the roof where a cupola let in some light and air. Two smaller cupolas were on each side of the central one in line with the peak of the roof. The wood floor of a haymow extended above them around all four walls. Ladders were conveniently spaced to get up to the hay. As Sam looked upward, he could see that the haymow was only about one quarter full, waiting for the end-of-summer and fall harvests.

"So, Mr. Trahern left you in charge, while he's at the show?" asked Sam.

"Yes, sir, " answered Jose, "I am his barn manager. If there were more horses here, I would still have my stable boys working, but I can handle the seven horses that are here. Mr. Trahern took Mr. Joe, the trainer, and three grooms with him, plus his wife and daughters. The girls are home from college and like to help with the horses."

"And you have Ms. Richmond, " said Sam.

"Si," Jose said, " We can both call Senor Trahern directly if something happens."

Sam had the feeling there was no love lost between Jose and Ms. Richmond, but he decided to let that go.

"Jose, has there been anyone else around here since Mr. Trahern left? Have you seen anyone out by this barn?"

"No, sir. We had feed delivery Thursday, yesterday, but he just unloads into the grain bin in the stable. He did not come out here at all. I don't look out toward this barn much, anyway. I'm almost always in the stable and there isn't a clear view, except if you are in the training arena. If the staff was here, a visitor would be seen, but not now."

"No guard dogs?" asked Sam.

"Only Senora Trahern's Corgis and she took them to the show," answered Jose with his first smile, "They would bark up a storm, if someone came, that's for sure."

"Did you hear a shot, about two hours ago?"

"No, Senor. I was cleaning tack and had the radio on," Jose shook his head, as if disgusted with himself.

"Do you live here on the grounds?" Sam continued.

"Only when the family is gone. There is a small bunkhouse with private rooms for me, or Mr. Joe, if one of us needs to stay over. 'Course, if we stay, it's usually to take care of a horse and then we're in the stable all night. The bunkroom is for stable boys and grooms, if they don't have their own place. I did stay overnight in my room since Senor Trahern left. I didn't hear anything and I am a light sleeper."

"OK, thanks, Jose, " said Sam, "I'm going to look up in the haymow. You can get back to work, if you want. If you see another deputy - her name is Mary Preston - she's been talking to Ms. Richmond – would you please send her in here?"

"Si, Deputy," Jose turned to leave, then looked back and added, "Be careful up there. The floor is still good, but there's no railing."

Sam climbed the nearest ladder on the side facing Blake's property. Hay was piled five bales high almost the length of the barn. There were gaps in front of every window, leaving a path through the hay. There were four windows on this side. Sam walked to the end window and began looking for evidence of tampering or an ejected shell, although he didn't expect to find a shell with only one shot fired. The window hadn't been opened recently and was stuck, so Sam moved to the next one.

"Hey, Sam, you in here?" shouted Mary from below.

"Come on up, " Sam called back.

When she reached the top of the ladder, he asked if she'd learned anything from Ms. Richmond. Mary said she didn't think so, but they could talk after their search. Mary moved toward a different window.

Sam stopped her, saying, "I think this is the one, Mary. Look at this."

He was sliding the window up and down jerkily, but it was easy to see it had been opened recently.

Mary stepped up next to him and said, "Yep. The sill is clean, but we'd better check for prints." Bending over, she came up with a 16" piece of 1" X 2" on the floor by the hay. They found marks in the soft wood of the window and in the frame that looked like they matched the ends of the 1" X 2".

"He held it open with this," said Mary, " I'll get the fingerprint kit, if you'll take pictures."

"Yeah, " answered Sam, " I'll check the other windows, but this one looks like the best angle for that shot. Just how in the hell did he get up here and gone without being seen?"

Chapter 6

Two hours earlier, at precisely 3:15 pm, a young man knelt at Knut Trahern's barn
window looking through the scope of a Remington 700 Tactical rifle. He
watched the big bay colt running in John Blake's pasture. It was a gorgeous creature,
sleek, muscular, powerful. It was perfect. He followed it with the scope as it ran.
Finally it stopped and lowered its head to graze. Just as he began to squeeze the trigger,
some movement in the background caught his eye. He zeroed in on a turquoise shirt
flapping in the breeze, partially hidden by a large drawing pad on a woman's lap. Her
head was down with her long auburn hair blowing across her face. She looked up at the
horse for an instant, then down at her work. His heart skipped. He sucked in air, let it
out and moved the rifle only an inch to focus on the horse again. He breathed in again,
slowly let the air out, and squeezed the trigger. But his heart was hammering. He knew
instantly the shot was off. He saw the colt spin and run back toward the gate and the
woman.

He quickly dismantled his rifle and tucked the pieces into his large backpack. He
quietly pulled out the piece of wood that held the window open, laid it on the floor partly
under a hay bale and closed the window. It was stiff, but didn't make much noise. With
the backpack over his shoulders he climbed down one of the ladders and walked to a

small door, which he opened and looked around before stepping outside. He pulled off thin leather gloves that he slipped into a pocket on the side of his backpack. Then he walked east, where there was a grove of fruit trees to help protect him from being seen. Once in the trees, he knelt down and lifted a camera from the top of the pack and snapped pictures as he walked. He was tall and thin with clean-cut sandy brown hair, wearing jeans, a blue button-down shirt and running shoes. He walked with confidence, as he'd taught himself to do, pausing briefly for each shot with the camera. Soon he was out on the road, headed toward a white Toyota Camry. Reaching it, he opened the passenger door. He put the camera away and placed the case on the floor.

He pushed his right hand down between the seat and seat back and pulled. The seat came up stiffly to reveal a space beneath that easily held the parts of his rifle. He had designed and built the space himself and was very proud of it. The cops would have to tear his vehicle apart to find the hiding place.

His hands were not shaking as he started the car, but he could feel his heart pounding. He drove carefully, keeping to the speed limit, coming to a full stop at the first crossroad. As he drove toward Belleriver, his mind raced. Was it her? That dark red hair wasn't that common. How could he have been back for so long and not seen her before? He hadn't thought of her in years. Mackenzie. Mackenzie Quinn. That summer. She'd almost gotten him caught. Now she had spoiled his plans again. He'd only wounded the horse. With such a powerful animal, would that still have an effect? He would find out when he got home. But he needed to find Mackenzie again.

Chapter 7

Sam Kincaid and Mary Preston divided up the neighbors within visual distance of
Robert Blake's farm. No one had seen anyone or anything unusual. By the time they
finished, it was after 9:00 pm, so they headed back to the office to write reports and
decide whom they were going to contact and when on Robert Blake's list of possible
enemies.

Sam had picked up the list after his last interview. Blake had explained each person's
possible reasons for wanting to hurt Cat on Fire. The obvious ones were the owners and
trainers of the horses that would be competing against Zeke in his next race, the
Breeders' Futurity at Keeneland in three weeks. The horse had come in first in four out
of five races the previous spring and summer and had just won the Iroquois at Churchill
Downs in September. There were nine other horses in the race, most of their owners and
trainers big names in the racing world. Sam sighed. They had no fingerprints, one bullet
and no witnesses, except artist Mackenzie Field. Since she had seen the shooting, but no
shooter, she wasn't much help. She was a beauty, but kind of touchy.

Sam checked with Mary about what they would do tomorrow, then headed out to his
car, a silver Honda Civic. He'd realized a few years ago that it was a waste of money to
drive his old Chevy truck from high school. He never hauled a trailer of any kind and
didn't need to carry big loads, so he traded for the very fuel efficient Honda. His buddies

teased him at the time, but he liked the car. He slid into the driver's seat, all six feet comfortably seated, although only a small child could fit behind him in the back seat. No kids in the picture, so that wasn't a problem. No wife, no kids. Just a somewhat crazy girlfriend, who was getting too serious for his liking. Mackenzie Field was a beautiful woman, he thought. That auburn hair was an unusual sight, long, down her back. Her green eyes had looked straight into his. He grinned when he thought of her reaction to his saying "ma'am". He'd picked up some "Southern" language in high school, a lot of which wasn't popular with independent women. Letty, on the other hand, would think it was cute.

Sure enough, as he pulled up in front of his house, he saw Letty's bright red Mustang convertible parked in his driveway, blocking the entrance to his garage.
The driver's door opened and Letty slid out, a cute blond in short shorts. She walked up to him, a grin on her perfect face. Throwing her arms around his neck, she whispered, "Welcome home, big boy!" Then she kissed him.

He pulled her arms off of his neck and said, "Hey, what are you doin' here?"

"Surprisin' you, " she giggled, "Didn't want to wait until your day off."

"Good things come to she who waits," he answered, "I'm tired, Letty, and I have to work tomorrow."

She had locked her arm threw his, as they walked back toward her Mustang.
She cocked her head and looked up at him.

"I'll bet I can help you sleep like a baby," she smiled.

"I'll just bet you can," Sam leaned down and kissed her gently, "Just not tonight." He gave her a little push down toward the driver's seat.

Letty's eyes flashed and she yanked the door shut.

"Maybe I'll just find someone who appreciates me more," she glared at him and started the engine. She did look over her shoulder before she backed out fast, narrowly missing his car. Letty didn't look at him again, just gunned it and roared down the street. Sam sighed, shook his head, and headed back to his car to pull into the driveway. After three months, the cuteness and perkiness was being worn off by the pouting and temper tantrums. That girl wanted a ring, the sooner the better. She was ten years younger than Sam. Maybe she'd thought dating an older man would get her married quicker.

"Not this old man," thought Sam. He pushed a button to lower the garage door, as he unlocked the side door to the house. He flipped on the kitchen light and turned on the TV. He was in luck. The Cincinnati Reds were in the eleventh inning, tied with the Cardinals. He unbuttoned the neck of his shirt, grabbed a beer and collapsed on the couch to watch the end of the game.

The ringing and vibrating of his cell phone startled him awake. Sam pulled it out of his pocket and answered without checking the screen.

"Sam?" said a man's voice.

"Yeah," answered Sam, rubbing his eyes and sitting up. He glanced at the TV, seeing an Andy Griffith rerun, so the game was over.

"It's Jeff. Did you see Letty Akers tonight?"

"Yeah," Sam glanced at his watch, "about an hour ago. What's up, Jeff? Is she all right?"

"I'm sorry, Sam, she's not. She was shot outside the Two Step. She's dead."

Sam felt cold, stunned.

"I'll be right there," he said quietly and ended the call.

Chapter 8

Sam pulled into the parking lot of the Two Step, a Western bar on the southwestern edge of Versailles. He saw Jeff Parker stepping outside the yellow crime scene tape enclosing a wide section of the lot. Jeff wore the Versailles Police Department uniform, his blond hair barely showing under his hat. He was on duty. Sam and Jeff had been friends for a long time. Jeff reached him as he got out of his car. Jeff's dark brown eyes looked worried.

"I'm sorry, Sam," Jeff said, with double meanings, "You can't go over there. The coroner's with her now."

"What happened, Jeff?" Sam stared at the small group of figures next to Letty's red Mustang.

"As far as we know now, she never even made it into the Two Step. She was shot in the head from a distance as she got out of her car. Two women came out of the bar to smoke and found her. They knew her by her Mustang and freaked out. Actually, one of the ladies worked with her at Buffalo Trace. They're inside being questioned now, along with all the other patrons. You said you saw her tonight?" As he talked, Jeff pulled out a small notebook, ready to write.

Sam closed the car door and leaned on it.

"Yeah, Jeff. I got home about 10:30 and she was waiting for me. She wanted to stay and I told her 'no'. She was pissed and left," Sam lowered his head, rubbing his forehead, "Aw crap, Jeff. If I'd let her stay, she'd still be alive."

"You two serious? I didn't think you'd been dating that long."

" Only three months or so. She was getting serious, wanting some kind of commitment, but I didn't feel that way. When she left, I figured we were at least half way to breaking up and I didn't mind. Now... damn."

"What did you do after she left?" asked Jeff.

"Started to watch the Reds game and fell asleep. Until you called."

"It's just after midnight now," Jeff sighed, "I'm sorry, Sam. We'll need you to come in and sign a statement tomorrow. You know you can't work this case."

"I know."

Sam climbed back into his Civic and slowly drove out of the parking lot. His mind felt foggy, tumbling over his brief conversation with Letty, wondering who could possibly want to kill her. She wanted attention and she wanted to get married, but she was also funny, daring, energetic and very attractive. He was sure she went to the Two Step to dance and flirt and try to make him jealous. It wasn't planned, so it was doubtful that anyone followed her there. Still someone could have been stalking her, followed her to his place, watched their conversation, saw her leave and followed her again. Then shot her? What the hell! That made no sense. If someone wanted to shoot Letty, there were other places and times that were less dangerous for the shooter. His neighborhood was quiet, mostly deserted after 10:00 pm, at least outdoors; everyone but him was sleeping. He kept going back to the "why". He believed the more you learn about the victim, the more you find out why someone would kill that person and that usually leads to the murderer.

Sam pushed the garage door opener and drove slowly into his garage. As the door closed behind him, his mind snapped to attention. Letty's murder wasn't the first long-range shooting of the day.

Chapter 9

Mac walked down Belle Street in the two block shopping area. Belleriver's downtown had one bank, two beauty shops, two combination bar-restaurants, a small grocery, a hardware store, a library and a general store. Everything but the bank and the library was family owned and run. The cross street, River Avenue (the town's founder had a one-track mind when it came to naming), held three antique and gift shops, a thrift clothing store, plus an insurance office and a real estate office. The buildings were mostly brick and old, but not shabby. The antique stores drew in antique hunters and tourists, which helped the other businesses, especially the restaurants.

Mac had just picked up some supplies at the hardware store that she needed to build a frame for her painting of Zeke. She had spent the morning at Blake's stable doing some sketches of Zeke's big, dark head. She was visualizing the composition in her head, as she walked back to her Jeep.

"Good morning, Mackenzie."

Mac focused on her surroundings and saw Kristopher Laska walking toward her.

"Good morning, Mr. Laska!" Mac smiled, happy to see her high school art teacher. He was a small man, just a little taller than Mac's 5'7''. He wore a suit, as always, had gray hair, bald and tan on top of his head and smiled warmly. He was in his sixties, but still painted and sold work all over the country.

"Please call me Kris, or at least Kristopher," he stopped in front of her.

"Old habits, Kristopher," Mac paused a little before saying his name. He had changed her life.

"What are you working on now?" Kristopher asked.

"A painting of Cat on Fire, Robert Blake's horse," she answered, "Actually, I've just finished all the sketches. Starting the painting this afternoon."

"Wasn't he shot? Weren't you there?" Mr. Laska would know, of course, as would everyone else in town. Jake at the hardware store had asked her too.

"Yes, but he's OK," she told the story again.

"Good. Good. I'm glad you're both all right. Good luck with the painting. I'm sure it will be beautiful."

Mac walked down the block to her Jeep, threw the paper bag of staples into her front seat and started the engine. It rumbled to life and Mac thought what a good car it had been, especially since her brother liked to keep it in shape. It wasn't Bud's original Jeep, but only a few years younger and dark green, like his. Mac had replaced Bud's with this one four years after his death. It was a good vehicle for the ranch, but she knew she couldn't keep driving the one she and Bud had used together. It was also the best deal she'd found when she went used 4WD shopping. As she drove back out to the ranch, she remembered Mr. Laska's help after Bud's death. Just like today, she ran into Mr. Laska downtown a few months after Bud's helicopter was shot down in Afghanistan. He had been to the visitation, but she hadn't seen him since. He mentioned that he would be teaching a summer painting class at the high school for ages 18 and up and that the sign-up began the next week. She said "maybe" and "thank you", still in a fog of grief. She had been working on the ranch and drawing in all of her other free hours. She drew all of the animals on the ranch more than once, especially the horses. She did watercolors too. Focusing on the lines and values that turned into the forms and textures of living beings was her only way to forget for a while. A couple of days after she saw Mr. Laska, she decided that a structured class would help. It would be another distraction and she could improve her oil painting. He had helped her start in oils in high school and she'd finished a beginning class at the University of Kentucky, but she'd dropped out after Bud's funeral. She signed up for the class.

It had been life changing. Mr. Laska had always encouraged her, but he was an insightful critic as well. Once in high school when they were drawing portraits in pastels, he had pulled a dark blue stick of chalk down the whole side of the face she was drawing. She was stunned.

"You need the dark values or the face will not look three-dimensional, " he said softly, " Now add your colors over this. Look for the darkest shadows. Look for the contrast."

Her drawing had improved noticeably after that. This class was an eye-opener as well. He encouraged her to let her brushstrokes show, which added both form and movement. He told her to look at the work of Van Gogh, Manet, Degas and John Singer Sargent. She took a special trip to the Cincinnati Art Museum to see works by Childe Hassam, Mary Cassat, and Sargent. She was enthralled for hours, because she could see how the artist painted, each brushstroke and color choice, so different from a slide or reproduction in a book. She especially liked the American artists who painted or drew from the old West. The Indians and their horses were vivid, alive, not stiff like photographs she'd seen.

Mac worked from sketches she'd made at home of one of her dad's mares, a beautiful black quarter horse running in a field, head up, mane and tail streaming. About three weeks into the class, Mac noticed a stranger in attendance, a big man with a round, red face, ginger hair with a little white in the sideburns, a dark blue suit and alligator-skin cowboy boots. He walked around the room quietly, while people worked, standing behind Mac for a good five minutes. At first it annoyed her, but since he didn't say anything, she quickly forgot he was there. She did notice that he shook Mr. Laska's hand before he left, both men smiling. He was back two weeks later, accompanied by a tall, thin white-haired man. Mac had finished the black mare; it was drying on an easel in the back of the room. She was starting another painting of mares and foals in their pasture from that spring. When she saw other students cleaning up, she began to as well, swishing her brushes in turpentine and wiping them on a rag. Mr. Laska always walked around the room at the end of class, making constructive comments on people's work and saying good-by for the day.

When he came to Mac, he softly asked her to stay after and meet their two guests, if she had time. She wondered if they were other artists or teachers, and agreed.

The two men and Mr. Laska were standing in front of her black mare painting, talking quietly, when she washed her hands and walked over to them. Her teacher introduced her.

"Mackenzie Field, I would like for you to meet Frederick Martin and Paul Noffsinger. These gentlemen are interested in your work."

Mac shook hands with both men, thinking their names sounded familiar.

"You can call me Ace, " said the large, red-faced man, Frederick Martin, " I own racehorses on a farm by Lexington and I'd like you to paint a portrait of my stud."

Now it clicked. Ace Martin was an owner of some renown, colorful in personality, language and positive support of his horses, their trainer and jockeys. Paul Noffsinger was an owner as well, following in the footsteps of his father and grandfather. He wanted her to paint his stud too.

"I'm flattered, " said Mackenzie, "but I've never painted for money."

Mr. Laska jumped in, "Maybe Mrs. Field needs a little time to think about this. One of us will get in touch with you both in the next few days, if that's all right."

Ace Martin looked like he wanted to object, or at least say something else, but he and Mr. Laska exchanged a glance and the big man simply shook her hand again and said he liked her work very much. Mr. Noffsinger did and said much the same and the two wealthy men left.

That was the beginning. Mr. Laska urged her to at least try the two jobs and helped her decide on an asking price for the final piece ($5,000, if the buyer was happy, $2500 to cover her time and expenses, if he didn't want the painting). Now she was up to $10,000 a painting and no one had ever turned down her work. She also charged varying prices for pencil or watercolor studies. It gave her an independent income and helped her deal with her grief. She owed Kristopher Laska more than a commission, which he refused, so she thanked him, loving her teacher dearly.

As she drove up the lane to the ranch, she saw a car in front of the house and wondered who was visiting. Soon she was close enough to see that it was a Woodford County Sheriff's car and a deputy was sitting on one of the porch chairs, drinking lemonade with her father.

Chapter 10

"Hi, Dad. Hello, Deputy Kincaid, " said Mackenzie, climbing up the wooden steps to the porch.

"Hello, Mrs. Field," answered Sam with a smile.

"Have some lemonade, Mac, " said her dad, "I was just takin' a little break with the deputy here."

He stood, poured her a glass from the pitcher and motioned for Mac to take his chair, "I've got to get back to work."

Mac took a few swallows of the tart lemonade and asked, "What can I do for you, Deputy?"

"I was just checking to see if you were OK after what happened yesterday," said Sam, "and if you remembered anything different."

Mac was a little puzzled.

"That's very nice of you," she said, "a little above and beyond, isn't it?"

"No, ma'am, we usually interview witnesses at least twice. So first, how are you?"

"I'm fine, thank you. I was fine as soon as I knew Zeke was OK."

"Have you thought about what you saw? Anyone in the distance? Anything different than what we talked about?"

"I have thought about it a lot, but can't remember seeing anyone. I did make a statement at the sheriff's office this morning right before lunch."

"Yes, they gave it to me. Thank you," Sam paused. Mac waited. She had a feeling there was something else. Sam sat quietly, looking off into the distance over the different pastures, some with cows, some with horses. He turned and looked at her seriously.

"There was another long-distance shooting last night, " he said, "A young woman was killed at the Two Step. In the parking lot, actually, getting out of her car. We don't have the ballistics back yet, but from what I've been told, it sounds like it's the same type bullet as the one shot at Zeke."

"That's terrible!" Mac said softly, "Who was she?"

"Her name was Letty Akers. Did you know her?"

"No, but you did. Right?" Mac watched him look away to the pastures again, calm, but his body was stiff.

"Yes, she was a friend. Because of that, I can't work the case, but I just have a feeling that her being shot like that, by a sniper, is related to Zeke being shot," Sam hesitated again, "and I want you to be careful."

"You think I was the target?" Mac exclaimed, "No. That's crazy. I don't have any enemies, at least the kind who would shoot me! And Zeke is a valuable horse! If he were killed or badly hurt, it would change the whole stakes of The Breeders Futurity!"

"I realize that, " Sam looked straight into her green eyes, "I don't have any proof. It just bothers me. Letty didn't have enemies that I know of, either. I'll keep you posted and I would like you to call me, if you notice anyone watching you or if anything unusual happens. Please, Mrs. Field."

"Sure. OK," said Mac, "and you can call me Mackenzie or Mac." She paused. "I'm very sorry about your friend."

Sam stared into the distance at the horses and cows, the slightly rolling horizon.

"This is a beautiful place," he said, "I can see why you and your brother still live here."

"Oh, you mean sponging off our dad?" Mac snapped, instantly irritated.

"Whoa, no, I didn't mean it that way," Sam looked at her curiously, "I'm sorry. I guess it's none of my business. I was just thinking what a great place to come home to."

Mac flushed, wondering why he set her off like that. He was still looking at her and a corner of his mouth started to turn up in a little smile. She looked straight back at him, then out at the horses.

"I'm sorry, Deputy, " she said, "I guess that's my problem, thinking I'm too old to still be living at home. Connor will probably take over the place and the business eventually, so he stays. Dad couldn't run it without him. I was gone for a while at college, but once I came home, there just wasn't a reason to leave. If there ever is, it will have to be some place in the country. I guess that's what I'm saving for. And we do pay my dad room and board."

"Believe me, Mackenzie, no one would ever mistake you for anything but an independent woman." Now he was grinning at her and she smiled back.

"I'd appreciate it if you'd call me Sam."

"OK, Sam."

"Thank your father for the lemonade. I'd better get back to work."

"Me too."

Mac watched him walk back to his car. He looked back and waved before he pulled out of the driveway. She thought, "That is one handsome man." then smiled at herself and went into the house.

Chapter 11

"Friday night, same as ever," thought Mac, as she walked along the sidelines of the Woodford County High School football field. She scanned the crowd for her friend Sarah, who had invited her. Mac hadn't been back to her high school for a football game, or any event, since Bud died. Her friend Sarah's nephew was on the varsity, and Sarah had been bugging Mackenzie to come with her to a game. She claimed she got tired of sitting with her sister and other family members. Mac thought she heard her name, and saw dark-haired Sarah standing and waving at her from the bleachers. That started a chorus of greetings from friends and acquaintances in the stands, as Mac climbed about half-way up to where Sarah had saved her a seat. Mac smiled, responded or gave little waves to as many people as she could single out in the crowd. She sat down next to Sarah with Mr. Wilfred, her mailman in Belleriver, on her other side. He was with his wife, and after saying "hello", they let Mac and Sarah visit.

"Did you come with Connor?" asked Sarah with no subtlety whatsoever, since she'd had a crush on him for at least a year.

Mac grinned at her friend and said, "Oh, you haven't seen him yet? He's been here a while with his friends. They wouldn't miss the kick-off."

"No, I haven't seen him," Sarah sighed.

"Why don't you ask him out? It's the 21st century; you don't have to wait for him. You know he's always been shy with women."

"I've been thinking about it. He's certainly had enough opportunity."

"Seriously, " said Mac, "do it."

Sarah Wells was not originally from Kentucky, but her sister and husband had moved to Versailles, where he worked in a brewery. Sarah had gotten her first teaching job at Belleriver Elementary and stayed for the next seven years. She and Mac had met when Sarah came to the ranch shopping for a horse four years ago. Mac helped her look at the horses for sale; and by the time Sarah had chosen Gus, a dark bay quarter horse gelding, Mac and Sarah were friends. In fact, Sarah was Mac's only close friend. Mac knew it was her own fault, and she didn't really mind. Bud had been her best and only friend after her mother died. She and Bud had been in a world of their own; they'd had friends to hang with, but not close ones. They'd unintentionally saved that closeness for each other. When Mac lost Bud, she was lost as well. She focused on her art and the ranch, which included her dad and Connor. Her friendship with Sarah had come easily with the horses being their initial bond. Sarah asked if she could board Gus at the ranch, which seemed logical and convenient. At first Mac helped Sarah brush up on her riding skills and confidence. Soon Sarah was invited to Sunday dinner and sometimes she helped around the ranch. She and Mac rode together, went to movies once in awhile, and Mac was often in the audience for Sarah's school activities. Neither one was much of a bar person, so this football game was the biggest social event Mac had been to in years.

"Did you eat?" asked Sarah, "They've got grilled pork chop sandwiches at the concessions."

"Sounds good," answered Mac, "Let's go before half-time, so it won't be packed."

They watched the game for about ten minutes, cheering when the Yellow Jackets scored, tying the game. Sarah pointed out her nephew Paul when he came in on defense: number 77. They both laughed when Sarah's sister and other family members screamed his name, guaranteeing his embarrassment. The defense held, and when the offense came back on the field, Mac and Sarah climbed down the bleachers and headed for the concession stand. Standing in line, Mac recognized a blond head almost at the front. She elbowed Sarah and nodded her head toward Connor. Sarah flushed and looked down at her purse.

Mac called to her brother, " Hey, Connor, wait for us."

Connor looked back, saw Mac, then Sarah, grinned and nodded.

Sarah rolled her eyes at Mac and said, "Oh my gosh. Sixth grade."

"Uh, no. I wouldn't have even thought to do that then. Connor would've killed me. Maybe in high school."

When they got their food and found Connor, he was alone, leaning on the chain link fence and eating a pork chop sandwich.

"Where are Jake and Pat?" asked Mac.

"Not hungry, " said Connor, taking a big bite of pork sandwich.

Mac and Sarah said simultaneously, "Since when?" and "What?" then smiled at each other.

"They ate before we came. I'm sure they'll be over here pretty soon."

They ate in silence and Mac looked around her old stompin' grounds. Ten years ago, she'd left Woodford High School. It looked about the same, cared for well. She saw a lot of familiar faces among the adults. Suddenly she saw the dark hole of a telephoto lens pointed her way. As soon as she looked directly into it, it swung away and she could see the head and upper body of a tall, thin photographer wearing a baseball cap and a dark jacket. She watched him turn back toward the football game and he disappeared in the sideline crowd. Mac had a feeling that he'd been watching her. She told herself that he was probably just scanning the whole scene for good shots and turned back to Sarah and Connor.

They seemed engrossed in conversation. For once Connor was talking. Mac listened unobtrusively and smiled. They were talking about cattle. Connor was explaining the difference between their beef cattle (Black Angus) and other breeds. Sarah had asked the right question. Mac listened absent-mindedly and went back to checking out the crowd. She looked for the photographer and finally saw him behind the end zone, training his camera on a player chugging down the field toward him. Mac looked more closely at the player. Number 77!

" Sarah! It's Paul! Sarah, look!" Mac tugged Sarah's jacket and pointed toward the running player clutching the football to his chest. Everyone was on their feet screaming. Paul was almost to the end zone when an offensive lineman grabbed his legs and brought him down. The crowd was still going nuts. The Woodford County Yellow Jackets' offense came on the field and scored in two plays. With only two minutes to play, the defense came back, held the Wildcats and secured the win. Sarah had been jumping up and down screaming, and when the buzzer sounded, she jumped on Connor and hugged him around the neck. He hugged her back; they stepped apart and looked at each other.

"Gee whiz, it's about time!" said Mac. Sarah and Connor both turned red, but then smiled at each other.

The three stood at the fence, watching the players trailing off the field and the fans climb down the bleachers and stream to the parking lot. Mac was thinking about where the Woodford people would go to celebrate when she saw the black lens pointed her way again. She looked quickly away, hoping the photographer hadn't caught her watching him.

"Hey, Sarah, " she touched her friends' arm, "do you happen to know the guy who's been photographing the game? I assume he's with one of the papers."

"Yeah, there is a guy usually here taking pictures. In fact, there should be two. One is from the Herald-Leader and the other free lances, I think. I've seen his pics in the Woodford Sun once in awhile. I can't think of his name. Why?"

Connor said, "He's in the end zone now, taking pictures of the crowd."

"Don't look at him, " said Mac, "I've caught him taking pictures of me twice tonight."

"Sister, I hate to say it, but you are pretty photogenic," Connor laughed.

"He's right, " said Sarah, "Besides, maybe they're going to run a hometown-girl-makes-good story and he's getting ahead of the game."

"Oh, they did that a few years ago, before you moved here, " said Connor, "Mac has moved up a tax bracket, but I don't think they'd be doing another story just yet."

Connor walked with them to Sarah's car, which was closest.

"Hey, why don't you two come with Jake and Pat and me to the Good Time for a drink?" he asked.

Mac didn't really want to go, but she saw the look on Sarah's face and said, "Sure. I'll drive, Sarah. Let's meet at your place first, leave your car and one of us can bring you home. Whoever drinks the least!"

When Mac put the key in the Jeep's door lock, she glanced back over the lot toward the field. Standing in front of the rec center was a tall, thin man with a baseball cap, leaning against the gatepost. He had a large bag over one shoulder and a camera with a long telephoto lens in his hand, hanging at his side. As Mac looked at him, he raised the camera, pointed it her way and she could imagine the click as he took another picture. This time she didn't look away, but stared at him, wishing he wasn't in the dim evening light. He turned slowly and walked around the side of the building, as if heading back to the football field, deftly taking apart the lens of his camera as he went.

Chapter 12

The clean-cut young man unlocked the back door to his house, a three-story, old Victorian on a street of older, well-cared-for homes with big yards in front and back. His had a carriage house remodeled into a garage. A six-foot wooden fence ran from the house to the garage and continued from the back of the garage around the backyard, returning to the far back of the house. Privacy. The young man liked privacy.

He stepped into a small, but efficient kitchen, and walked through a larger dining room with a long, mahogany antique table surrounded by eight chairs. He continued down a narrow hallway with a stairway on his right and turned into the living room beyond the stairs.

"I'm home, Mother," he said.

"Hello, Son," answered a white-haired woman who looked to be in her 60's, sitting in a high-backed chair next to the fireplace. She was simply sitting, a magazine in her lap, but she had not been holding it when he walked into the room.

"The Yellow Jackets won," said the young man.

"That's good, " she answered without looking at him. She was staring into the dark, unlit fireplace.

"I'm going up to shower, " her son continued, "Then I'll probably just go to bed. I'm tired."

"Good night, Son."

"Good night, Mother."

The young man left the room and walked up the stairs to the third floor. He had lied to his mother. He was not tired at all. He was energized. He walked quickly down another narrow hall to the room at the far end. He opened the door, dropped his equipment bag by the door and locked it behind him. He walked into the room, and stepped to the left where a large wooden crib sat under a large curtained window that overlooked the backyard.

"Hello, Marcus," he said, smiling down into the crib.

"Hello, Brother," came the answer from large brown eyes.

"Are you feeling stronger today?" asked the light-haired man.

"Yes, " said Marcus's eyes, "but I do need more."

"I'll get you more, don't worry. I have to be careful not to attract attention, you know. We're getting close though. I can feel it. Can you?"

"Yes."

"We'll get you well and whole soon."

The young man leaned over the crib and touched the face of his dearly loved brother. It was the soft rubber face of a large boy doll. Above the head, leaning against the crib's headboard, was a framed photograph of a live boy lying in the same crib.

Chapter 13

Sam finished the report of his interviews with the owners and trainers on Thomas Blake's list. Most had been offended; a few understood and all of them had alibis. That didn't mean one of them hadn't hired someone to shoot Cat on Fire. Overall, Sam was frustrated. Almost every deputy sheriff and policeman in Woodford County was working on Letty's murder. They'd even taken Mary away from him. Worst of all was not being able to investigate the murder. He knew the sniper element wasn't enough to connect the horse shooting with the human one, but Sam was convinced they were related in some way. He also felt rotten about Letty's death. She'd been way too young and hadn't done anything to deserve it.

Sam rubbed his hands roughly over his face and through his hair and sighed. He needed a lead. Or he needed a contact within the horseracing community. "Oh, crap," he thought. He did know someone, but he didn't want to go there. He really did not want to go there, especially to ask for help.

"Shit," he said softly and pulled out his cell phone, scrolled through his contacts and hit one. The phone didn't ring many times before someone answered.

"Hey, it's me," said Sam, "You busy? OK if I come over and talk to you? No, it's business. Racing business. I'll be there in half an hour." He hung up and left the Sheriff's office.

Sam drove to Lexington on the Versailles Road. In less than thirty minutes, he was pulling into the driveway of a red brick ranch house. A tulip tree cast shade over the entryway, which was also covered by a small wooden porch that extended half the length of the house. He tapped lightly on the front door, and walked into the family room. A gray-haired man in jeans and a black t-shirt met him and put out his hand.

"Hello, Sammy. Good to see you," he said with a grin.

They shook hands and looked at each other. They were old-young mirror images of each other, the same height, same blue eyes and thick hair, the same muscular frame, just about thirty years apart in age.

"Hey, Dad," said Sam, "Is Mom at work?"

"Well, yeah. She's got second shift. Aileen is at a friend's. Come on out to the kitchen. That's where I'm working," answered Bill Kincaid.

Sam followed his father to a long oak table in the dining area connected to the kitchen and took a seat. There was a laptop and racing forms spread out at one end of the table.

"What do you need?" asked Bill.

"I've got a problem at work that you might be able to help me with."

"Be glad to, " said Bill, sitting down behind his laptop.

Sam told his father about the shooting of Cat on Fire three days before, the evidence of a sniper in the neighbor's barn and Blake's suspicions. He didn't mention the list of possible suspects.

"I know Cat on Fire, " Bill stated and started typing on his laptop, "He's a good horse. Just won the Iroquois at Churchill and is scheduled to run in the Breeder's Futurity in October."

"I know that, " said Sam, "What I'm wondering is if you know anyone who might go that far to stop that horse."

"The mob would," answered Bill, smiling and shaking his head, "No, Sam, I'm not serious about that." He paused, typing and looking at his computer, "Cheating still happens in racing, but this is pretty extreme. Usually it's a jockey on the take or a groom slipping something to a horse. Shooting a horse, even just to wound it, is risky and blatantly obvious. I'm looking at the list of other horses in the Futurity and none of those owners or trainers would do something this stupid. I also think Blake is mistaken about the racist angle."

"Well, whoever did it was smart enough not to get caught," said Sam, "and we don't have any leads."

"Did you get the bullet?"

"Yep. Hit a tree. It looked like a .308 Winchester, but we don't have ballistics back yet."

"You already talked to those trainers and owners, didn't you?"

"Yes, and I didn't get a bad feeling from anyone, although a few were pissed off at being questioned. I just thought you might know them better and could tell me if someone was crooked or desperate." Sam was leaning on his knees, head down, staring at the linoleum floor. He straightened up, stretched back in his chair, looking out the windows at the green back yard. A border of colorful flowers surrounded the edge, perennials that his mother had planted. A rope swing with a wooden seat hung from the high branch of a maple tree.

"Did you put that up for Dave's kids?" Sam nodded toward the swing.

"Yep. Aileen still uses it. She's only ten, going on sixteen. Tara can just manage it," answered Bill, "Matt's a bit small yet." He paused, looking steadily at his son.

"I thought you'd be busy with that murder investigation down there."

"I can't work on it. The victim was a girl I was dating."

"I'm sorry, son. That's rough."

Sam sighed and put his elbows back on his knees.

"We weren't serious, but she was a nice girl. A little crazy. Fun, but not wild. She didn't do anything that should have led to someone shooting her."

"A sniper," said Bill, "Just like the horse."

"That's what's bothering me. We know it was a .308 cartridge, but don't know if it was from the same gun. So far, the only people I've mentioned the possible connection to think I'm crazy. We'll have a better idea when we get the ballistics reports."

"It's not as crazy as thinking any of those owners or trainers would hire a sniper to shoot Cat on Fire," said Bill, "I do know those people, some just by reputation, but none of them fit that kind of profile. As far as I know, none of them have money troubles. I don't know why someone would shoot a horse and then shoot a young woman. Was he practicing with the horse? That's crazy too."

"Well, thanks, Dad," said Sam, "I'd better get back to work."

"Sure you don't want to stay for dinner? You can watch Aileen and me cook."

Sam grinned, "That would be something. What are you having – hot dogs?"

"We'll see what she wants. Probably pancakes."

"Sounds great. Maybe some other time."

Bill walked Sam to the front door and stood on the porch for a minute.

"Come back soon, Sammy."

Sam waved from his car window and backed out of the driveway.

"That wasn't so bad," thought Sam. He looked back at the house before he put the car in drive. Not a mansion, but it was a big step up from where they'd lived when he was growing up. Evansville, Indiana. Nice town on the Ohio River where Sam and his family had lived in one side of a big wooden duplex in a blue-collar neighborhood. The house had once been handsome, built for a large Irish Catholic family like its neighbors. By the time Bill Kincaid's Irish Catholic family moved in, it had become a weathered duplex with a black family living in the other side. The whole neighborhood was a mix of poor laborers and factory workers. There weren't any gangs yet, just poverty. Bill moved from job to job, and lost a lot of his income playing poker or any kind of gambling he could find.

In 1995, when Sam was 13, Casino Aztar opened in a riverboat on the Ohio. Bill thought his future was made. It wasn't. More and more of his earnings were lost in the casino. Bill didn't drink and he wasn't abusive. He loved his wife, Jenny, and his two boys, Sam and David, but there was always another game, another chance to win big. Jenny worked as a nurse and kept her income in a separate account. Both boys had paper routes and helped out with chores, but it was Jenny's nursing that kept the family afloat. Sam loved his dad, who was so much fun when he was at home, but Sam and David both hated the gambling. They promised each other they would never gamble.

In the summer of 1999, Bill went with a few buddies to Ellis Park racetrack across the river in Henderson, KY. He won $154, and came home obsessed with horseracing. He stopped going to the casino. He read everything about thoroughbred racing that he could find. He bet small at first and never did worse than lose twenty or thirty dollars on any given day. He usually came out ahead every week. He stopped going to the casino completely. When the track was closed, he continued his research and followed racing all over the country. He also worked hard at his factory job and spent more time with his family. Jenny and the boys were wary, but happy. The following year, Sam left to attend the University of Kentucky. He had a small wrestling scholarship that paid tuition. He worked his way through with some help from his parents to cover the rest. He rarely went home and when he did, everything seemed to be going well. While Sam majored in History and minored in Psychology, his father had become a successful horseplayer. When Sam graduated and couldn't decide what to do with his degree, Bill and his family moved to Lexington to be closer to Keeneland and Churchill Downs. Bill was earning enough to support his family, which was growing. Jenny was pregnant, a happy surprise. David started at the University of Kentucky. Bill was asked to work part-time on Racehorse Television, which fit well with his true career as a horseplayer. Sam was uncomfortable with his father's choice, but he had to admit his parents were happier than they'd ever been, especially when baby Aileen was born. Jenny felt secure enough to stay home with her little girl, until she started first grade. Meanwhile thanks to a friend with the Versailles Police, Sam had accepted a job as a Sheriff's Deputy in Woodford County, which he gradually discovered was perfect for him.

"Maybe it's time to forgive the old man," thought Sam, as he drove back to Versailles.

Chapter 14

Mac let herself be dragged to the Fall Fling by Sarah and Connor. It was an annual barn dance sponsored by the two churches in Belleriver, the United Methodist and the Belleriver Baptist. For sixteen years it had been held at Frank Miller's huge, eighty-year-old barn with a hog roast outside, and tables inside full of homemade side dishes and pies, thanks to the church ladies. The ten-dollar charge covered everything and the proceeds went to the churches and the Shriners Children's Hospital. No booze was allowed and most people honored that rule. There was some square dancing, but mostly it was Country Western slow dancing, line dancing and two-step.

Mac, Sarah and Connor found seats at one of the long picnic tables near the large, open door of the barn. Their plates were loaded and for a few minutes they ate in silence, just pausing to smile and wave at friends and neighbors passing by. Mac saw her dad leaning against the wall with some other ranchers and farmers; most of them had wives busy taking care of the food. It was a perfect September night, just cool enough to keep the bugs at bay.

Connor finished first, straightened up and patted his flat belly.

"That was good," he said, dragging out the "good" to about four syllables.

"I'm stuffed," said Sarah, pushing her nearly empty plate away.

"Let's dance," Connor looked at Sarah, "Work off some of those pounds."

"I'm not sure I can move," answered Sarah, but she smiled and got up, "We'll be back soon, Mac."

"Don't hurry. I'm still eating."

Mac watched them walk away, Connor's hand lightly on Sarah's lower back. It was a slow dance. Mac smiled to herself as she watched them curl into each other naturally, as if they'd been dancing together for years.

"Hello there, pretty lady," said a male voice beside her. Mac started, then looked into unusual light brown eyes and a smiling, handsome face.

"Oh, sorry to startle you," said the man, "Do you remember me?"

Mac thought he looked familiar, but she didn't remember him. She was uncomfortable and couldn't seem to find her voice. The young man didn't have the same problem.

"I can see that you don't, or you're not sure," he looked at her intently, and continued, "We were in Belleriver Elementary together, but I was a couple years behind you in school. I'm the obnoxious photographer who was taking your picture at the football game last night. Randy Bayard at your service."

Mac tried to stop the gasp of surprise that escaped her mouth, and she found her voice, "I didn't appreciate that. I don't like having my picture taken, especially by strangers. Please don't do that anymore."

Randy leaned back and threw his arms out, and then bowed theatrically, "I beg your forgiveness, milady!"

He looked up with sparkling eyes and a wicked grin, "I couldn't resist the most beautiful woman I'd ever seen. My camera couldn't resist. It has a will of its own."

The man was charming, Mac had to give him that. And he was good-looking in a clean-cut, all-American boy kind of way. She still felt uncomfortable, but managed to say, "I forgive you. Just get control of your camera. I see you don't have it tonight. That's good."

"I left it in my car. I may take some shots later for the Sun, but I promise I will not take any pictures of you."

"Thanks."

"Say, could I get you a piece of pie, you know, in reconciliation?"

"No, thank you. I'm too full right now."

"Would you like to dance?"

Mac was getting a little annoyed, but told herself she was being ridiculous.

"Sorry. I'm waiting for some friends."

"We could dance while you wait."

Randy held out his right hand. Suddenly someone slid onto the seat across from Mac.

"Sorry I'm late, Mackenzie," said Sam Kincaid with an apologetic smile, "I had to change out of my uniform."

Mac smiled at him with relief, "That's OK, Sam."

Randy's hand fell to his side and his face turned coldly blank.

Sam looked up at him and said, "Hello. You're Randy Bayard, aren't you? You here for work or play, Randy?"

"A little of both, Deputy," Randy's expression changed from chilly neutral to a big, fake smile in an instant, " If you two will excuse me, I think I hear some cherry pie calling my name."

He gave a little bow, looked up at each of them briefly, and walked away.

"Oh my gosh, thank you," said Mac.

"You looked like you might need a little help," grinned Sam.

"It was weird. He was not going to take no for an answer," Mac blew out a big breath she hadn't known she was holding.

"Do you know him?" asked Sam.

"Not really. He said we were in grade school together, but I don't think I remember him. How do you know him?"

"I saw him taking pictures around town, so I checked him out. He does sell photos to the Sun and the Herald-Leader, but doesn't actually work for either paper."

"He was taking pictures at the football game last night. I caught him taking some of me. Today he said I was pretty, and he couldn't resist. When I told him that I didn't like it, he said he wouldn't take any more."

"You were supposed to call me if you noticed anyone watching or following you."

"Well, it was just last night, and he was taking a lot of crowd pictures, not just the game. I thought I was being paranoid."

"What do you think now?"

"I don't know. He was flirting just now, but he made me feel uncomfortable. When I was in the parking lot after the game, he was staring at me and he took another picture. It creeped me out."

Sam didn't like the sound of any of it, but decided to let it go, and check out Randy Bayard more tomorrow.

"Are you on duty?" asked Mac.

"Not really. Sheriff let me go early, since I've put in some overtime this week.

I think he knew I'd come out here and could keep my eyes open. Most of the police and deputies are working Letty's murder fulltime."

They both paused.

Finally Mac asked, "Have you eaten? The food is great."

"I haven't had dinner. I guess you have, though," he was looking at the scrap-covered plates between them.

"I could eat a piece of pie," smiled Mac and began picking up the paper plates.

Soon they were back, Sam with a piled-high plate and Mac carrying two pieces of pie, blueberry for both of them. Mac watched him dig into the food and she smiled. He noticed. He chewed, swallowed and said, "I'm hungry."

Mac threw her head back and laughed, "That's legal, I think. You remind me of my brother Conner. When food's in front of him, he's focused. I mean totally into it. Sorry. You go right ahead. I'll eat my pie."

Sam smiled and went back to eating. Mac tried to eat, but she found herself looking at him while she slowly chewed. He glanced back every now and then, gave her a little smile, and went back to his food. By the time he got to his pie, they were staring at each other and still managing to get bites of blueberry pie into their mouths. Mac couldn't help it; she liked his bright blue eyes and the black hair that fell over his forehead. Suddenly Sarah plopped down next to her and Connor sat across the table next to Sam.

"Hello, Deputy Kincaid," said Sarah, "Connor, this is Sam Kincaid."

"How do you know him?" asked Mac, surprised.

"A couple of years ago, Sam came to my 6th grade class and talked about being a deputy sheriff," explained Sarah, "The kids loved him. All of the girls had crushes and everyone wanted to see his gun and hear stories. How do you know him?"

"I told you about Cat on Fire," started Mac.

"Well, you didn't tell me the deputy was Sam."

Connor switched the conversation to the high school football team, Sarah's nephew's helpful interception and other Belleriver news. Then the band switched songs to the boot-scootin' "Footloose", and Sam reached across the table, took Mac's hand and said, "Come on."

They headed for the dance floor, where lines were already forming. Sarah and Connor followed. Mac had not danced in years, but she picked it up quickly. Sam was surprisingly good. Sarah and Connor were excellent, turning, spinning and stomping. Mac was breathless, grinning at Sam. The music ended abruptly and immediately swung into "Ring of Fire". Sam grabbed her back with his right hand and her right hand with his left and led her in a flying two-step around the floor. He was a confident dancer, his hand firm and guiding on her back. His strength was flowing through her and all she had to do was relax and follow. She stopped looking down at their feet and focused on his blue eyes looking into her green ones. The music flowed into "My Favorite Mistake". Sam gathered her closer and they danced. Mac rested her head on Sam's shoulder and decided she didn't care if this was a mistake.

Chapter 15

As the song's final chords floated over the dance floor, Sam surprised Mac by dipping her back. Once again his blue eyes were locked on hers. She started to smile. A scream pierced the air. They both looked behind them. A young man lay on the floor with a young woman bending over him, screaming.

"He's bleeding! He's bleeding!" she shrieked and began crying.

Sam and Mac went to either side of the prone figure. They could see blood dripping from just below his collarbone. Mac had her arms around the woman and Sam was examining the wound. Then he saw blood pooling on the floor beneath the man.

"He's been shot," he said, and looked directly at Mac, "Stay low and get behind the bandstand. Take her with you." Mac pulled the sobbing woman away from injured man.

Just then a shot rang out and the crowd ran, except for the lead guitarist, who fell to the floor, half his head blown away. People were running in every direction, looking for friends, family and a place to hide. Most of them had the sense to run to the back of the barn.

"Close the barn doors," yelled Sam, but no one heard him over the screams of the fleeing crowd. Sam ran toward the front of the barn, right in the open. When he reached the big doors, he saw Connor already there pushing on the twelve-foot high sliding door. A big, ruddy-faced man was leaning on the door on the other side. The door wouldn't budge, while Connor's door was screeching toward the middle.

"Pull up on the lock," yelled Connor. The man's red face looked startled, then he pulled on the hook that was holding the door open. A plump young woman ran up next to him and the two of them pushed the door closed. The crowd was much quieter, except for muffled sobbing.

"Everyone, stay down, " yelled Sam, "I'm a deputy sheriff and I'm calling for help."

"I already did," called a woman's voice from the back of the barn. Faintly, they heard sirens, proving her words.

"OK. Stay where you are, but get tables down in front of you. If you don't have anything for cover, crawl to the back of the barn behind the bandstand. Is anyone here a doctor or an EMT?"

"I am," called an older man, coming out from behind a table.

"I'm a nurse," said a soft-spoken black woman behind Sam's back.

"I'm an EMT," yelled three voices from different parts of the barn. One of them was the plump woman who had helped close the barn door. Sam, Connor and the medical personnel were making their way down the sides of the barn, converging on the young man still lying on the dance floor.

"Connor, could you go check on Sarah and Mac? I told Mac to go behind the bandstand," Sam looked up at a tall, freckled redhead who was standing behind the doctor, "Could you go check the guy on the stage? I don't think we can help him, but could you look?"

The redhead and the plump woman turned toward the stage. The nurse had pushed someone's shirt under the young man's back and an EMT was holding a thick wad of napkins on the wound. The shirt and napkins were soon bright red.

Connor came back with Sarah, Mac and Gabe, their dad. Sam was on his phone with the dispatcher, trying to find out who was coming. The sirens were getting louder.

"Connor, can you find the lights and shut them down. He still has targets through the windows." Connor and Gabe went behind the stage. Soon the bright overhead lights and the spotlight on the stage went out. The battery-powered fake candles on the tables gave a faint glow. Sam saw one of the EMT's huddled with the doctor grab a couple of them to take back to give them some light with the injured man. Someone else pulled out a cell phone that had a flashlight.

"Don't make yourselves targets," called Sam, "Can you move him?"

The doctor shook his head, then said something to the people around him. They all moved away, except the doctor and the nurse, their faces lit by the fake candles. Suddenly

Connor and an EMT appeared, carrying one of the long tables. They lay it down on its side in front of the wounded man, the doctor and the nurse, blocking them from view.

"I made the call," said Sarah, "but I think they got several calls. Sheriff and police. I told them the shot came from outside, probably a sniper."

"Good," said Sam, "They're forewarned." Sam's phone rang and he started talking immediately, "Pete, I'm inside. The shooter was definitely outside. Yeah, two down, one wounded, one dead. You guys should not come up to the barn until you clear the area. Fan out around the buildings and parking area. The son of a bitch has plenty of places to hide. I'm guessing he shot from the parking area, but I could be wrong." He paused, then said, "No. I left my gun in the car." He ended the call and put the phone back in his jeans pocket.

"Excuse me. Can I help?"

Sam looked to his left and saw Randy Bayard standing next to him.

"No. Thanks. Just stay back behind the stage," answered Sam.

"I went out to get my camera, but I didn't even make it to the car, when I heard a shot, so I came back," Randy explained, as if he'd been asked.

Sam looked at Randy, frowning, and asked, "Where were you when you heard the shot?"

"I went out that small side door beside the bandstand and walked along the side of the barn. I didn't even get to the front of the barn. I heard the shot and ran back. It seemed to come from out front, the sound of it, you know," Randy rambled nervously, "I suppose I should have gotten my camera anyway. Not much of a hardcore news photographer, am I?"

"So you didn't see anyone?"

"No. I really didn't look around. I just came right back inside."

"OK. You'll be questioned again once things settle down. Just go back behind the stage for now."

When Randy had gone, Sam turned to Mac, Sarah, Connor and Gabe.

"Would you all get behind some cover? I have to go back up by the front doors for when the sheriff and the police get here."

"Be careful, Sam," said Mac, as Gabe and Connor led her and Sarah away.

As Sam walked toward the front of the barn, he heard the sirens' loud whoops. They had to be at the road at the end of the lane leading to the old farmhouse and outbuildings. Through the few windows he could see the blue and clear lights flashing faintly. Suddenly the sirens stopped. The silence and dim light were eerie. Minutes passed. Sam heard whispers now and then, but for the most part, the people in the barn remained quiet. Finally someone banged on the barn doors and called out Sam's name.

"It's Sheriff Dade, Sam," the rough voice added.

Sam pulled open the door, saw the Sheriff, and opened it wider.

"We've got two ambulances waiting," said Sheriff Dade, "We didn't find anyone out here. He's long gone, I'm afraid. Or he came inside and is in here."

The ambulances were brought up to the barn and the injured man was loaded. The young woman who had been dancing with him wanted to go in the ambulance, but the Sheriff told her that she could go in a few minutes after she had been questioned. The ambulance pulled away with sirens blaring. Deputy Mary Preston spoke quietly with the Sheriff and then led the young woman away to some chairs. The Sheriff had everyone find chairs and wait to be interviewed. Soon deputies and several Versailles police were conducting the questioning. The coroner was examining the body on the stage, while a deputy and an EMT moved a table on its side to block the body from view. Another deputy had taken photographs before the coroner began his work. Sam told the Sheriff what had happened. Sheriff Parker Dade was in his late fifties, grey-haired and tough. He was a little shorter than Sam, but stood military-straight, his bearing that of the Marine he had been.

"This is bad, Sam. Three shootings in four days. I want you to work this one. I imagine they are all connected. Maybe the horse, too, like you thought. We'll have ballistics in two weeks or so. If we find the bullets tonight, we'll be pretty damn sure, even without testing."

"Yes, sir," said Sam, relieved that the Sheriff was considering his idea.

Sam walked over to where Mary was talking with the sobbing young woman. He quietly sat down in a chair on the other side of the witness. Mary looked at him, lifting her eyebrows, and pressing her lips into a thin line.

"Pam," said Mary, leaning toward the dark-haired woman, who couldn't seem to stop crying, "Pam, this is Deputy Kincaid. Deputy, this is Pam Donovan."

Pam looked at Sam briefly, then buried her face in her hands and cried harder.

"Ms. Donovan, we need your help," said Sam.

Mary added softly, "Her dance partner's name is Elliot Ferris."

"Pam," Sam tried again, " Elliot needs your help. We'll let you go to the hospital as soon as you tell us exactly what happened."

Abruptly, Pam Donovan sat up, wiped the tears roughly from her cheeks and pushed her dark brown hair back from her face. She was a pretty girl, in spite of her red eyes and splotched face. She wore a swirly Western skirt, pink and brown boots and a pink and turquoise plaid shirt with blood smeared all over the front. She took a deep breath and spoke in a shaky, but clear voice.

"Elliot and I have only been dating for a couple of months, but I really like him and he seems to like me. We were having so much fun tonight. I didn't even know he could dance. I don't know what to tell you. One minute we were dancing, then he was down. He was bleeding. I screamed and screamed. I wanted to help him, but I didn't know what to do. Then that nice girl pulled me away."

Her lip was trembling and another tear rolled down her cheek.

"You did fine," said Sam, "We got medical help for him and we had to get you out of danger. I know it's hard, but think back. Did you notice anything at all before Elliot was shot? Or after, when there was another shot?"

"I was looking at Elliot, when I heard the second shot. But before," Pam paused, little frown lines appearing between her eyes and she looked back at Sam, "I saw the couple in front of us. The guy was dipping the girl down and I was thinking that was so sweet."

Chapter 16

Sam left Pam Donovan with Mary and looked around the large open space for Mackenzie, Sarah, Connor and Gabe. Finally he saw them sitting together at the end of one of the long tables. He hurried over to them.

"Have you all been interviewed?" he asked abruptly.

"Yes," they answered, almost simultaneously.

"Connor, can you follow Mac home? In fact, maybe you could all go to the ranch and stay tonight."

"Sure," Connor said, looking at Sarah.

"Why?" asked Mac, "What's wrong, Sam?"

"I'd just feel better if you all went home. I'm hoping everyone will go home and stay there for tonight."

"Sam, I know something else is wrong," answered Mac. She was looking at him half-puzzled, half-irritated, staring at his face.

"Look, I have to help question people, you know, do my job," said Sam, "If I get done early enough, I can come out to the ranch later."

"Sam's right," said Gabe, standing.

Connor stood up, Sarah and Mac following. Connor took Sarah's hand.

"Come on, ladies," he said, "Let's swing by Sarah's and pick up some overnight stuff for her. We need to get out of the way."

As they walked away, Sam could hear Sarah protesting that she'd be fine at her apartment. Mac looked back at him over her shoulder, gave him a little nod, then took Sarah's arm and began convincing her to come to the ranch. Sam blew out a big breath, but still felt agitated. He walked back across the room toward the Sheriff. He heard a familiar voice and, looking to his left, saw Randy Bayard, being questioned by Jeff

Parker. He slowed his walk, coming up behind them, and heard "...camera, but I didn't even make it to the car, when I heard a shot, so I came back." Sam stopped a few feet away, out of Randy's peripheral vision. He saw Jeff look at him and Sam shook his head just enough. Jeff looked down at his notebook and asked Randy, "Where exactly were you when you heard the shot?"

"I went out that small side door beside the bandstand and walked along the side of the barn. I didn't even get to the front. I heard the shot and ran back. It seemed to come from out front, the sound of it, you know," answered Randy.

"Could you show me where you were beside the barn?" continued Jeff.

"Uh, sure. Pretty close, I guess. I suppose I should have gotten my camera anyway. Not much of a hardcore news photographer, am I?"

Sam turned away, so they wouldn't see him when Randy and Jeff went outside. He would talk to Jeff later and tell him about the repetitive dialogue, so close it sounded memorized. He would make sure they searched Mr. Bayard's car before he left.

* * *

Almost three hours later, Sam drove the country roads that led to the Quinn ranch. At nearly eleven p.m., he wasn't sure if it was too late to call, but he could take a look, and make sure everything was OK. As he turned in the lane, he could see the downstairs of the two-story wooden house was lit up and the porch lights were on by the front door. By the time he reached the top step of the porch, Mac was holding the screen door open for him.

"Come on in, Sam. We're in the kitchen."

Gabe, Connor and Sarah were seated around the well-worn kitchen table. Everyone greeted him in subdued voices and he took a seat. The table sat eight, but they all sat closely at one end. A plate of chocolate chip cookies with only a few left was in the middle of the table.

"Want a beer or homemade lemonade?" asked Mac.

"Lemonade, thanks," replied Sam.

"What can you tell us, Sam?" asked Gabe.

"There's a little good news," he began, "Elliot Ferris, the man who was shot, is going to be fine. It went through, just under his left collarbone. He'll probably get to go home tomorrow. I can tell you that it's the same bullet as the one that killed Letty Akers and Brad Jenkins. It's a .308 Winchester, which is pretty common around here with hunters. It's also the same make as the one that nicked Cat on Fire."

Sarah gasped, Gabe and Connor leaned back in their chairs and Mac just stared at him.

"We don't have the ballistics back yet, so we don't know if the bullets came from the same gun. We're leaning toward thinking the shootings are all related, but we don't have a clue as to why."

"It's some crazy person, mad at the world," said Sarah, "You hear about it every day. Someone who's been fired. Or his wife left him. Or a soldier with post-traumatic stress. It's finally come to our part of the world."

Connor reached across the table and took her hand.

"There's more," said Mac, watching Sam's face.

"I'm worried about you, Mac," Sam said, "I sat in on the interview with Pam Donovan. She said that right before Elliot was hit, she noticed the couple dancing next to them. She said she saw the guy in front of them dip the girl at the end of the song. That was us, Mac. If you look at the bullet's trajectory, you could have been shot."

"It could just as easily have been you," Mac shot back, "I don't think he cares who he shoots, as long as someone dies. Poor Brad…" She trailed off.

"You were in the line of fire when the horse was shot, too," Sam continued.

"No, if he'd wanted to hit me, it should have been easy. I was just sitting there."

"Maybe Cat on Fire got in the way," said Sam.

"Oh, good grief! Why would anyone want to kill me? Also I wasn't there with Letty Akers and I don't look like her, so he couldn't think she was me," Mac argued, "This isn't going to help you find this guy."

"We have to look at everything," said Sam, "and everyone. What about Randy Bayard? He certainly wasn't happy when I interrupted tonight."

"Kill me for turning down a dance?" Mac was incredulous.

"You said he made you uncomfortable. Taking pictures of you at the game. And he told you he knew you from grade school. You still don't remember him?"

"No," said Mac, "not at all. That still doesn't sound like grounds for suspecting him of murder."

"Trust your gut, Mac," said Sam, "I just want you to be careful."

Gabe, Connor and Sarah watched their interchange in silence. Sarah and Connor exchanged a few glances. Gabe looked seriously at his daughter.

"Mackenzie, he's right," Gabe stated, "You should be careful and pay attention to your surroundings. Even if this Bayard guy just has a crush, he sounds pretty immature."

They talked for a few minutes longer, mostly about Brad Jenkins. They'd all known him from the band. He'd been a class ahead of Connor in school. He had a wife and two sons, only 2 and 4 years old. His wife Jessie had taught at Sarah's school for a year before Jessie had the first boy and decided to stay home. Jessie had family in Belleriver and Lexington, but it was going to be rough. Brad had worked construction and brought home decent money, plus frequent gigs for the band. Sarah thought Jessie would have to go back to teaching, if anything was available. No matter what, raising two boys would be tough for a single, working mother. Connor wondered out loud about the funerals for Brad and Letty, but Sam didn't know when the bodies would be released. Gabe excused himself at midnight to turn in. Connor said he would show Sarah the guest room and they headed upstairs too.

"I'd better go," said Sam.

Mac walked him to the front door. Sam looked directly into her green eyes.

"Take care, Mac," he said softly.

"You too, Sam," she answered, watching him walk out into the night.

Chapter 17

The young man slumped at the bar was almost asleep over his glass of Buffalo Trace. He was on his third bourbon straight up. Carl, the bartender and owner, kept an eye on him. His name, as he had informed Carl months ago, was Robert Ezekiel Lee, commonly called Bobby Lee. He said his father was a Civil War re-enactor and wanted his only son to remember the South's most famous general. After that introduction, Bobby Lee hadn't talked much. Carl learned a little more about him from other bartenders and patrons.

Bobby Lee sat by himself and rarely talked, unless someone approached him. Word was that he had been in the Army in Afghanistan for several years. He was from Frankfort originally and lived there now. He worked at the Buffalo Trace distillery. At first Bobby Lee only came in once or twice a week. Carl's Place was small and off the beaten path, definitely not a tourist bar in Frankfort. Bobby ordered one beer, then one Buffalo Trace neat. He would nurse those over two or three hours, not looking around or even watching the television. He was handsome in a hard way with a thin, rough, unshaven face. He had dark blond hair cut short, light gray eyes and a thin, wide mouth. He usually wore jeans and a black tee shirt that stretched over his muscled back. His arms were muscular too, tan with blond hair, and he held his drink with long, strong fingers. Every now and then, a girl would be stupid or drunk enough to try to pick him up. Bobby Lee would look at her, say something softly, like "Not now." and she would back off.

Gradually, Bobby Lee started coming in more often, not just on the weekends. He still just had one beer followed by one bourbon and kept to himself. Carl liked the guy. He felt a connection, because Bobby Lee had come back unnoticed from a war overseas. Carl had served in Vietnam, had come home physically undamaged, but mentally lost. He would not have made it, if he hadn't had an unbelievably stubborn wife. Elaine had helped him start the bar with small inheritances from his mother and her father. She stayed with him for twenty years, until his bad dreams decreased in intensity and occurrence. Then she died from uterine cancer. Carl missed her every day, but he kept working, and volunteered at the Leestown VA Medical Center in Lexington once or twice a week. What he saw in the PTSD ward, he saw in Bobby Lee. He wanted the young man to get help, but hadn't figured out how to reach him. Carl had noticed a big change over the last two days. Bobby Lee had upped his intake to three or four beers, which he drank quickly, then three bourbons, the first one thrown back and the last two nursed. His eyes were red rimmed and his hands trembled on the glass. Tonight Bobby Lee came in later than usual, close to 10:00 pm, and he'd gone straight to bourbon. When Carl asked Bobby if he was all right, Bobby Lee glared at him, his gray eyes darker than usual. Carl was used to angry and emotional drunks, so he said calmly, "I'm here, if you want to talk". Bobby's eyes softened a little, and he shook his head slightly before staring back into his glass. Carl went back to wiping down the bar and taking orders. The bar was crowded, even for a Saturday night. A lot of people were coming to the bar to order, instead of waiting for Carl's one waitress.

Suddenly someone yelled, "You cocksucker!" There was the popping sound of someone being hit, followed by a crash. The crowd pulled back from the bar and the fight. Carl could see Bobby Lee on top of another man, both on the ground, pounding each other. Carl pushed a few people aside and grabbed Bobby Lee around his upper torso, pinning his arms to his body. Bobby Lee was wiry and strong, but Carl was much bigger and he held on fiercely. Two other guys pulled back the man who had been on the floor. He stood up shakily, one side of his face swelling and his nose bleeding. Carl recognized him anyway: Frank Boudreaux and his two drinking buddies, Jack Hunniker and Pete Nelson. They were regular customers, not usually troublemakers, but not the brightest good ol' boys.

"Sonofabitch came from nowhere," growled Frank, wiping the dripping blood from his nose with the back of his hand, smearing blood across his cheek, "I didn't say nothin' to him." He stood up a little straighter, pulled out his wallet and threw a few bills on the ground, "Let's get outta this dump, boys."

Just then everyone heard the sound of sirens coming closer.

"You're not going anywhere, Frank," said Carl, "The police will be straightening this out." Carl no longer held Bobby Lee, who stood next to him, looking steadily at Frank. Carl didn't know who had called the cops, but he wasn't sure he was glad. Bobby Lee's body was rigid, as though he would take on all comers.

"OK, everyone, take a seat," announced Carl, "The cops will probably want to question everyone. Y'all can have free sodas till they're gone." He turned to Bobby Lee and motioned him back to his seat at the bar.

The bar door opened and two Frankfort policemen walked over to where Carl and the combatants stood.

"What's up, Carl?" asked the older of the two. The younger man was looking from Frank to Bobby Lee, easily identifying the participants.

"Just a little misunderstanding, Officer Franklin," answered Carl.

"Misunderstanding, my ass," snarled Frank, "That sonofabitch broke my nose. I probably have a concussion from hitting the floor. Broke that chair, but it's his fault."

"Do you want to press charges, Frank?" asked the policeman.

"Damn right I do. As soon as I go to the hospital," Frank said, holding a wad of napkins to his still bleeding nose.

Franklin leaned in closer to Carl and said softly, "I'd like to wrap this up quickly, if possible. There's trouble over in Belleriver with that sniper. They may want extra help. Do you know what happened here?"

Carl shook his head "no". His waitress Missy appeared at his side.

"I heard what Frank said, Carl," she whispered, "I was at the next table takin' orders. Frank and his buddies were talkin' about the war and how glad they were not to be there. They'd never make it in the Army. Buncha cowards. They'd been talkin' kinda' normal, but then Frank says real loud that anyone who got killed over there just wasted his life. That's when Bobby Lee punched him and I don't blame him one bit." Missy stopped, looking from Carl to Franklin. She was only five feet, two inches tall, with curly short brown hair, and brown eyes that were spitting fire at that moment. She was curvy enough to attract attention from male customers and tough enough to keep them away.

"Thanks, Missy," said Franklin, "Can you come down to the station and make a statement tomorrow?"

"Sure. But I don't think Bobby Lee should be in trouble for this," she said, then went back to serving Cokes and sweet tea to the customers.

"Will he be in trouble?" asked Carl.

"We'll see. It will be up to a judge, if Frank Boudreaux presses charges," said Franklin, "Right now, I think I'll talk to a few more people, have Pete run Frank to the hospital and I'll take Bobby Lee into the station for the night."

Later, when Officer Franklin approached Bobby Lee at the bar, Carl was surprised that Bobby left quietly with the policeman. As he turned to go, Bobby looked Carl in the eyes and gave a little smile. Carl had never seen Bobby Lee smile before, but Carl thought Bobby's gray eyes were the saddest he'd ever seen.

Chapter 18

When Mac walked downstairs in a dress on Sunday morning, her dad, brother and Sarah stared at her in shock.

"You look nice, Mackenzie," said Gabe, "You comin' to church with us?"

"I am today," she answered, "Do I have time for breakfast?"

"Sure, it's on the counter, still warm. Eggs, bacon and blueberry muffins."

"I'm going to take Sarah home so she can change," said Connor, "We'll see y'all there."

Mac ate quickly, feeling her dad watching her.

"It's been awhile, Mac," he said, "People might make a fuss."

"I hope not. That's a good way to keep me from coming back."

"Well, it's good to talk to the Lord with all this craziness goin' on."

"Dad, I never stopped talking to the Lord. But back then, when I lost Bud, church didn't help. Everyone telling me it was God's will and that Bud was in a better place. It made me furious. I think God helped me, but He did it in a different way."

Her dad looked down at his cup of coffee. Mac knew he had loved Bud like a son. Gabe had felt her heartbreak like his own. Perhaps it was worse for him. He'd lost Bud and he didn't know how to help his little girl.

"That's how I felt when your mother died. I didn't want to live. I was angry with God. If it hadn't been for you and Connor, I wouldn't have made it. But the people from church helped, too. Bringing food for weeks. Helping with work here. I took you two to church, just to have something to do on Sunday. And because I knew your mama would've wanted it. Anyway, I'm glad for you to come anytime."

Mac looked at her gray haired father. He still had some black running through his hair and black eyebrows, and his face was tan and lined. He was sixty-two years old, still a tough, hard-working cowboy, but he had lived without her mother for sixteen years. Tears welled up in her eyes. She hadn't seen much of him the summer Meg Quinn was dying from brain cancer. She had lived with Aunt Tina that summer. Three or four times a week Aunt Tina would drive her to the hospital in Lexington to visit her mother.

Her dad was always there. Sometimes he would hold her on his lap and rock her a little, while they both looked at her mom. At first Mom was awake a lot and talked with Mac. She didn't tell her little girl that she would be home soon. She tried to reassure Mac with the thought that Mom would always watch over her from heaven. Mom asked her to be strong and to help take care of Connor and her dad. Mac promised that she would. She thought now that she probably hadn't done a very good job of that. Maybe going to church wasn't such a hard thing to do for her dad, whether it helped her or not.

When they arrived at the Church of Christ in Belleriver, they waited in the truck for Connor and Sarah. The four walked in together. Mac saw a few people take notice of her presence, but she didn't see any whispers passed down the pews. They sat in the middle row on the left, where her family had always sat. She didn't recognize any of the hymns, all modern ones, with a big screen in front that had the words displayed so that everyone could sing. Old Lester Millhouse stood off to one side, playing an acoustic guitar, and his wife Mary sat behind a keyboard, also accompanying the congregation. Mac sang along softly on the choruses, which seemed to repeat a lot. There was a new, young pastor, who asked everyone to pray for the "gunman's victims" and for the police in finding this evil man. He even asked for prayers for the gunman, that he would repent and turn himself in to the law. Mac doubted that would happen. She joined in wholeheartedly though when they closed the service with "Amazing Grace". After they left the church, the parishioners milled around in front, many of them speaking to Mac, simply saying how glad they were to see her. Quite a few had been at the barn dance the night before, and the shootings were the major topic of conversation. Mac gently pushed through the crowd toward her father, hoping to get him to take her home. Just then, someone touched her arm and said, "Hey, Mackenzie."

She looked to her right and was startled to see Randy Bayard smiling at her.

"Hi, Randy," she answered, startled and bothered by his presence, "I didn't know you belonged to this church."

"I don't, really. Just every now and then I go to a church here or in Versailles. See if I'm missing anything."

"Well, you'll have to excuse me. Time to head home," Mac said and turned to look for her father. She didn't see the angry flash in Randy's eyes, but she heard him say, "See you later."

Mac thought to herself, "I hope not." She knew Randy had every right to be at church, the barn dance and the football game, but he made her uncomfortable. Part of her thought she was being unreasonable, but she also knew she couldn't help not liking him. Mac had not had to deal with dating men for much of her life. In high school, she'd been Bud's girlfriend. In college, she'd had the ready answer that her boyfriend was in the Army, which seemed to stop most boys in their tracks. She and Bud were married over her first Christmas break. His helicopter was shot down the following spring. First her grief kept her unavailable. When she started painting for income, most of her clients were men old enough to be her father, or wealthy women, and Mac had no problem keeping their relationships businesslike. Whether she knew it or not, she was more than reserved; she was unapproachable to men who tried in the slightest way to get close. Nine years was a long time to be celibate, but Mac just felt empty. She didn't want any entanglements. She put her heart into her paintings. She felt safer living at home with her dad and Connor. Sarah became her one close friend. Meeting Sam Kincaid was the first crack in her wall. As she joined her father, who was talking to the young minister, Mac wondered what Sam was doing.

Chapter 19

Sheriff Dade motioned Sam to come to his office. The Sheriff sat back down behind his desk.

"I just got a call from the Franklin police, " he said, "They've got a guy in custody who aroused their suspicions. I'd like you to head over there and talk to him. They arrested him for starting a fight. He's ex-Army. Name's Bobby Lee. Robert Ezekiel Lee to be exact."

"Yes, sir," Sam nodded and turned to leave. He made no comment on the name or its variation. Namesakes of the famous general still abounded in the South.

"Sam," Dade spoke again, "Lee was a sharpshooter."

"Yes, sir." Sam answered and left.

It took Sam about twenty minutes to get from the Sheriff's office to the Frankfort Police Department. He parked in the lot and walked quickly into the simple, concrete building. He was a little surprised to be greeted by Todd Franklin, the cop who had made the arrest and should have been off duty by 9:30 am. The two men shook hands.

"I wanted to fill you in myself and watch the video again," explained Franklin, "Besides, I'm a little jacked. I'm thinking this could be your man."

Sam nodded and followed Franklin to a small room where they could watch the interview of Bobby Lee in privacy. Sam first saw Bobby Lee seated near a small table. Lee was thin and muscular, with his elbows leaning on his knees, his head hanging forward. He straightened as Todd Franklin walked into the room and sat in a plastic chair. The camera angle was from above, but Sam could clearly see Bobby's calm, angular face. He didn't look drunk or upset, even with blood splatter on his neck.

Officer Franklin stated the date, his name and Bobby Lee's name for the record. He also read Bobby his rights again, even though he'd done it at Carl's.

"Could you tell me what happened tonight at Carl's place?" asked Officer Franklin.

"I was having a drink at the bar, and I heard the men behind me talking about Afghanistan," answered Bobby in a husky, soft voice, "One of 'em said it was a waste for a guy to die over there. I turned around and hit him. I'm a vet. I was in Afghanistan for six years. I lost some friends over there."

"What did you do over there?"

Bobby Lee's face tightened in anger at first, then he sighed and relaxed.

"I killed people."

Franklin wasn't fazed and asked quietly, "How? What was your rank and job?"

"I was an E7 most of the time. Came out an E8. First Sergeant. Sniper."

"When did you get out?"

"2010."

"What have you been doing since?"

"I work at Buffalo Trace."

"Doing what?"

"Drive a forklift in the distribution center."

"Good job?"

"Yeah. Decent. Good pay. Good boss."

"Do you miss the Army?"

"No. What's any of this got to do with a bar fight?"

"Just background. Waiting to see if Frank Boudreaux presses charges. You got anyone you can call, if we let you go? Can't let you drive."

"Mmmmm, no."

"No friends from work?"

"Not anyone I'd call at 2:00 in the morning."

"Carl said you seemed kind of down tonight, drinking more than usual. Anything happen recently?"

Bobby's head went down and he shook it slowly from side to side.

"What were you doing before you came to Carl's Place?" asked Franklin.

"Not much. Drivin' around."

"Driving around where?"

"Just around. I don't remember."

"Have you had any problems since you got out of the Army, Bobby? You don't have an arrest record here. That's good. It's tough, though, changing from the Army to civilian life," Franklin waited.

"People don't respect the military anymore," stated Bobby flatly.

"What do you mean? What people?"

"Lots of people. Like that shithead in the bar tonight."

"Yeah. That was a stupid thing to say," agreed Franklin. He paused, then asked, "Anyone else give you a hard time?"

"Not for awhile. There was an idiot at work, but he got fired."

"For giving you a hard time?"

"No. For being lazy. Late all the time. Stuff like that."

"Anyone out there nice to you? Respect that you were a soldier?"

Bobby Lee nodded and stared over Franklin's shoulder. Franklin was patient and waited silently.

Finally Bobby said, "Yeah. Letty. She gave tours and worked in the gift shop. She was impressed when I told her I'd been over there, in Afghanistan. I was going to ask her out, but she had a boyfriend."

Bobby Lee sat quietly, looking past Franklin, and tears rolled slowly down Bobby's cheeks. Franklin still didn't speak. Finally Bobby mumbled, "Now she's gone."

"Do you know what happened to her?" asked Franklin.

"Some asshole shot her."

"Do you know anyone who was angry with her? Someone at work, maybe."

"No. No one, " Bobby sat up straight, no longer crying, "She was cute and funny. Everyone liked her. A lot of the guys had the hots for her, but no one hated her. Can I go now? I'm tired."

"Sorry, Bobby, you're going to spend the night here, or at least until we hear from Mr. Boudreaux."

Franklin stated the time and date again, ending the interview. He froze the screen and looked at Sam.

"What do you think, Sam?"

"I'm not sure," said Sam," He fits the profile, and we've got to follow through. Have you submitted his name to NCIC?"

"Yeah, first thing. We should get something soon. Do you want to interview him? He's still asleep. Boudreaux declined to press charges, but I haven't told Bobby Lee that yet."

"Yes, wake him up. Let's give it a shot."

Fifteen minutes later Sam walked into a small interview room and found Bobby Lee sitting across a small table. Bobby's eyes were red and his beard was scruffier, but he sat straight in the chair and looked steadily at Sam. His hands rested on his knees.

"Hello, Mr. Lee. I'm Deputy Kincaid," said Sam, sitting in the other plastic chair, "Are you feeling OK this morning?"

"I'm all right," answered Bobby.

"I need to ask you some questions, if that's OK with you," said Sam.

"You told Officer Franklin that you were in the Army in Afghanistan. Is that correct."

"Yes, sir."

"You were a marksman, a sharpshooter?"

"Yes, sir."

"Do you own a rifle now?"

"Yes, sir."

"What kind?"

"An M24, like I had in the Army."

"Why?"

"Why?" repeated Bobby Lee. He actually looked a little confused.

"Why do you own a sniper rifle? What do you do with it?" asked Sam.

"Thought I'd hunt with it, but I haven't. I've shot targets a few times."

"Where?"

"Couple of places in Lexington. I'd have to look up the names."

"How'd you do? Get rusty at all?"

"Did OK. No problems," Bobby Lee looked intently at Sam and said, "I'm not stupid. I know why you're asking all these questions. I didn't shoot Letty. I couldn't. She was pretty and sweet and funny. She was straight up with me. She knew I wanted to ask her out and she made sure I knew she had a boyfriend."

"That didn't make you mad?"

"No. Just thought I'd wait and see. She wasn't wearin' no ring, so I thought I had a chance," Bobby's eyes teared up again and he looked down.

"Where were you the night she was killed?"

"At Carl's. I was there until it closed. I heard the next morning at work. You can ask Carl."

"I will," said Sam, "Where were you last night before you went to Carl's?"

"I had a burger at the drive-in. Drove around."

"Drove around where?"

"Just drove around in the country."

"Why?"

"It relaxes me. Lookin' at the fields and horses. I was tired."

"Tired like upset?"

"Yes, tired like upset," Bobby looked directly at Sam again, "I was thinking about Letty. I'd like to get my hands on whoever shot her, but I don't know how. That's your job. So why don't you get to it, instead of wasting time on me?"

Bobby Lee's body was rigid and his hands were clenched into fists on his knees.

"This is part of that," answered Sam, "Maybe you can help us. Maybe you saw something without knowing it. Where did you drive?"

"I have no idea," said Bobby Lee, "I don't remember."

"Did you see any houses or barns that you could describe?"

"No. They're all beautiful around here. Black fences. Red barns. Green ones. White and green. Green grass. Brown horses. Actually not too many horses. They're put away in the evening. It's all peaceful and quiet."

"Did you hear anything?"

"Like what? A gunshot? Was someone shot last night? Is that what you're digging for?"

"Like music."

"I just said it was quiet. I didn't have my radio on and I had the windows down. I didn't hear music. I didn't hear a gunshot. I just drove around the country outside Frankfort, until I felt like going to Carl's."

" You didn't head to Lexington or Versailles or anywhere?"

"No. Listen, man, I don't know what you want, but I can't help. Either charge me with somethin' or let me go home."

"Bobby, would you be willing to let us have your rifle for elimination purposes?" asked Sam.

"Sure. I don't care. I'll give it to you tomorrow."

Sam looked at Bobby Lee. Bobby wasn't angry any more. He just looked beat down. Sam sighed.

"OK, Bobby Lee. I'll go get Officer Franklin."

When he got outside, Todd Franklin was waiting.

"What do you think?" he asked.

"I don't know," said Sam, "He's got a rifle and the skill to use it, no alibi for last night before he was at Carl's. I don't think it's enough to hold him. I'll check his alibi for the Akers killing. We'll have to keep an eye on him. Maybe we can get a warrant for his rifle for when the ballistics reports come in. Let him go. Thanks for calling us."

Sam left the Frankfort Police Station, thinking that Bobby Ezekiel Lee had probably cared more for Letty than he had. But that didn't mean Bobby hadn't killed her.

Chapter 20

Mac fumed, as she and her dad drove home from church.

"What's got you all riled up?" asked Gabe.

"Did you see that guy I was talking to right before I came to get you?"

Gabe nodded, "Yep."

"Have you ever seen him at church before?"

"Not that I remember," Gabe answered.

"That's Randy Bayard, the photographer from Friday night's game. He was bothering me at the barn dance last night too. Now he suddenly shows up at our church."

"Maybe he just has a crush on you," said Gabe, "Not the worst reason for going to church."

"Dad, he's pushy. I told you how he took pictures of me at the game and after. He was over the top from the start. Coming to our church is too much, and showing up the first Sunday I've been in years is just plain spooky. He makes me very uncomfortable."

"Well, you don't have to go out with him. If he asks, just say "no". Trust your instincts."

Mac looked at her father. He grinned and winked at her. She blew out a deep breath.

"Sorry, Dad. He's not worth worrying about. Do I have time to paint this afternoon?"

"I don't see why not. Connor and Sarah are going go for a ride, then fix supper. You should have some lunch, but you'll have all afternoon to paint."

"I am so lucky to have a father and brother who cook," Mac laughed.

"Why don't you invite Sam for supper?" suggested Gabe.

"I'm sure he's busy, Dad. Probably with work," Mac answered, "There haven't been multiple murders around here in forever. At least not that I can remember."

They arrived home to find Connor and Sarah putting wrapped sandwiches and water bottles into saddlebags.

"We made extra," said Sarah, "Ham and cheese on the counter. Sure you don't want to come with us, Mac?"

Mac smiled at her friend's disingenuous offer and the relieved look exchanged by Sarah and Connor when she said, "No, thanks. Work to do."

"We'll be back in time to bake chicken. Just a couple of hours out to the creek and back," said Connor, as they headed out the door.

Mac grabbed a sandwich and a glass of milk and headed upstairs. She quickly changed into old jeans and a tee shirt already splattered with paint, then climbed the narrow staircase to the attic. Her father had helped her clear half the floored attic to use as a studio. He'd cut out a skylight in the roof and added insulation and finished the sloped roof walls. Even with only two heating ducts, it was amazingly warm in winter. Mac stood in front of the large 3' x 4' canvas that John Blake had requested. She had already penciled in Cat on Fire running across a pasture, head and tail up, looking as though he was flying. She studied the sketches and watercolors taped on the wall next to her easel, as she chewed. With the last bite in her mouth she picked up a brush and began mixing a wash of pale blue for the sky. For the next hour Mac was lost in the colors and basic shapes of the composition. She was distracted by the sound of tires on gravel and hurried over to the open window under the peak of the roof. She hoped it was Sam, but the bright yellow sports car was unfamiliar. She watched a stocky man in jeans, a cowboy hat and boots climb out and look around. He walked as if his feet hurt and was soon knocking on the door. He paused a few seconds, then knocked louder. Mac sighed and put her brush in turpentine. She hurried down the stairs as the visitor continued knocking more loudly.

Mac pulled the door open and the man looked startled. He started to drop his hand, but pulled off his tan cowboy hat instead. He looked to be in his late thirties or early forties, and did not have much blond hair left under his hat.

"Is this the Quinn ranch?" he asked.

"Yes. May I help you?" Mac answered.

"I'm sorry to drop by unannounced, but John Blake recommended you and I'm leaving town tomorrow for a few days. I just thought I'd take a chance."

"A chance on what?"

"Oh, sorry," the man's round pink face flushed, "I'm Jeremiah Bagley from Lexington. I'm interested in buying a riding horse. I saw John Blake at the track yesterday and he said the Quinns have good quarter horses for sale. I'm very sorry that I didn't call ahead."

"You'll want to talk to my father. He's probably out in the barn now, so if you'll follow me."

Mac was irritated, but used to the rudeness of many potential horse buyers. Quite a few seemed to think that it was a 24/7 open barn and appointments were unnecessary. She headed to the barn, but had to slow her long stride for Mr. Bagley to keep up. He winced with every other step. His pointed-toe black boots looked new and obviously too small. Her dad would be dealing with a novice rider and owner, which he didn't like.

They found Gabe brushing a chestnut mare in the aisle. Mac introduced Mr. Bagley, and told her dad that she was going back to work. She hurried back across the yard, but before she reached the porch she heard galloping hooves. Turning, she saw Gus, Sarah's gelding, tearing down the path between pastures. At the same time she saw dust at the end of their road. Someone else was coming to visit. Mac ran toward Gus, who slowed as she neared. She grabbed his long rope one-piece rein and he stopped. She walked him in a circle, until his breathing slowed. She saw her dad running toward her, Jeremiah Bagley standing in the barn door and Sam's car pulling into the yard.

"Dad, I'm going to find Sarah and Connor," she yelled, pulling herself into Gus's saddle, "Tell Sam I'll be right back."

She gently nudged Gus into a trot and headed out on the long pathway that ran between the pastures. She had only gone a half-mile or so, when she saw a horse and rider coming toward her. No, two riders. It was definitely Connor's big grey gelding Pistol with Connor and Sarah on his back.

"We're fine," called Connor when he got closer, "I knew you'd come."

"What happened?" asked Mac as she turned Gus next to Pistol and they headed home. Sarah had grass stains on her cheek and sleeve and her dark brown naturally curly hair had grass in it, but she grinned at Mac.

"Guess I'm almost a cowgirl," Sarah said, "Something spooked Gus. He went left and I went right, but I'm not hurt. Just my pride."

"It was a gunshot, Mac, but don't panic," said Connor, "It was definitely a shotgun. Probably someone hunting doves. And it was pretty far away, but too close for Gus."

"We'll have to desensitize him to loud noises, Sarah," said Mac, "That's two falls. One more and you're a cowgirl."

"Can't I just become a better rider without falling off?" laughed Sarah, "That ground gets harder every time."

Gabe and Sam were waiting in front of the barn with Mr. Bagley.

"Everyone looks OK," said Gabe, as Sarah slid off Pistol's back and Connor and Mac dismounted, "You need to ride him around some, Sarah, before he starts getting' ideas."

"Is that one of your horses?" asked Jeremiah Bagley with wide eyes, "Did he throw that young lady?"

Sarah explained what happened again, which didn't seem to reassure Mr. Bagley at all.

"I think I'd better rethink this," Mr. Bagley's face was bright red.

"Take some riding lessons," suggested Gabe, "Find out what you're getting into. A horse's instinct is to run when it's afraid. They can be taught not to, but it takes time and they have to trust their rider."

"I want to trust the horse!" Bagley snorted, "Thanks for your time, Mr. Quinn." He shook Gabe's hand quickly and headed toward his bright yellow car.

Sarah mounted Gus and they followed Connor and Pistol to the corral. Gabe headed back into the barn. Mac looked at Sam and turned back toward the house.

"Want something to drink?" Mac asked, "Lemonade, tea, water?"

"Water would be fine. Want to sit out here?"

"I'll be right back," she answered.

Sam was sitting in one of the wooden chairs, so Mac sat in the other after handing him a glass of ice water.

"Been working?" she asked.

"Yeah," he said, "Hope you don't mind me stopping by. I'd had enough for today."

"Anytime."

"What were you doing before the runaway?"

"Painting."

"Oh, sorry. I didn't mean to interrupt. I can go."

Sam started to rise, putting his glass on the small table.

"No, please stay. Mr. Bagley was the one who interrupted, then Gus being a goofhead. I'll probably be helping cook supper pretty soon. Why don't you stay and eat with us?"

"Sure. Thanks. Do you usually cook?"

Mac smiled, "No. I can, but Dad and Connor are much better at it. I just cut veggies or make the salad. I'm not your typical homemaker."

"How'd that happen?"

"When I was little, I helped Mom bake cookies and pies and cakes, but I didn't do much with the meals, except set the table. Mom died when I was twelve and I just never got into cooking after that. Dad or Connor fixed meals. Connor loves to eat, so he taught himself all kinds of things from recipes. He experiments too," she ran out of words.

"I'm sorry, Mac," said Sam.

"Just what happened," she said softly, "Can't be helped. We're doin' ok."

Connor and Sarah climbed the front steps just then.

"Stayin' for supper?" asked Connor.

"I hear you're a mean cook, so I couldn't resist," Sam said.

"I am indeed, and Sarah will be helping, so it should be a feast."

Sam asked Mac to show him around the property, so they walked and talked about the horses, how he got into law enforcement and how she got into painting. He asked if he could see what she was working on, so she took him up to the attic.

"I've barely started this one, but I can show you photos online of some of the commissioned paintings I've done."

They went down to the computer in her dad's study and she started a slide show of her work. Sam watched intently. After about twenty photos, he said, "Wow, Mac, you are really good at this."

"Thanks," she said, "I love it. I'm pretty sure I drew and painted more than I rode as a kid. And I was crazy about horses and riding too. Mom and Dad had my drawings up all over the house."

Just then Connor yelled, "Come and get it!"

It was a feast: baked chicken, roasted red potatoes, green beans and biscuits. While they ate, Connor asked Sam if there were any leads in the sniper shootings. Sam told them about two confessions they'd had from the same two sad men who confessed to every crime in the area that wasn't solved within a few days. In fact, he said, they'd even confessed to crimes that had the perpetrators in jail already.

"We're kind of overwhelmed with helpful calls right now. People who saw a neighbor carrying a rifle. People who have a neighbor they think is crazy. People who heard shots. A lot of people suspect their spouse or a relative. We do check everything plausible, but I can't talk about specifics."

"Speaking of odd people, " said Connor, "Didn't I see you talking to Randy Bayard at church this morning?"

Mac described the brief incident again and felt her anger return. Sam looked irritated too.

"Does he belong to your church?" asked Sam.

"No. That's what annoyed me. Why is he following me around?"

"He's just immature," said Sarah, "He wants to ask you out and doesn't know how."

"Well, the answer is 'no' if he ever does!" Mac said.

After supper, they played Hearts with the Steelers-Panthers game on in the background. Around 10:00 Sam said he had to go. Mac walked with him out on the porch.

Sam turned to her and said, "I am going to ask you out as soon as we catch this guy. I feel like I've been imposing on your hospitality."

"I'll hold you to that, Sam, but we're happy to have you anytime."

"Well, thanks. Good night."

He hesitated, but then turned and walked down the steps.

"Good night, Sam," Mac answered softly.

As she went back into the house, she smiled to herself and thought, "Damn! I wanted him to kiss me!"

Chapter 21

Sam had found everything he could on Bobby Lee and Randy Bayard online, in county records and in the NCIC (National Crime Information Center). Neither of them was in the NCIC and Bobby's records were just as he had told Officer Franklin. He wanted to follow up on Randy, but knew Bobby Lee was the more likely suspect, so he began checking records in Frankfort where Bobby was born.

Bobby Ezekiel Lee was born in Frankfort in 1984. He had attended Elkhorn Elementary School and Elkhorn Middle School, followed by Franklin County High School. Sam decided to visit the schools to see what staff remembered about Bobby Lee. He went to Elkhorn Elementary first, although he doubted anyone on the staff was old enough to remember Bobby. He was wrong. Principal Wanda Pearson said he could speak to 5th grade teacher Bob Hardin in ten minutes, while his class was in Art.

Mr. Hardin did not seem disturbed by the presence of a sheriff's deputy or the interruption of his day. He was a medium-sized man with thinning brown hair that he made no attempt to hide. He wore copper-colored metal-framed glasses that almost matched his brown eyes. He looked to be in his 60's and wore a light gray suit with a royal blue shirt and a navy blue and red striped tie. They met in his classroom that held about fifteen desks and brightly colored posters and photos of striking landscapes from around the world.

"How can I help you?" he asked immediately, "We have about twenty-five minutes before the kids come back."

"I'd like to ask you about Bobby Lee, who went here several years ago," began Sam. Mr. Hardin was nodding before Sam even finished.

"What do you want to know? Is he in trouble?" asked Mr. Hardin.

"I can't go into detail in an ongoing investigation, but he isn't in trouble that I know of," said Sam, "Why would you think that?"

"Because you're a deputy sheriff," smiled Mr. Hardin, his lined face looking suddenly boyish, then serious again, "You realize his school records are sealed unless you have a warrant."

"I just want to know what he was like in fifth grade," said Sam, "I'm not trying to hurt him, just find out more about him. I already know that he served in the Army and that he works at Buffalo Trace now with an excellent work record."

"Good. Good. I would expect that," said Mr. Hardin. He lowered his head for a few moments, then looked up at Sam and spoke quietly, "I don't know why I'm hesitating. He was a reserved boy in class, except in history, which he loved. Maybe that led him to the military. He was an average student, except for history, where he excelled. He wasn't popular with the other kids, but he wasn't ridiculed or bullied either. I think that's why I remember him. He was on his own, but he didn't seem lonely. No, that's not right. He probably was lonely, but he didn't act out like many kids on the fringe do."

"Didn't he have any friends?" Sam asked.

"Not in his class. But the younger children liked him. He was one of the fifth graders who helped in other classes at the end of the day. He would help fourth graders during their study hall or help the teacher. He was decent at sports, so he wasn't the last picked for a team and he played hard. He also defended the little ones on the playground against bullies."

"What about his family?"

"They were reserved as well, but one or both of them always came to the Open House and meetings with his teachers. His mother was a waitress and his father was a mechanic. I believe his father served in Vietnam, but managed to come home without any overt problems. There was never any hint of abuse or alcohol or drug problems."

"Thank you very much, Mr. Hardin," said Sam.

"I hope he's all right," answered the teacher, "He stood out to me. He seemed quite self-contained for a fifth grader. Not exactly confident, but okay with who he was. Maybe

it was his research in history, especially the wars. I'm a history buff myself, so perhaps it
was the shared interest."

Elkhorn Middle School provided less information, because the principal and teachers
were too young. The office secretary remembered Bobby, because he was so polite and
rarely absent.

Sam pulled into a drive-through and ate a hamburger, fries and a sweet tea before
visiting Franklin County High School. He was lucky again. He didn't have to wait long to
see the principal, Jeremy Coldiron, who was tall and thin with wispy gray hair, piercing
dark eyes, a long nose and a thin, wide mouth. He shook hands firmly with Sam and
asked how he could help. When Sam explained about Bobby Lee, Mr. Coldiron motioned
him to a chair and he sat down behind his large, wooden desk, a scarred relic of many
years ago. The large screen iMac computer looked out of place on it.

"I was still a History teacher when Bobby Lee was here," began Mr. Coldiron, "Bobby
took every history class we offered, so I actually taught him for three years. Except for
his love of 20th Century History, I can't say that I knew him well, but I can give you my
impressions."

Sam waited. Mr. Coldiron moved some papers and a pen on his desk, then folded his
hands and looked steadily back at Sam.

"Bobby Lee was quiet, an observer. He wasn't a joiner, except for History Club. I
think he only joined that because we went on field trips to battlefields and historical
museums and sites. His attitudes toward war changed as he went through school. As a
sophomore, he was very patriotic, looking at war as part of the United States' glorious
history. He loved Teddy Roosevelt, although he was nothing like him. He was like a
sponge his junior year, reading every book I recommended, plus others that he found,
even historical literature that Mrs. Henry our English III teacher pointed out to him. As a
senior, he was almost a pacifist. His father had served in Vietnam and it troubled Bobby
to learn the horrors of that war in particular. At one point I asked him if he'd ever talked
with his dad about the war and he said no, his dad never talked about it."

"Did he have any friends, a girlfriend, do any sports?" asked Sam.

"He talked a little with the other kids in the History Club. I think he was friends with
Kyle Franklin and Terri Laws. Terri was a girl, one of only two in the club. Kyle was

much more outspoken than Bobby, but I got the feeling that they agreed on a lot of things, at least historical issues."

"You remember a lot about these kids from over 10 years ago," said Sam.

"I remember all of my serious students. I came up with Kyle and Terri's names, because they're married and run a real estate business here in Frankfort. I know that Bobby Lee went into the Army after graduation, which surprised me a little. I wondered how he squared that with his new pacifist leanings, but of course, I didn't get to ask him. If you'll excuse me, I'm going to call our librarian and get my memory some more help."

He lifted the receiver, pushed a button and spoke, "Ms. Simmons, could you please find our yearbooks from 2001 and 2002 and send them to my office?"

He looked at Sam and said, "Mrs. Henry is retired, but she might remember more about Bobby. Would you like me to call her and see if she can see you?'

Sam thought for a moment, then said, "Sure. Thank you."

Mr. Coldiron pulled out his cell phone and dialed, waited, then said, "Liz, I have a Deputy Sheriff Kincaid here from Woodford County, wanting to know what Bobby Lee was like in high school. Care to help?"

He listened for a while, then said, "I'll tell him. Thanks, Liz. Bye."

"She can see you in an hour and I'll give you directions to her place. She and my wife are in a book club together. Her husband and I used to be in it as well, but he passed away and I'm too busy these days. Oh, good, here are the yearbooks. Thank you, Tracy."

A young girl with long, brown hair had knocked on his door and stood holding two slim volumes. She handed them to Mr. Coldiron, and smiled shyly at Sam, revealing colorful braces. Sam smiled back at her, wondering why blue and gold. When Mr. Coldiron walked around the desk with the yearbooks, their covers supplied the answer. He soon found the few pictures of Robert Ezekiel Lee in both books. Bobby had been in the History Club, on the wrestling team for four years and didn't smile in his school pictures.

"Maybe I should talk to his wrestling coach," said Sam.

"That will be difficult, since Mr. Pitt is no longer here. He retired and moved to Florida, I believe. I can look up Bobby's records, if you think it would help."

"No, that won't be necessary. You've been very helpful," said Sam.

"I don't remember hearing anything about Bobby's wrestling, so he wasn't a star. He would have tried hard, though," said Mr. Coldiron, handing Sam a piece of paper, "Here is Mrs. Henry's address and directions. It's not far."

Sam shook the principal's hand and thanked him. Back in his vehicle, he read the directions, which were simple. He was there in five minutes. The small one-story brick house was only about four blocks from the high school. Sam wondered if she had lived there when she was teaching. He rang the doorbell and waited. A small, white-haired woman answered the door and asked to see identification. She was the epitome of an English teacher with her intelligent gray eyes behind wire-rimmed bifocals and her fine gray hair brushed up into a French twist. Her lips were pressed into a thin line as she studied his ID. However, she was dressed in a Chicago Cubs tee shirt, jeans and red Nike tennis shoes, and when she handed back his ID and opened the door, her smile was welcoming and her eyes were warm.

"Come in, young man. Please sit anywhere in the living room. Hope you don't mind cat and dog hair."

"No, ma'am, " answered Sam, as a brindle Corgi sniffed his feet, and wiggled his bottom in hopes of a pet.

"Spencer, leave the officer alone," said Mrs. Henry. She led Sam into a comfortable living room of stuffed chairs and a long plaid couch. The furniture formed a U in front of a full-screen TV, but it was surrounded by bookshelves that were overflowing with hardback books. Beyond the living room, Sam could see a breakfast nook and part of a kitchen decorated in yellow and blue. A sliding door was behind the table that led to a fenced-in back yard. Sam sat on one end of the couch and Mrs. Henry sat at the other. She was promptly joined by a black and white cat that folded into her lap and the Corgi jumped a few times before achieving couch-height and lay next to her.

"As you can see, I won't be getting up for awhile, so ask away," Mrs. Henry smiled, petting one animal with each hand.

"Mrs. Henry, I'd like to know what you remember about Bobby Lee," said Sam, "What kind of student was he? Did he have friends? Date anyone?"

"I don't suppose you'll tell me why," she let her hands rest on each animal's back and waited.

"No, ma'am. Bobby Lee is not in trouble, but he is a person of interest in an ongoing investigation."

"I hope it isn't those horrible sniper shootings," she said.

Sam didn't answer, so she continued.

"Bobby Lee was an average student. He wasn't interested in any subject except history, especially 20th century American history. His English work was adequate, unless he had the option of writing about any of the 20th century wars. Those papers were quite good: well written with his research documented. I looked him up in the yearbooks I have to jog my memory. He was a wrestler, although not exceptional. He was in the History Club all four years. He was friends with Kyle and Terri Franklin, who own Franklin Real Estate here. You could talk with them as well. Actually, I think Bobby took Terri to a few dances. Kyle was dating a cheerleader back then. I don't know what happened, but after graduation, Bobby went into the Army. Kyle and Terri went to the University of Kentucky, after which Kyle went into the real estate business with his father. Eventually he and Terri married and share the business."

"What kind of person was he?" asked Sam.

"Do you mean was he a loner, hot-headed, spiteful, vengeful? The kind of person who would kill people if he didn't get his way?" Mrs. Henry shot back.

"No, ma'am," answered Sam.

"I'm sorry," said Mrs. Henry, "You haven't been pushy or antagonistic. It's just that I'm fairly sure that you're looking for a murderer. I know Bobby Lee was in the Army and may have killed, but I don't believe that he's a murderer. Still, I only knew him in high school and haven't seen him since." She paused, sighed and continued, "Bobby Lee was a quiet boy. He didn't have a lot of friends and wasn't in the popular crowd. He only excelled in the study of history, which isn't likely to make you Prom King. He wasn't a class clown. He was an only child of hard-working parents. There was no evidence or rumors about problems at home. His parents came to the annual Open House. I don't know if they came to his wrestling matches."

"I'd still like to know what you thought of him, his character," said Sam.

"Bobby sat in the back of the room and didn't participate, unless I called on him. The other kids seemed to accept him; they certainly didn't tease him. He was private, but not in a conceited way. He seemed content within himself, if you know what I mean. That is quite unusual in high school students. Is any of this helpful, Deputy Kincaid?"

Sam nodded. Suddenly Mrs. Henry sat up straighter, disturbing the cat, which turned around and lay back down.

"I just remembered something. About why I liked him," she said, looking at Sam, "There was a new boy midyear, who sat in the empty seat in front of Bobby. He called him by name: Jamal. The boy was black. That shouldn't have been a problem back then, but it could have been. Our percentage of black students was even smaller than it is now. Plus Jamal had moved from Mississippi and might have been expecting problems. At any rate, Jamal came out of his shell and moved on to the popular crowd, partly because he could play basketball. He and Bobby sat in those same seats for the rest of the year and always nodded hello to each other when they came into class. It might not seem like much, but it showed me Bobby's convictions were real."

Sam thanked Mrs. Henry. She walked with him to the door, Spencer and the cat in attendance. Sam reached down to pet the animals and asked the cat's name.

"Hemingway," she answered with a smile, "What else?"

Chapter 22

Since it was only 3:00 in the afternoon, Sam decided a visit to Franklin Real Estate was in order. With any luck either Kyle or Terri Franklin would be in the office. He used his cell phone to find the address and directions. The office was in an old brick building just off Main Street. It was a beautifully restored building to blend in with the downtown restoration, an appropriate advertisement for Frankfort real estate. The title was painted in gold Edwardian Script lettering on the opaque glass window in the wooden door.

Sam walked into an abruptly modern office with pale gray walls and darker gray carpeting. Photographs of beautiful properties in Frankfort lined the walls. He walked up to a glass-topped desk where an attractive fortyish woman with streaked blond hair and French-tipped nails was typing on a metallic red laptop. The nameplate at the front of the desk read Mrs. Alma Willoughby.

"May I help you?" Mrs. Willoughby flashed bright white teeth between red tinted lips.

"I'd like to speak with Mr. or Mrs. Franklin or both," said Sam, showing his ID.

"Mrs. Franklin is in. Let me tell her you're here," the receptionist replied. She picked up her phone, pressing a button and said, "A Deputy Kincaid is here from Woodford County."

She hung up without saying anything else and a dark-haired woman in a burgundy suit appeared from a hallway in the back of the room.

"Hello, Deputy. I'm Terri Franklin. Would you like to come back to my office? Would you like coffee or a soda?"

"No, thank you, Mrs. Franklin."

Sam followed her to an office that was obviously done by the same decorator as the entryway, only with dark green carpeting and pale green walls. Her desk was light gray metal and glass-topped with a metallic blue laptop and a few personal photographs that Sam couldn't see. He sat in an unexpectedly comfortable dark green leather chair with a metal frame. The walls were covered in more photographs of Frankfort homes and landscapes.

"How may I help you?" Terri Franklin asked.

"Are you friends with Robert Ezekiel Lee?"

"Wow! That would be going back a few years," she looked surprised, smiled and leaned back in her chair, "I was friends with Bobby Lee in high school. I hope he isn't in trouble."

"No, ma'am, but I'd like to know what he was like, or is like. Are you friends with him now?"

"My husband and I lost track of him after he went into the Army. Kyle and I were both friends with Bobby in high school."

"I had hoped to speak with both of you, but would you mind sharing what you remember about Bobby Lee?"

"Okay. Let me think. Where to start? We were in a lot of classes together. Same age and all. But we really became friends in History Club. We were different from the other kids, being interested in history. Believe me, there were not many kids in History Club. We three were the most loyal. Bobby and I were very shy. Kyle was more outgoing and outspoken. Mr. Coldiron was very good at starting controversial discussions and even Bobby would join in. He couldn't help himself, because he felt so strongly."

"About what?" asked Sam.

"War. Any war at first, but eventually World War I, II, Korea and Vietnam. What caused the war. U.S. involvement. Isolationism. Nuclear warfare."

"What were his views?"

"Those changed over the years, as did Kyle and mine, although not always at the same time. At first Bobby was very gung ho patriotic. Gradually, he became more of a pacifist. But he wasn't an isolationist or neutral. He didn't see how the United States could avoid being involved in the problems of the rest of the world, even if it meant military involvement."

"Were you surprised when he joined the Army?"

"Yes and no. I was surprised at first and a little hurt. I thought we would all go to U of K together. But after he left and I went to college, it made a weird kind of sense. I think he felt he had to take action, that he'd studied enough, read enough books, and needed to do something."

"Were you two dating in high school?"

"Kind of. Not in the way I wanted, but he took me to Homecoming and Prom. We were just friends, and we went because I wanted to go. Kyle was dating other girls, mainly Mandy Samson, a cheerleader. She didn't like to hang out with Bobby and Kyle and me, because we'd get into serious discussions. We still would do stuff together, go to movies, just hang out at one of our houses, go on hikes."

"Did you try to keep in touch with Bobby?"

"I only wrote to him once and he didn't answer. Kyle and I went our own ways too in college, at first. I was scared to death, but I had the best roommate freshman year. Louisa Newton from Chicago, Illinois. She was a pistol and brought me out of my shell. We're still friends, although she lives in New York now. Anyway, I changed my major from history to business and saw Kyle in one of my classes. He still says he was completely blown away by the new me. We began dating, and moved back here after graduation. He went into his dad's real estate business, but I was determined to do something on my own. I worked in at least three businesses here in town. I learned something at each place, but I wanted a chance for advancement. I finally gave in to Kyle's pleas and came here to sell real estate. I was their best salesperson that first year, even better than Kyle, but he didn't mind. He was proud of me and proposed. Two years later his father retired and we took over the business as partners. And here we are."

"Have you heard from Bobby Lee?" asked Sam.

"No, not directly," answered Terri, "Kyle and I talked about getting in touch when we heard Bobby was back, but it seemed awkward. Oddly, I've never even run into him."

Just then there was a soft knock on the door. One second later, a tall, blond man peered around the door and stepped inside.

"Excuse me, but Alma said the Deputy had asked for both of us, so I thought I'd see if I was needed," Kyle Franklin smiled. First he shook hands with Sam; then he walked around his wife's desk and bent over to kiss her on the cheek.

"Hi, honey," he said.

"Hi there," answered Terri, "You'll never guess who we've been discussing. Bobby Lee."

Kyle had taken an identical chair next to Sam. His eyebrows went up and he blew out a sigh.

"Why are you asking?" Kyle looked at Sam.

"Bobby is a person of interest in an ongoing investigation," Sam repeated his standard response, "He's not under arrest. I'm just gathering information."

Kyle looked at his wife.

"How far did you get, hon?" he asked.

"History Club. Friends in high school. Bobby going into the Army. College. You and me getting married and working together."

"Do you have any thing to add, Mr. Franklin? Have you seen Bobby lately?"

"Sounds like Terri covered it. No, I haven't seen Bobby recently," he answered.

"Thank you both for your time, " said Sam, standing.

"Let me show you out," said Kyle.

When they got in the hall and Kyle had gently closed his wife's door, he said, "Would you like to see my office?"

"Sure," answered Sam, thinking it was an odd request.

A little further down the hall, Kyle opened a heavy wooden door to a much different office. It was as large as his wife's, but with an old, wooden desk, one wall of wood bookshelves, filled with books on history, real estate and fishing. In front of another wall was a long, brown leather couch with a large painting of a lake hung above it. A small fishing boat with two fishermen sitting in it was near a pier. On the far wall hung a flat screen television with two comfy armchairs facing it.

"I'm here so much that I like it to be more like home," said Kyle, motioning for Sam to sit down in one of the padded wood chairs in front of his desk.

"It's nice," said Sam, "Is that painting one of our lakes?"

"Not that I know of," answered Kyle, "I got it at a charity auction. It just looked peaceful." He paused, looking at the painting, then said, "Officer, I wanted to talk to you a little more about Bobby Lee."

Sam looked at him and waited. Kyle Franklin fiddled with a pen on his desk, and finally continued.

"First of all, I did see Bobby Lee several weeks ago. Neither of us had seen him in years, not while he was in the Army or when he came back. We did hear that he was back and that he got a job at Buffalo Trace. Both Terri and I felt awkward contacting him, partly because we're married now. Terri said they were not serious when she and Bobby dated in high school, but we weren't sure how he felt then or now. We decided we'd let him get in touch with us. Anyway one evening about three months ago, I had a business dinner at La Fiesta Grande. I happened to notice a guy at the bar who reminded me of Bobby. I walked past to get a better look and it was him. I almost said 'hello', but he seemed preoccupied, looking down at his drink. He looked terrible, grubby clothes, unshaven, except for his military haircut. I guess I chickened out, and I never mentioned it to Terri either."

"How did you and Bobby get along in high school?" asked Sam.

"We became friends of a sort in History Club. Bobby and Terri and me. We liked to talk about historical issues, kind of debate. What started a certain war. Why the U.S. was involved. Did we handle our side well? Were we honorable or practical or imperialistic? Stuff like that. I'll tell you one thing: Bobby never joked around. Sometimes Terri and I would see the funny side of something, but Bobby never did. He never laughed and rarely smiled. I asked Terri once before we were married why she went out with him. She said she liked him, of course, and they were really just friends. She liked that he was different. I asked her if she ever heard him laugh. She said rarely, but he did, kind of a soft chuckle. I liked him too, but I don't think I knew him well. He was smart about history and could make an argument for any viewpoint. He'd stay calm, no matter how strongly he felt. I was surprised when he went into the Army. He'd become such a proponent of non-violent tactics in civil disobedience and in world diplomacy. I always felt there was something in him that he never let anyone see."

"Did you ever go hunting together?"

"A couple of times sophomore or junior years. I'd forgotten that. Once we went out for target practice. He was good, a crack shot. He said his dad taught him, but his dad didn't like to hunt. Bobby is the only person I knew in high school who got a wild turkey. By senior year, neither of us mentioned hunting. He wrestled. I played baseball and was on the golf team. Just busy."

"Do you remember what kind of rifle he had?"

"No. Mine was a Remington. His might've been too. That was a while back."

Sam thanked Kyle Franklin and left. As he drove back to Versailles, he wondered about a successful man who was afraid to say hello to an old friend in a bar.

Chapter 23

Mac didn't hear from Sam on Monday or Tuesday or Wednesday. In spite of painting most of those three days, she was disappointed. And irritated with herself for being disappointed. The Lexington paper and radio rehashed the shootings and emphasized the fact that no one had been arrested. She knew Sam was busy and under pressure, especially from himself.

At 3:00 on Wednesday Mac decided to text Sarah and ask her to come out for a ride after school. Just as she picked up her cell, the house phone rang. If she had still been painting, she would have ignored it, but being in the kitchen right next to it, she picked up the receiver.

"Hello," she said.

"Hello," said a male voice, " Is this Mackenzie Field?"

"Yes, it is."

"Um, my name is Robert Lee. I knew your husband Bud in the Army."

Mac was stunned. She had received several letters and a few phone calls after his death and funeral from men who had served with Bud, but nothing in years.

"You did?" she answered, at a loss for words.

"Yes. I know it's been a long time, but I wondered if I could see you and just share a few things. Maybe we could meet for coffee somewhere."

"OK. When?"

"I live in Frankfort, but I could come to Versailles or Belleriver, wherever you like. I could come now, if that was convenient."

Mac could see her dad and Connor walking from the barn toward the house.

"Listen," she said, "why don't you come out to our ranch? My father and brother will be here, but we could speak in private, if you prefer. I can give you directions."

"I don't want to be any trouble," said Robert Lee.

"You're not."

Mac gave Robert directions and walked out to meet her dad and Connor to tell them about their visitor.

Forty-five minutes later an old, dull red pick-up pulled in front of the house. Mac was waiting on the porch with a pitcher of lemonade and two glasses on the wooden table. She watched the wiry, blond-haired man climb out of his truck and walk up the steps. He reached out a hand and said, "Hello, Mrs. Field. I'm Robert Lee."

Mac shook his large hand, returning the firm grip.

"Call me Mackenzie, please."

"Mackenzie. Thank you," he answered, sitting in one of the wooden chairs next to the table.

"I know this seems odd after all these years. I was over there six more years after Bud died and it's taken me awhile to get settled since I got back. Well, no, that's not it exactly."

He looked down and shook his head, obviously uncomfortable.

"Why don't you just tell me how you knew Bud," said Mac.

"He was a helicopter pilot. I guess you know that," he looked at her and gave her a brief, small smile, "I was a mechanic, mainly for the helicopters. Bud knew as much as I did. A few times we worked on his Chinook together. He was a great guy. He told stories, mostly funny ones, about back home. He told me about you and showed me your picture. He had it on his instrument panel, so he could look at you any time he was flying."

Mac felt her eyes filling with tears and her throat choking up. Robert glanced at her, then away, but didn't apologize or stop talking.

"He was a great pilot. That's why I knew when they said it was an accident that it wasn't true. Is that what they told you?"

"At first," Mac answered, "but I kept asking."

She had to stop. The lump in her throat made it too hard to talk.

"So they did tell you he was shot down by enemy fire?"

When Mac nodded, Robert continued, "I knew the Chinook was OK, because we did a pre-flight check together. I always wondered if they told his family the truth. I planned on visiting you and his parents when I came back, but after six more years, it kind of went out of my head. Then I read about you being there when that racehorse was shot. Other stuff happened, but I finally decided to call you. Are his parents still alive?"

"Yes. They live in town, in Belleriver. I'm sure they'd like to meet you," said Mac, "What are you doing now, Robert?"

"You can call me Bobby. I live in Frankfort and work at Buffalo Trace."

"What job?"

"I'm in shipping. I mostly drive a forklift."

"Do you like it?"

"Yes. It's a good job. Good pay," Bobby looked away, out at the pastures.

Mac felt there was something else he wasn't saying, but didn't know how to ask. Just then the screen door opened and Connor stepped out. Mac introduced Bobby and the two men shook hands. She explained that Bobby had known Bud in Afghanistan.

"Fried chicken for supper," said Connor, "Would you like to stay?"

"No. No, thank you. That's very kind, but I've got to go. My mother is expecting me."

"Thank you for coming over," said Mac.

Bobby nodded, then walked down the steps and out to his truck. Connor stood next to Mac on the porch, watching him leave. They heard the screen door open, as their dad joined them.

"What did he want?" asked Connor.

"Couldn't you hear through the window?" said Mac.

"Some. You both talked pretty soft."

"He told me about being a mechanic on Bud's helicopter and what a great guy Bud was. What he really wanted, I don't know."

* * *

Mac's cell phone rang at 8:05 that evening. When she saw it was Sam, she stuck her brush in turpentine and answered.

"Hey, Sam."

"Hey, Mac. What are you doing?"

"Painting. How are you?" She thought he sounded tired.

"Still working the case. If we're getting anywhere, it's not obvious. How's the painting going?"

"Pretty well. Background is about finished and Zeke is blocked in."

"Zeke?"

"Oh. That's his barn name. Everyone at Blake's calls Cat on Fire 'Zeke'. Almost all registered horses have a barn name. Something shorter, usually affectionate."

"Like a nickname."

"Yeah."

"Is it too late to come out? Thought I'd call first."

"It's fine. Come on out."

Sam knocked on the door twenty minutes later. Mac opened the door and asked, "Porch or living room?"

"Porch, if that's OK with you."

"Want some chocolate chip ice cream?"

"Sure. Thanks."

Sam was sitting on the porch swing, gently pushing it with his boot. Mac handed him a bowl heaping with ice cream and chocolate sauce. She sat in the swing too, and began eating her smaller helping.

"Always feeding me," muttered Sam with a smile.

"You can thank Connor for that. He loves to cook and bake. He did not make the ice cream, but he bought it. Actually he loves to eat, so he makes sure we always have goodies around. Luckily we all seem to burn it off."

"Do you always paint in the evening?" asked Sam.

"Sometimes. I got interrupted this afternoon, so I needed to do some more after the dishes were done."

"Interrupted?"

"Yes. An unexpected visitor."

"Oh," Sam wasn't sure what to say. He looked at Mac's beautiful face, soft in the shadows. She looked sad. The only light was the moon, which didn't reach too far onto the porch.

"I was married, Sam," she said, "Bud and I grew up together. I was 18 when we were married and 19 when he was killed in Afghanistan."

"I'm sorry," said Sam.

"I don't know what you know about me," Mac began.

"Enough to start. Thought I'd find out for myself," Sam wanted to hold her and kiss away the sadness in her face, but he waited.

"I'm just telling you, because that's how I was interrupted. One of Bud's Army friends called and stopped by. It's been a long time since anyone did that, so I was surprised. Bobby was a mechanic who worked on Bud's helicopter."

"Bobby?" Sam straightened and stopped pushing the swing.

"Yeah. Bobby Lee. Probably named after…"

"What did he look like?" The urgency in Sam's voice startled Mac.

"Thin, short blond hair, kind of craggy and rough, needed a shave, muscular. Why? What's wrong, Sam?"

Sam leaned on his knees and ran his hands over his head, blowing out a deep breath.

"Damn," he said, "What did he want?"

"He just wanted to tell me about working with Bud. He was over there six more years after Bud died. What is wrong?"

"It took him this long to come and see you?" Sam was furious. Why was Mac tied up in this?

"I don't know, but being over there can really mess you up. Look. Nothing happened, so either tell me why you're so angry or just calm down. No. Calm down anyway."

"Mac, he's under suspicion for the shootings. Sorry. It freaked me out that he would come and see you. Can you remember what he said?"

Now Mac was stunned. She told Sam her conversation with Bobby Lee as well as she could remember it.

"Doesn't sound suspicious," said Sam.

"No, and he seemed like a nice guy, just kind of lost. I actually felt like he wanted to tell me something more, but he didn't. Just a feeling."

"Sorry I lost it," Sam sighed, "I liked the guy when I talked to him. He just didn't seem right for this, but isn't that what they always say about serial killers? Nice guy. Quiet. Maybe a little odd, but a good neighbor. Or a good tenant. Or a good soldier."

"Let's talk about something else. Or do something. Want to play checkers?"

"I haven't played since I was a kid."

They headed into the house, where there was more light. An hour later, Mac had beaten him twice and it looked like she was going to do it a third time, when his cell rang. He answered, listened, then said, "I'll be right there."

"Mac, I'm sorry. It's work. I have to go," Sam stood, bent over the checkerboard and kissed her forehead. Mac followed him. She stood behind the screen door, watching him run to his car and tear down their lane.

Chapter 24

Sam's call had been from the Sheriff, alerting him to a possible hostage situation in Versailles. There was definitely a shooter. Someone was holed up in his house taking potshots at his neighbors. A young policeman stopped Sam as he turned onto the street. Sam rolled his window down, showing his ID.

"Hey, Sam," said the officer, who Sam saw was Phil Patterson, a newbie to the department, "They're calling in everyone."

"How is it?" asked Sam.

"He's still in there. Hasn't shot at anyone in awhile. Name's Heck Martin. Just got laid off. Has a wife and little girl, but we don't know if they're in there."

Sam pulled in as close as possible to the police barricade and took his gun out of the glove compartment, slipping on the holster and making sure he had his ID in his hand. A small, yellow-sided house was lit up with car lights and two spot lights on either side. Other police cars in the alley behind the house lighted the back of the house and yard. Crouching low, he approached the barricade, where several police officers were behind their vehicles. Even with the strobe lights, he recognized Sheriff Dade, Mary Preston and Todd Lakewood to his left, so he headed toward them.

"It's not good, Sam," said the Sheriff as soon as Sam appeared behind him, "The police were called over an hour ago and they brought us in. A Patrick Johnson who lives next door was shot at when he took his dog for a walk, and he called the police. The immediate neighbors on all sides have been cleared out. An elderly woman who lives across the street thinks the wife and daughter are in there. The little girl is only four."

"Do you know the guy?" asked Sam.

"I don't, but some of the police do. His name is Heck Martin. He was in the military in Afghanistan or Iraq. Been home for five or six years. He worked at Pilkington, but was fired recently. Neighbors have called a few times in the last six months about loud fights between him and his wife. Evidence of abuse, but she would never press charges."

"No evidence of child abuse," broke in Todd Lakewood, "I asked one of the cops and they had checked that at her pre-school."

"Did someone call?" asked Mary.

"One of the teachers actually called about the mother being banged up, black eye, cut lip, bruised cheek. The teacher checked the kid, who didn't have anything worse than a skinned knee," Todd had been a deputy for almost twenty years. He was plump with a round, pink face that was normally disarmingly jovial. Tonight he looked angry and worried, like everyone else, " I will never understand guys who beat up on women. Never."

"I don't understand why the women stay with them," said Mary.

A male voice on a bullhorn broke the stillness.

"Heck Martin, answer your phone. We'd like to settle this without anyone getting hurt."

A rough male voice yelled, "Too late."

"Oh, shit," said Mary and Todd together.

Sam could see the Chief of Police Williams on a bullhorn behind the police car nearest the small yellow house.

"What do you mean, Heck? Are Lynnette and Colette OK?"

"You know what I mean. It's too late for talk."

A shot cracked the stillness and one of the spotlights shattered. They heard swearing from the cops huddled near the spotlight.

"Anyone hurt?" called the Chief without using the bullhorn.

"We're OK, Chief," an older male voice responded.

In the silence that followed, they could faintly hear a phone ringing inside the house. It was silenced abruptly. Sam could see a policeman holding a cell phone to his ear, looking at the Chief, and shaking his head "no". The Chief lifted the bullhorn to his mouth again.

"Heck, this is Trent Williams. We're here to help you."

"Bullshit!" yelled the man in the house.

"Come on, Heck. I've known you for years. I know you're angry. Tough times. No way for a soldier to be treated. But hurting your family won't help. Shooting at your neighbors won't help. You need to send Lynnette and Colette out. Get them out of harm's way."

The silence dragged on for five minutes that seemed like five hours.

"Get my mother over here. I want to see Colette going to someone safe," Martin's voice carried, but it was calmer, softer.

"OK, Heck. We'll get her."

The Chief turned to a woman officer nearby and motioned her over. After a brief conversation, while the male officer with the phone used it to find Mrs. Martin's address and number, the two police officers headed to the other end of the street.

"I hope she's not too far away," whispered Mary.

They waited a long half-hour. The police and deputies talked softly, watching the brightly lit house, readjusting their stiff bodies to different positions. Then the two officers returned with a little woman of about sixty in between them. Her hair was unnaturally brown, pulled into a long ponytail, and her face was lined with worry, but she walked steadily to the Chief. After a few words between them, he handed her the bullhorn and showed her the button to push.

"I'm here, Heck. Please send Colette out to me. I wish you would put the gun down and come too."

"I can't, Mom. Let me see you."

Before anyone could stop her, Mrs. Martin stood up as tall as she could and waved the bullhorn over her head, yelling, "I'm here, Heck!"

The Chief and the female officer grabbed her shoulders and pulled her down. There was no shot. Everyone breathed in relief, except Mrs. Martin, who was struggling with Chief Williams.

"Let me go! He's not going to shoot me!"

Just then the front door opened a crack and a tiny little girl with waist-length chestnut brown hair was pushed forward. She stumbled and blinked in the bright lights. There was still a slight opening in the door and they could tell Martin was talking to her, but not what he said. Colette looked back toward the door and then out toward the lights, saying softly, "Nana."

"Run to the cars, Coley," they heard Martin say, "Nana will get you."

The little girl was coming down the steps. Mrs. Martin hissed something unintelligible at the Chief and he led her to the end of the squad car, blocking her body with his. When they reached the small break between the cars, Mrs. Martin knelt down and called her granddaughter.

"Colette. Come here to Nana, baby."

Colette turned her way, walking uncertainly. She could hear her grandmother, but not see her in the bright lights. Suddenly, an officer in a bulletproof vest broke from the side, running toward Colette. At the same time, Mrs. Martin jumped over the bumpers of the two cars, and reached the little girl first, wrapping her in her arms. The officer, who was a very large man, swooped them both up and ran back to the car barrier on the side. Officers immediately surrounded them. There were no shots or sounds from the house. The Chief sagged behind his vehicle briefly, then pulled the bullhorn up to his mouth again.

"Thank you, Heck. Your mother has Colette. She's fine. Now, why don't you send out Lynette?"

"Maybe later. Would you please tell me when someone has taken my mother and Colette home?"

"Yes, I will. I think they will be going to the hospital first, unless an EMT checks her out here."

"I think the hospital would be best," answered Martin, "I'd like a doctor to check Coley. I didn't hurt her. I couldn't. But just to make sure she's not too scared."

The Chief spoke to the female officer again and she walked quickly through the other officers and cars to an ambulance parked on the perimeter. Soon the ambulance siren wailed, diminishing as it turned the corner and disappeared.

"Is she alright?" called Martin anxiously.

"Yes, Heck. She's fine. They turned on the siren just so Colette could hear it. Why don't you send Lynette out?"

There was no answer. Minutes passed. The Chief was raising the bullhorn to his mouth again, when a shot cracked.

"Heck!" called the Chief, "Heck Martin. Answer me."

Another rifle shot was his answer.

They waited five minutes with Chief Williams calling out to Martin every few seconds. Finally he signaled to officers on both sides to move in to toward the house. There were two on each side, all wearing bulletproof vests. One was the big guy who picked up Mrs. Martin and Colette. Sam thought he was Pete Jenkins, a veteran cop and brother to Brad Jenkins, the guitarist who was killed at the barn dance. Jenkins moved up to a side window, glanced in, then headed toward the front door. His partner had checked another window and was moving quickly to the back of the house. A cop from the west side of the house met Jenkins at the door. The second cop held the screen door open, while Jenkins backed against the wall on the other side and banged on the door with his fist.

"Open up! Police!" he yelled. He hit the door and yelled again, then grabbed the handle and pushed, keeping to the side. The door swung open and stayed there. No shots. No one appeared. The two men crouched low and entered the house, their weapons held straight-armed in front of them. Simultaneously everyone heard the loud knocking and yells of "Police!" at the back door. Three very long minutes of silence followed. Suddenly Jenkins appeared at the front door, gun holstered.

"Clear, Chief. We need two ambulances," he called.

Chapter 25

Almost two hours later Sam and the other eight Woodford County deputies present were manning the perimeter. Neighbors had trickled back or never left, but were not being allowed back into their homes yet. The press had arrived from Lexington and the Woodford Sun. Sam looked for Randy Bayard, but didn't see him. He listened to Mary Preston tell the reporters that the Chief of Police would not be making a statement for several hours. The ambulances had left before the Lexington press arrived, which an elderly man in the crowd helpfully told the reporters. They surrounded him and heard what Sam remembered: one ambulance left in a hurry with its siren blaring, while the other departed quietly. Just then Sam heard his name called and saw Phil Patterson hurrying toward him.

"The Chief wants to see you up at the house, Sam," relayed the young officer.

Sam followed Patterson back up the street. When he got to the porch of the Martin house, another cop gave both of them booties and latex gloves to put on. They walked through a very small vestibule and into a living room that was messy with furniture pushed out of position, magazines and toys on the floor, a spilled drink from a plastic cup staining the beige carpet. To his left through an open door, he could see a bedroom, where a female officer was dusting for prints and another cop was taking photographs. It held a queen-sized bed and a tall dresser that he could see, so he assumed it was the parents' bedroom. Sam followed Patterson into the kitchen. Blood pooled on the linoleum floor in two different areas. A white wooden chair was tipped on its back in one pool. Bloody slide marks ran down the lower cabinets to the other pool. More blood and brain matter splattered the cabinets and walls. Chief Williams and Jeff Parker stood to one side, blocking the door to the back porch.

"Hello, Sam," said the Chief, "Jeff here tells me you've been working the sniper case from your end, the horse shooting and the barn dance."

"Yes, sir," answered Sam.

"I might have some evidence for you," Chief Williams stepped back from the door. Jeff Parker nodded grimly at Sam and stepped into the enclosed back porch, flipping on the light. Sam followed him out into the small, cluttered screened-in area. It was filled with a cushioned glider, lawn furniture, a small grill and a long, wooden box about 5' x 2' x 2'. The box had a metal hasp and had been padlocked. The lock lay on the floor, obviously removed with bolt cutters. Jeff lifted the lid. Inside were two heavy-duty plastic rifle cases. Jeff lifted out the top one, and showed Sam that it was empty.

"The rifle that Heck used today has already been loaded up to go to the lab," said Jeff, "It was a Remington Tactical. He also has this beauty."

Jeff opened the case, so that Sam could see the Kimber 84M Classic rifle inside.

"We'll send them both to the labs and see if we can get a match for the bullets we've all sent," continued the Chief, "Find out if Heck's the sniper."

Sam was still looking down into the large box. Underneath the cases the entire bottom was lined with boxes of ammunition, including Remington .308.

"Looks like he turned himself in," said Jeff Parker, "Better than killing any more innocent people."

Sam looked up at the two policemen.

"How's Lynette? Heard anything yet?" he asked.

"In surgery. He shot her in the chest," said Jeff, "It's a miracle she didn't die outright."

They stepped back into the kitchen. Jeff handed the second case and rifle to Patterson and instructed him to take it to Samson.

"What happened here?" Sam asked.

"Some kind of scuffle, maybe over the gun. Lynette got shot in the struggle. Or maybe he just shot her. She bled a lot, as you can see. EMT said she was hit in the upper right chest, just off center, near her collarbone. She was unconscious, when Dunn and Fugate came in the back. She remained unconscious the whole time. Then it looks like Heck braced the stock of the gun against that table and ate the barrel. He stood with his back to the counter. The table is on the wall and that far counter fits into the angle made by the doorframe and the wall, so it braced the gun pretty well. What was left of Heck slid down the cabinets and was semi-upright when we arrived. The gun was on the floor pointing toward his body. Ramsey took about a million photos, which you can see tomorrow."

"We should get out of here, so Lester can do her work," said the Chief. The three men walked into the living room and a stocky, brunette female officer came out of the bedroom, carrying a large, black plastic case.

"Finished in the two bedrooms. May I have the kitchen now, Chief?" she asked. Her large brown eyes passed briefly over Sam.

"Yes, Officer Lester," answered Williams, "Patti, this is Sam Kincaid from the Woodford County Sheriff's Office. Lester here just finished extensive forensics training with the state police, but luckily, she's returned to us."

Patti Lester nodded at Sam, and gave her boss a big smile. She immediately headed for the kitchen.

"What do you know about Heck Martin?" asked Sam.

"I wasn't lying when I said I'd known him for years," said Chief Williams, "Let's go out in front. I could use some fresh air."

They regrouped on the front porch. The Chief turned his back to the street, and rubbed his face with one hand.

"There's over twenty years difference in our ages. His dad was a friend of mine from high school football. John was three years older than me, but when they put me on varsity my sophomore year, he took me under his wing. We've been friends ever since. I watched Heck grow up. His real name was Hector after a great-grandfather, but no ever called him that. He was their only child and they spoiled him some. Still, he was mostly a good kid, no trouble with the law. They were real scared when he went into the military, but proud. John died while Heck was in Iraq. Heart attack. They let Heck come home for the funeral. He came home for good five or six years ago, married Lynette, had Colette. He changed jobs three times, but I didn't think there was a serious problem until this past year," Williams paused. He leaned against the post supporting the small front porch with his arms crossed, and looked down the street toward the police perimeter. He was a big, barrel-chested man. He had dark brown hair, laced with silver, round cheeks and a double chin, but he wasn't fat, just large. His warm brown eyes looked into the distance, seeing only sadness.

"I wasn't in for the first call, but told my people to call me if they got any more. So I came to this house for the second call. Heck looked stunned when he saw me at the door. He let me in and was obviously embarrassed when I saw Lynette straightening up the living room. Her hair was a mess and her face was red with bruising on her jaw. She excused herself to check on Colette and when she came back, I could tell she'd put on make-up, fixed her hair. She absolutely refused to admit that Heck had hit her. She was a good actress. Insisted that she slipped on a toy and hit her head on the coffee table. Said the yelling the neighbors heard was the TV. I pulled Heck out here and tried to talk to him. I told him I'd listen any time if things were tough. He refused to admit anything either. Job was fine. Marriage was fine. Everything was fine. I didn't believe him and I think he knew that. I told him to call me first if he had any problems at all. He said he would. But this is what we get."

Chapter 26

Word spread fast that the police suspected Heck of being the sniper killer. Sam knew that would happen, but he didn't like it. He also knew Baptist Health Hospital wouldn't give out Lynette Martin's status, unless he could prove that he was a deputy sheriff, so he drove to Lexington late Thursday morning. After running a gauntlet of nurses, he got lucky and was allowed to speak to her doctor who was doing rounds.

Dr. Stephen Timmons was fortyish, dark-haired and olive skinned. He didn't look as tired as he should have after a two-hour surgery and probably as much sleep.

"I just left her, Deputy Kincaid," he said, "She's very lucky physically. The bullet went under her clavicle and out her back, but missed her spine entirely. I'm sorry, but I'm not giving you or any of the police permission to interview her before tomorrow. Family only. She needs rest."

Sam took the elevator downstairs to the lobby and walked outside. He followed the sidewalk around the huge building just to walk and think. He knew he was in the minority, but he didn't think Heck was the sniper. He half hoped that he was, so this could be over. Earlier in the week, he'd contacted the State Police's Intelligence Branch and given them Robert Ezekiel Lee and Randy Bayard's names. He hadn't heard back, but was hoping that they could find what he couldn't. He hadn't found anything on NCIC, or anywhere else, that he didn't already know about the two men. When he thought about Bobby Lee going out to the Quinn ranch and Randy following Mac, he worried. What was she, a magnet for messed-up men? Then he snorted and shook his head. What did that make him?

Sam walked back to his Woodford County vehicle and sat behind the wheel, putting the windows down. It was a warm fall day with a light breeze, but dim inside the parking garage. He pulled out his notebook and flipped through the notes he'd taken so far. He had bare bones on Bobby Lee and Randy Bayard. He'd tried to keep his interviews with their employers low key, so they wouldn't get fired for being under suspicion.

* * *

Bobby's boss Jesse Dunn liked Bobby. Said he was hard working and reliable. Apparently almost everyone at Buffalo Trace knew that Bobby had a crush on Letty, but it didn't seem like anyone teased him about it. Letty was nice and up front with him, so everyone else let it go. Jesse Dunn said there was no way he'd believe that Bobby would hurt Letty and that's what he told the Versailles police too.

When he talked to the editor of the Woodford Sun, Ms. Carrie Anderson told him that she hardly knew Randy Bayard. Three years before he'd brought in some photographs he'd taken around Belleriver and Woodford County, and she'd liked his work. He was strictly freelance and she did not give him assignments. The Sun had its own photographers, after all. Randy brought in photos about twice a month and she bought the ones she could use in that Thursday's edition. She said they had a business relationship and they didn't chat about anything but his photos. When Sam asked her what she thought of Randy, she looked startled and finally said, "He's young, polite and a decent photographer. To say anything else would be supposition." Sam thought she was an unusual newspaperwoman and he asked her to keep his visit to herself. She agreed. The Lexington Herald Leader's editor knew even less and said they rarely published Randy's photos. They had their own photographers, after all.

Sam had Bobby Lee's birth date, school records, doctor and dental records. Bobby had voluntarily requested his military records, but that would take weeks. Bobby's mother was living, but Sam hadn't interviewed her yet. Jeff Parker from the Versailles Police said that Bobby Lee lived in his mother's home in a small, separate apartment. Mrs. Lee had told Jeff that Bobby Lee was home the night Letty was shot. They'd had supper together, like they usually did. They had watched TV all evening and she couldn't remember what time Bobby left to go to his adjoining apartment, but it was after the late news. She was honest about Bobby going to Carl's Place most evenings, so that night had been a special treat for her.

He had less on Randy Bayard: birth certificate and school records up to mid-6th grade. Randy had been withdrawn from Belleriver Elementary during his 6th grade year and there was no record of him in the county until he began free-lancing for the Woodford Sun three years ago. He wasn't even registered to vote. No parking or speeding tickets. Neither paper had asked for his education or work records. They did have his Social Security number, a Kentucky driver's license and his home address in Belleriver. Sam found Mrs. Felicity Bayard owned the home and he assumed she was Randy's mother. He hoped the state police could find a lot more information on Randy Bayard.

Sam remembered what Dr. Timmons said about Lynette's family. He called Mary Preston.

"Hi, Mary. What are you up to?" he asked.

"Eating lunch at my desk. Very ritzy," she replied.

"Do you have time to find out about Lynette Martin's family for me, especially her parents, siblings, the people close enough to visit her in the hospital?"

"I can tell you a little right now," answered Mary, "Her mother works at Piper and James, her husband's law firm. She's a secretary and office manager. Mr. James still works there and is an equal partner."

"That's great. Can you get me their vehicles and license plates and the phone number of the firm, please?"

"Why don't I find the cars and you look up the phone number. You do have a smart phone, Sam. I'll call you back."

He did have a smart phone and used it to get the law firm's number. When he called, he asked to speak to Mrs. James and was told she had taken the day off. He got an incoming call just as he hung up.

"Mrs. Rose James drives a light blue Lexus and her husband has a silver BMW," said Mary, "So not too shabby. In fact that's his plate: NT2SHBY. Hers is normal." She read the number to him.

"Thanks a lot, Mary."

"Happy hunting, Sam. I have to deliver some papers, but then I'll see what I can find on the rest of the family."

Sam drove through the parking garage without seeing either vehicle. He finally parked where the empty spaces began, backing in so that he could watch new cars arriving. He didn't have to wait long. The blue Lexus with the correct plates passed him and parked just around the curve on the next level. A rail-thin blond woman with a pixie-cut emerged from the car. She faced the door to lock it and Sam saw her fiftyish face did not match her youthful frame and hair. He didn't want to startle her, so he stood next to his car, held up his badge and called her name. She did seem startled, but stood still and looked at him carefully.

"I'm Deputy Sam Kincaid, ma'am, from the Woodford County Sheriff's Office. Could I possibly speak with you now or after you see your daughter?"

"Could you come around and let me see some identification?" she asked.

Sam walked up the ramp and around the corner to the back of her car, holding out his badge and ID. She took the ID and looked it over, then looked Sam up and down.

"Have you had lunch, Deputy?" Mrs. James asked.

"No, ma'am."

"Then let's go talk in the cafeteria."

They walked in silence. Mrs. James was tall, about 5'10" and stood very straight, her shoulders back. She seemed confident, very much in control. When they got to the cafeteria, Sam chose a sub sandwich and an iced tea and Mrs. James got a chef salad. She led the way to a table in the back of the large room with no one sitting nearby. Mrs. James spread her napkin in her lap and took a sip of her bottled water.

"I imagine you'd rather be talking with my daughter," she said, taking a bite of salad.

Sam ignored his food and asked her how Lynette was doing.

"My husband and I stayed all night, but she was sleeping. She woke up about 6:00 am, when a nurse came in. We talked briefly, then we left to clean up and let her go back to sleep. Ken went in to work for a little while. I came here."

"What did you talk about this morning?" asked Sam.

"Just how she felt. If she was in any pain. We didn't try to talk about Heck or what happened. She was too weak," Mrs. James looked down at her salad and put her fork down.

"Can you tell me how you felt about Heck?"

"He was my son-in-law. I loved him. He was a good man and a loving father," she paused and sighed, "I know what you want. Was he the sniper? Two years ago, I would have said absolutely not. Now…" Her eyes filled with tears and she brought her napkin up to her trembling lips.

"I'm sorry, Mrs. James. I know this is hard. Can you tell me what their marriage was like?"

She wiped under her eyes with the napkin and sighed deeply.

"They met right after Heck left the Army and they married about a year later. They seemed very happy. Once Lynette told me that Heck had nightmares about Afghanistan, but he didn't want to talk about it. He worked at 84 Lumber for a while, then at Woodford Feed. He liked manual labor and was very good at fixing things around the house. Lynette worked checkout at the Kroger, so they were doing fine. Then she got pregnant and they were so happy. There were some difficulties with her pregnancy and she had to stop work and stay home for the last two months. She only had enough time to be paid for three weeks, so that was worrisome. We told them that we would be glad to help, but Heck said no. When Colette was born healthy, everything seemed wonderful again. They adored her. Heck wanted Lynette to stay home until Colette went to school, but she didn't think they could afford it. I'm pretty sure they argued about that. Lynette stayed home for two months, which was her maternity leave. They had Heck's mother to babysit, so that was the compromise. Heck was still working at Woodford Feed, but when Colette was two, he got laid off. Not fired. Cutbacks. His boss felt terrible and gave Heck a great recommendation. After about three months, he got on at Pilkington. That was a rough three months and he still refused to take any help from us. Lynette seemed very stressed and we didn't see as much of them as usual. I saw her with a bruise on her cheek once at Kroger. I was horrified, but didn't want to embarrass her at work. I tried to talk with her about it, but she laughed it off and said she tripped at the playground and hit her face on the ladder to the slide. Ken was furious, but I talked him out of confronting Heck. Now I wish I hadn't. Maybe we could have convinced him to get counseling."

Mrs. James teared up again. Sam handed her a clean napkin. The strong, confident woman had disappeared, leaving a grieving mother.

"How have they been in the last year?"

"Not seeing them as much has continued. We only saw them for special occasions, like holidays and birthdays. Heck wouldn't let us take them out for dinner anymore. Actually, I'm assuming it was Heck. Lynette always made some excuse. She stopped confiding in me. She'd only talk about Colette. And Heck was very quiet when we were together. I think he was only happy when he played with Colette."

"Has Colette seemed different?"

"Do you mean toward her father? No. They were crazy about each other," Mrs. James looked over Sam's shoulder into the distance, remembering some scene, "She was quieter. She used to be very active, kind of showing off for all of us, the center of attention. She would be playing with a toy, singing to it, then look at one of us and grin. The biggest smile ever. She loved to climb on us, the furniture, dance around the room… She's become much quieter in the last six months or so."

Mrs. James looked directly at Sam.

"Is that all? I need to see my daughter now."

"Yes, ma'am. Thank you. I'm sorry for your loss," answered Sam.

"When you talk to Lynette, will you try to be…" she paused, searching for a word, "… gentle."

"Yes," said Sam, " I will."

Chapter 27

On the drive back to Versailles, Sam put in a call to Jeff Parker, who answered.

"Jeff, it's Sam Kincaid. Any chance we can talk to Lynette Martin together tomorrow? I hate putting her through too many interviews when she's this fragile. Plus I'd like your input."

"Sure, Sam," answered Jeff, "I've been thinking this should be a joint investigation, anyway."

"Let's see where your Chief and the Sheriff stand on that, but I imagine they're leaning that way too."

Next he called Mac.

"Hi, Sam. Aren't you working?"

"Yes, but I have a minute to ask you to dinner."

"We'll have longer than a minute to eat, I hope."

"Me too. Pick you up at 6:30?"

"That would be great. See you later."

When Sam walked into the office, Mary Preston waved him over. She handed him one sheet of typed names and information, and looked at him quizzically.

"What are you so happy about?" Mary asked.

Sam hadn't realized he was still smiling. He tried to clear his face and said, "Just naturally cheerful, I guess. What do you have for me?"

"Right," Mary said skeptically, but she continued, "The James family is small. Lynette has one sister who lives in Lexington. She's a paralegal working on her law degree. Her name is Alicia Bennett and her phone number and address are at the top. Home and work."

Mary pointed to the information at the top of the sheet.

"The other names are possible friends and acquaintances from Lynette and Heck's respective jobs. I also included Heck's mother, Carolanne Martin. As far as I know she still has Colette."

"Would you talk with Lynette's friends on here? Do you have a copy?" asked Sam.

"Of course," said Mary, "That may add some names to the list."

First Sam called Jeff Parker again. He asked if Jeff wanted to interview Carolanne Martin with him.

"Sure, except you'll be joining me. I just called her and set up an appointment for thirty minutes from now. I was just about to call you. By the way, Chief Williams is going to call Sheriff Dade about the joint investigation."

Jeff gave Sam Mrs. Martin's address and Sam agreed to meet him there. Jeff's Versailles Police cruiser was parked in front of a small pale blue frame house, when Sam pulled in behind the car. Jeff got out of his vehicle; he and Sam headed up the concrete walk. A narrow strip of garden surrounded the house. The flowers were a mix of perennials and wildflowers, some dying, and some still colorful. Jeff knocked on the door, which had one small decoratively glazed window at head height with a peephole below it. He waited a minute and rang the doorbell, which played the standard chimes. The door opened on a chain. Jeff introduced himself and Sam and both officers held up their ID's. Mrs. Martin closed the door to take off the chain, reopened it and let them in, as she stood behind the door with Colette clinging to her leg.

Mrs. Martin picked up Colette and waved them into the front room straight ahead. The woman was very thin and short, about 5'2" and she looked exhausted, but not too tired to hold the little girl. Mrs. Martin sat on the worn gold brocade couch, pulling

Colette close to her side. Again she waved them toward two matching armchairs on either side of the couch.

"We are very sorry for your loss," began Jeff, "How are you and Colette getting along?"

"Fine. We're fine," Mrs. Martin answered.

Sam and Jeff looked at each other, wondering how they could question Heck's mother with Colette there. Mrs. Martin's hair was shoulder length, brown and wavy, held back from her face with a plastic headband. Her large, hazel eyes were red-rimmed with dark circles beneath them. Her thin lips were pressed together and turned down. She stroked Colette's long chestnut hair. The little girl leaned against her grandmother, looking down at her small hands in her lap.

"My neighbor will be here soon with her son," said Mrs. Martin, as though she had read their minds, "She's bringing Billy over to play with Colette in the back yard."

Just them the doorbell rang, and the woman and girl got up to answer it. Mrs. Martin moved as if every bone in her body ached. Sam and Jeff could hear soft voices and a small voice saying, "Hi, Colette." She must've taken the neighbor and son through a different path to the back door, because she returned in a few minutes to the living room and sank onto the couch.

"I'm sorry, but we need to ask you some questions about Heck," Jeff began again.

"Go ahead," said Mrs. Martin.

"Could you just tell us about him, what kind of boy he was like growing up?"

"Heck was a good boy, " she sighed and looked up at them, "I'm sure every mother tells you that. But Heck was. He was full of fun. He loved sports. He and his dad would go hunting; throw the football or the baseball. When he was little, I played too. I even went hunting with them a few times. In high school, he played football and baseball. Didn't make the basketball team, but he didn't mind. He wasn't the best student, but he got mostly B's and nothing lower than a C. After high school he enlisted in the Marines. He thought he'd just serve one tour, but he loved it and reenlisted. His father died when Heck was in Afghanistan and they actually let him come home for the funeral. It broke his heart to lose his dad. He went back over there to finish his tour, but then he came home. He probably felt he should take care of me, although I tried to let him know I was fine. I'm a bookkeeper, so I can always find a job; I work freelance now for a lot of the small businesses here in town."

Suddenly she stopped and said, "Would you please excuse me? I need to get a glass of water. Can I get you anything?"

"I'll take some water, thank you," said Sam, and Jeff added, "That would be nice."

When Mrs. Martin returned with a tray holding three glasses of ice water, both men worried that she wouldn't make it to the coffee table, but she put it down carefully. They each took a glass and drank. Mrs. Martin held her glass on her lap, taking a sip now and then. She looked at the wall behind Sam and Jeff, which was full of family photographs. They were mostly of Heck from infancy through family pictures with Lynette and Colette.

"What happened after Heck came back?" asked Jeff.

"He got a job at 84 Lumber right away, but didn't get along with his immediate boss. Frank Tomlinson was a little guy who had a chip on his shoulder. He was the kind of guy who resented military men, because he never would have made it in the service. He ragged Heck constantly. Heck could've joked or ignored it, if it was another employee, but he had no recourse with Frank. So he looked around and got a job at Woodford Feed. He'd met Lynette by then and they dated for a year and got married."

She got up from the couch, put her glass on the table, walked slowly past them and took two pictures off the wall.

"Here's their wedding picture," she said, handing it to Jeff, "and here's their family picture after Colette was born. It's a candid taken in their house, but I just love it." She passed him the second photo and he handed the first to Sam. Mrs. Martin sat back down on the couch. Her eyes were full of tears when she looked at them again.

"They were so happy," she said and tears rolled down her cheeks. She reached for a box of tissues on the end table and wiped her face.

"When Colette was two, Heck lost his job at Woodford Feed; laid off, not fired, but that was a blow. It took him three or four months to get on at Pilkington, so they struggled financially. He didn't like his boss there. He couldn't seem to please the guy. I don't know what the problem was."

Her voice trailed off. She took a sip of water, put the glass down and went back to kneading her hands in her lap.

"How often did you see Heck in the last year or so?" asked Jeff.

"Oh, almost every day. Every weekday, anyway. I take care of Colette. Lynn went to work later than Heck, so she would drop of Colette. Heck would pick her up around 5:30 or 6:00. Sometimes I would invite them all over for dinner too."

"How did Heck seem?"

"Quiet. OK, but serious. Except with Colette. She would run to him and he'd throw her up in the air. Or over his shoulder. He would hold her and hug her and carry her out to the car. Sometimes they would go for a walk and she would hold his hand. She would be talking a mile a minute, telling him what we did that day. I don't know what went wrong. I didn't see this coming."

Mrs. Martin was crying again, sobbing, with her face in her hands.

"Is there anyone we can call to come over and be with you?" Sam was leaning forward, almost rising to join her on the couch.

"I'm sorry," she said, grabbing more Kleenex and blotting her eyes, "I'm so sorry." Abruptly she straightened and sighed deeply, "I'll be alright. I have to be. For Colette."

"We're very sorry for upsetting you," said Jeff, "But if you think of anything we should know, please call either Deputy Kincaid or myself."

Mrs. Martin rose as the two men did and looked at them steadily.

"I'll be thinking about this for the rest of my life," she said.

Chapter 28

Sam pulled in the long gravel lane and looked at the now familiar ranch house, as he drove toward it. White wood with green shutters, three stories, five tall windows along the second floor front, a lot of windows on every side except the north, a porch around the front and the east side, a mix of perennials, forsythia and burning bushes along the base of the porch, evergreen bushes along the west side. The big barn and out buildings were white with green trim as well. It all looked warm, comfortable and well kept. The people who lived here loved this place. It surprised Sam that it felt like he was coming home.

Just as he stopped in front, Mac opened the door and waved.

"Come on in," she yelled. She was grinning at him as he climbed the steps and she held open the door.

"Do I need to change?" she asked. She had on dark jeans, the bootlegs over black and silver Western boots and a turquoise shirt with black snaps and black and silver scrollwork on the yoke. Her long auburn hair hung in soft waves past her shoulders and down her back, held back from her face with black and silver barrettes. Sam thought she was beautiful, but was puzzled by her question and frowned a little.

"Whoa," she reacted, "I guess that's a 'yes'. Where are we going, so I can be appropriate?" She turned to head upstairs, looking at him over her shoulder. Her green eyes sparkled at him and Sam almost grabbed her.

"You're fine," he said instead, "I mean, you look great! Ready to go anywhere. I'll let you know ahead of time, if we're heading for Paris."

Mac grinned at him again. He'd never seen her smile so big. As he held the door for her, she called, "We're leaving, Dad."

From another part of the house came, "Have fun!"

He held the car door for her too, which she mentioned when he settled in the driver's side.

"I haven't had anyone hold a door for me since high school," she said, "Except going in or out of a store. I'm never sure what I think about it. I'm perfectly capable of opening my own door, but it still seems nice."

"It's a gesture of respect," said Sam.

"Maybe. But you wouldn't do it for a guy," Mac responded.

"No," Sam laughed, "I guess it's old school from when women were meant to be pampered and taken care of."

"Yeah, like when they made all their own clothes, churned butter, baked bread, washed clothes in a tub…"

"All that easy stuff, not like men's work. Plowing fields, chopping wood, hunting…"

"Oh, and having babies!"

"That's not fair. Men can't do that!"

They were both laughing and continued to compare men and women's roles as they drove into Versailles.

"I think the women who were pampered were few and far between," said Sam, "Different time periods and usually upper class. Like Marie Antoinette."

"Well, look what happened to her!" exclaimed Mac.

Sam had stopped the car and Mac smiled again when she saw where they were.

"Addie's! I love Addie's! Haven't been here in ages."

"We can come anytime," said Sam, "Maybe we can convince Connor and Sarah to come with us sometime."

"No problem there," smiled Mac, "Sarah is going to be jealous."

A lovely white-haired woman greeted them and turned them over to a young, black-haired waitress with huge brown eyes accented with eyeliner and a silver nose ring. She also had three earrings in each ear, all silver rings with varying engraved patterns. In spite of her youth and taste in accessories, she turned out to be a very good waitress named

Cari. She seated them at a table for two by a window that looked out on lawn and trees. She brought them glasses of water and asked if they would like drinks from the bar first. Sam and Mac both said they'd wait until they ordered their meals. As soon as they folded their menus, Cari returned.

"I'd like the chicken breast with wine," said Mac,pointing at the menu, "and house dressing on my salad. White wine, please. A Riesling, if you have it."

Cari handed her the wine menu and Mac found what she wanted.

"I would like the sausage and kale pasta, please," said Sam, "House dressing and a glass of this burgundy."

"Very good," said Cari and disappeared with the menus.

"How's the painting going?" asked Sam.

"Very well," Mac smiled at him.

"Why?" he asked, so she would keep talking.

"I've never had anyone ask that before," Mac said, "Do you really want to know?"

Sam nodded and answered, "Yes."

"Well, partly it's that I have a lot done. The background is finished and I'm working on Zeke."

"Is it more fun to work on the main part of the painting?" asked Sam.

"Maybe. When I paint anything, the image becomes lines and shapes and colors, brushstrokes. It isn't grass or bark or skin or mane. I'm up close for the actual painting, then I step back and I can see if it's becoming what I want it to be. So for part of the time, I forget the horse and his pasture, then I look from a distance and there they are."

"Wow," said Sam, "It sounds a little like magic. I don't see how you can forget the images."

"I suppose they're in the back of my mind, but every brushstroke has to be alive or the horse won't be. Up close the images disappear. I'll show you sometime."

Their salads arrived and they ate in silence. Sam felt completely comfortable. He just kept looking up at Mac, enjoying what he saw, especially when she had to push a piece of lettuce into her mouth with her finger.

Sam had nearly finished his salad, when he asked, "What's the other part?"

"What other part?" asked Mac, looking up at him.

"You said the painting was going well partly because you had so much done," said Sam, "What's the other part that's going well?"

"Oh my gosh. You really listen!" Mac sat back in her chair and looked back at Sam in astonishment, "I haven't had to repaint anything yet. It just seems to be flying out of my brush. The colors. The textures. The movement. It's been fun and it feels alive. Every brushstroke. That's what I always want, but it isn't always easy."

She flushed and looked down at her salad.

"That's wonderful," said Sam, "I don't know that I've ever felt that way about my work. Or anything."

"Well, how did you become a deputy?" Mac asked.

"That's actually thanks to Jeff Parker," said Sam, "He's with the Versailles police. I met him at college. My family is from Indiana and didn't move here until I was at the University of Kentucky."

"Why did you go there instead of to Indiana?" interrupted Mac.

"Wrestling scholarship. Jeff was on the team too, one year ahead of me. He was really good. We wrestled at the same weight and he beat me most of the time. Anyway, when he graduated Jeff came right back here and went into police training. My folks were in Lexington, but I visited Jeff over breaks too. I had no idea what to do with history and psychology degrees, but Jeff said they were perfect for police work. After I graduated, the first opening was with the Sheriff's office. I applied and here I am."

"How long now?"

"Mmmmm… almost ten years. Whew! Hadn't thought about that."

"OK, " said Mac, "I'm going to ask the big question, even though it annoys me when people ask me. Why aren't you married? " Suddenly she sat bolt upright and her eyes widened, "You're not married, are you?"

Just them Cari returned with their food, placing the steaming plates on the table. She asked if there was anything else they needed, and Sam gave her a big smile and said "No".

"That's your answer, too," he grinned at Mac and took a big bite of pasta. Mac was looking down at her food and blushing. Sam chewed slowly and swallowed.

"To answer your first question, it's the same old answer. I haven't dated anyone who made me want to get married. So far."

They ate in silence for a while, only commenting on how good the food was. Then Sam paused and asked, "Why haven't you remarried?"

"Bud and I had been together for so long, but only married for a year and most of that time he was in Afghanistan. We had been friends since third grade, and then dated in high school, so it kind of felt like we'd been married longer. When Bud was killed, it was like an earthquake. It felt like my whole life, all of our plans had been ripped away from me. I thought nothing mattered, so I didn't go back to college. I stayed on the ranch and drew and painted. I groomed Sprint and rode a little, but mostly I just painted animals. I eventually started helping with chores. My dad and Connor were wonderful. So patient. And I know it hurt them to lose Bud too. About a year later, I ran into Mr. Laska, my high school art teacher. I started taking his adult painting class. A few months later, he brought a couple of horse owners to see my work and that started what I do for a living now. Since then, same answer: I haven't met anyone who made me even think about marriage. So far."

She looked at Sam and he looked back; both had soft, but serious expressions that they held for a few moments. Then they resumed eating. Sam's plate was soon empty. Mac pushed her plate away with just a small pile of noodles left. They both leaned back in their chairs, Mac rubbing her abdomen.

"Whew! I'm full!" she said.

Cari returned to take their dishes and asked if they would like dessert. Sam looked at Mac and cocked his head.

"I'm not sure," answered Mac.

"Could we have a few minutes?" Sam said to the young waitress. To Mac, he said, "Let's finish our wine and think about it."

Mac took a sip of her wine and asked, "Do you like being a deputy?"

"Yes," Sam answered, "It's not usually this stressful. There haven't been many murders during my ten years and they were all pretty cut and dried. Not this complicated with multiple deaths."

Sam paused. His hands were folded together on the table, his thumbs rubbing each other. His expression was serious, almost frowning. Mac waited.

"I went to Letty's memorial service on Tuesday morning. It was sad, of course. What a waste. And her poor parents. Another funeral tomorrow: Brad Jenkins. We'll have deputies there. I'll probably go, if I can. Heck Martin's will be next week, I imagine. Sorry. I didn't mean to ruin the mood."

Mac reached across the table and touched his big hands. He wrapped her small hand in his.

"I don't think I want any dessert," she said, "Let's go."

When they were back in Sam's car, he said, "I'm sorry. I didn't plan past dinner. Any ideas?"

"Let's go back to the ranch. I have something we can do there."

When they reached Mac's place and got out of the car, she took Sam's hand and lead him to the barn. Inside she grabbed a box of grooming tools and handed it to him, while she carried her own. She put her tote down outside Sprint's stall and took Sam into the stall next door. Inside was a huge (to Sam) black mare with no white markings at all.

"This is Mara, one of our broodmares. She's getting up there and we may not breed her anymore. She's imposing, but very sweet."

Mara had lifted her head up from her hay and smelled Sam's face. He slowly stroked her neck and she put her head back down to the hay. Mac pulled a rubber tool from the plastic box and showed Sam how to curry the mare's body in circles from the neck to the rump and up and down the legs.

"Just do that on both sides. I'm going to curry Sprint. Put your hand on her rump when you go behind her."

Mac left him in the stall with Mara and went to work on her buckskin. She peeked over his back now and then to see how Sam was doing. He seemed fine, rubbing firmly. She saw him change sides touching Mara as he walked around her. Suddenly he laughed.

"What's she doing?" he asked, staring at Mara's head, which was up in the air. Her neck was stretched and arched toward Sam. Her lips were open and rolled back, showing her stained teeth. Her eyes were closed in bliss.

"Don't stop," said Mac, "You found her sweet spot!"

Sam had paused and Mara's head came down, turned, and she looked at him. He began rubbing the base of her neck again energetically and she stretched up in pure joy. Sam continued, grinning at Mac.

"Easy to please," he said, "although my arm is getting tired."

"A big tough guy like you should be able to go all night!" laughed Mac.

Sam did stop then and looked directly at her, blue eyes gleaming.

"I can," he said with a smile.

Mac blushed furiously and hid behind Sprint.

"Groom your horse," she ordered, half-choking on laughter.

Sam did. A few minutes later, he asked, "What's next?"

Mac returned to Mara's stall and exchanged his rubber brush for a medium bristle brush. She showed him how to brush the loose dirt and hair off, stroking in the direction of the fur. Sam accepted the brush from her, then cupped her face in his other hand and gently kissed her. Mac closed her eyes and sank into his warm lips. When they separated, she stepped back, smiled, and went back into Sprint's stall. She kept smiling as she brushed his golden coat.

"Now what?" called Sam.

"Want to do her mane and tail?"

"Sure."

Mac gave him a regular hairbrush and showed him how to brush in sections, holding the base of the clump of hair so that it wouldn't pull.

"Next time we'll clean their hooves," she said, "but that's not as relaxing."

"This is relaxing," answered Sam, "So this is what you do when you're stressed?"

"This, or paint."

After a few minutes of silence and brushing, Sam said, "Would you teach me to ride? I can pay you."

"Sure. And don't be ridiculous. I don't let Sarah pay me anymore. It's fun. I used to give lessons for pay before I made enough money painting. Don't have time to do it as a business now. Dad and Connor and I all help beginners if they buy horses from us, but just to get them started. Then we refer them to some instructors we know."

"Want to refer me?"

"Nope. And you haven't bought a horse yet. We'll just try you out on Mara. When's your next day off?"

"Probably Sunday. If nothing else happens."

"OK. Come out about 1:30 or 2:00. You can have a lesson. Then we'll ride. If you survive, you can stay for dinner. How's that?"

"Sounds great!"

Chapter 29

The tall, young man started his car the instant he saw Deputy Kincaid and Mackenzie walk back from the barn to the deputy's car. He'd been using his rifle scope all evening to keep an eye on them from a distance. He couldn't see them inside the restaurant, but he watched them go in and leave. Now he watched them kiss and his hands trembled. Quickly he packed the scope in the base of his passenger seat and took one last look to see that the deputy was actually leaving. He was. The lights of the Civic flashed on and the car made a half-circle turn and headed down the lane. The young man had turned off his lights and he drove a good half-mile and made a left at the next intersection before he turned them on. He drove about 45 mph on the country roads, slow and steady if there were any observers. His palms pounded a rapid-fire beat on the steering wheel, although he had no music playing. He was muttering to himself around his clenched teeth, the same words over and over.

"You die. My brother lives. You die. My brother lives. My brother lives."

By the time he pulled into his garage, he had stopped the rat-a-tat-tat of his hands. He leaned back in his seat and let out a deep sigh. He closed his eyes and his jaw relaxed.

"Time for a new day, Marcus" he said softly and clearly.

Chapter 30

Sam heard from Jeff Parker first thing Friday morning. Since Brad Jenkins' funeral was that day, Jeff had scheduled their interview with Lynette Martin at 10:00 am, well before the afternoon service. The two men drove separately and met in the Baptist Health Hospital lobby. When Sam walked in, he saw Jeff at the information desk. As he approached, he heard Jeff say, "That's good news." Jeff saw Sam and said, "She's better, still in intensive care, but we can see her briefly."

"That's good," said Sam. They walked to the elevators and Jeff pushed the button for the fourth floor. A stern-looking desk nurse asked a young nurse to take them to Lynette's room. At the door she said, "You have five minutes. I'll be back."

Lynette Martin lay with the top half of her bed angled up about thirty degrees. Her long blond hair framed her pale face. Her blue eyes opened when they entered the room.

"How are you doing, Lynette?" asked Jeff.

"OK. The doctor says I'm doing fine," she answered softly, "He's going to let me see Colette this afternoon."

"We have to ask you some questions, " began Jeff, "The doc says we only have a few minutes, so can you tell us what happened Wednesday?"

"What happened was Heck got fired from Pilkington," Lynette said. Her lips trembled and her eyes filled with tears, but she continued in a shaky voice," He came home early, about 3:00. I was off that day, home with Colette. She was down for a nap, luckily. He was furious from the minute he walked in, but sad too. I got him to sit down in the kitchen and tell me what happened. I hoped Colette wouldn't hear us. He told me his boss Mr. Fredericks blamed him for getting an order wrong and fired him on the spot. Heck said it was Fredericks' mistake, but Fredericks wouldn't admit it. He was given two weeks' notice, but he was so angry, he walked out. He heard Fredericks yell at him not to bother coming back."

Lynette paused, wiped her eyes with a tissue and took a sip of water.

"Then Colette came in, squealing 'Daddy', and he just scooped her up. He was crying by then, but somehow he pulled himself together, and took her out in the backyard to play. I fixed dinner. We ate. Then we went in the living room and watched Little Mermaid for the hundredth time. Heck just held Coley on his lap. I saw him wipe his eyes now and then, but he held it together. We put her to bed about 8:00. I tried to talk to him. I told him everything would be all right, but he just stared at me like he didn't know who I was. Then he got up and went into the basement. Told me to leave him alone. So I did. Washed the dishes. Went upstairs and took a shower. I read for a while, but when he didn't come up, I went downstairs. Found him in the kitchen with his rifle, trying to brace it up against the table so he could..."

Lynette put her face in her hands and sobbed. Just then the young nurse walked into the room; as soon as she saw Lynette crying, she started to hustle the two officers out of the room.

"No. No," cried Lynette, "I'm all right. Please let them stay. I need to finish telling them what happened." She wiped her eyes again and blew her nose, giving the nurse a feeble smile. The nurse looked at Lynette steadily, nodded, and stared at Jeff and Sam sternly. Then she left.

"I tried to get the gun away from him," Lynette went on more strongly, "We fought over it, which was stupid, I know. I jerked it down as hard as I could and it went off. I don't know whose finger hit the trigger, but that's how I was shot."

Jeff and Sam glanced at each other and back at Lynette.

"You're sure, Lynette?" asked Jeff.

"Oh, yes," she answered, "I fell back and hit the cabinets or the counter and I was out. I don't know anything that happened after that, except what my mother told me. But I do know that Heck didn't shoot me on purpose. So please tell the Sheriff and Chief Williams and everyone. He didn't shoot me on purpose!"

Lynette's blue eyes were overflowing again.

"We'll tell them," Jeff promised, "I'm so sorry, Lynette."

"We'll let you get some rest," said Sam, "We will have to come back, Lynette, and ask you some more questions. We're very sorry for your loss."

As Sam and Jeff walked down the hallway together, Jeff said, "I'm getting tired of saying those words."

"Yeah," said Sam, "all day today."

When they reached the parking lot, Jeff asked, "Does what Lynette said change how you're looking at this?"

"Well, it makes it look like Heck was more suicidal than homicidal," said Sam, "But it's too soon. I'm still going to have to ask her where he was on the nights of the other shootings. I'm not looking forward to that."

"No, she's upset enough, but I'm sure she'll figure out what people are thinking, if she hasn't all ready," answered Jeff, "Listen, Sam, I'm going to call that Mr. Fredericks at Pilkington. Want to go out there with me?"

"Depends on when. I'm going to the Jenkins' funeral at 1:00."

"I am too. I'll see if I can arrange it for 3:30 or so."

Jeff walked away a few steps, talking on his cell phone. Sam waited, leaning on Jeff's police cruiser and watched cars coming and going in the lot. He saw a white Camry pull out of the lot and turn left. He knew Randy Bayard drove a white Toyota Camry. Trouble was so did a lot of other people. And there were a lot of white cars similar to the Camry. Oddly enough, Bobby Lee drove an old, white Ford Escort, but it was so banged up, it was easier to spot. Sam watched the white car until he couldn't see it anymore. Then Jeff walked back to him.

"We have an appointment at 4:00. Is that OK?" he asked.

"Should give us enough time," said Sam and walked the few rows to his car.

Sam and Jeff sat together at Brad Jenkins' funeral, along with several other men and women from law enforcement, including Sheriff Dade and Chief Williams. The tiny Church of Christ was packed; people, black and white, stood in the back and the side aisles, leaving only the center aisle free for the casket and the minister. Several people spoke about Brad, especially his uplifting guitar playing. Lester Millhouse spoke last, simply saying, "This is for Brad. We'll miss you." Then he played a lively, bluesy version of "Sing Low, Sweet Chariot" with his wife Mary and two middle-aged black men singing the well-loved verses. Soon the whole congregation was singing, as six men, three white and three black, carried Brad's casket from the church. Sam found himself unable to sing as the casket passed by, from a lump closing his throat. Everyone liked Brad and loved his music; this was an irreplaceable loss and a terrible waste. He knew hundreds of people felt the same way about Letty Akers. Anger welled up in him again and settled in his gut like a burning coal. Somehow, he didn't think he'd feel that way, if he was sure Heck Martin was the killer.

Sam and Jeff drove separately to Pilkington off Highway 60 in Versailles. Preston Fredericks' office was on an upper level of the warehouse with large windows on three sides. His secretary, a middle-aged brunette with too much makeup (in Sam's opinion), sat at a large wooden desk that took up most of the room in front of Fredericks' office, which was clearly labeled Manager and his name below that. The secretary said he would be right with them and he was. His office door opened and a short, stout, balding man with dark-framed glasses motioned them in. He didn't shake hands, but moved behind his much newer desk, and began without preamble.

"I understand you're here to discuss Hector Martin. Unfortunate. Very unfortunate. He worked here in the warehouse and was fired that day. We here at Pilkington have expressed our condolences to his family. We sincerely hope his being fired had nothing to do with his decision to… to end his own life."

"Why?" asked Sam.

"Why? What do you mean 'why'?" spluttered Mr. Fredericks.

"Sorry," said Sam, "I meant why was Mr. Martin fired?"

Mr. Fredericks wasn't pleased with that question either.

"That's private Pilkington business," he answered.

"Not anymore," said Jeff, "Mr. Fredericks, we are investigating a suicide and we need for you to tell us why Heck Martin was fired. I don't think he'll mind."

"It had been a long time coming," huffed the perspiring, little man, "I tried to prevent it, but it was one thing after another with him. Broken glass – an order ruined. Coming in late without a legitimate excuse. Not getting along with other workers. Being disrespectful to me. On and on. When he first came, I thought he could move up to assistant manager, but that didn't happen. It was very discouraging. And that last day, he mislaid an order. It was supposed to have gone out the day before and it took us all day to find it. It was the last straw."

Preston Fredericks' face was red, dripping with perspiration, and he was breathing heavily.

"Would you like a drink of water, Mr. Fredericks?" asked Jeff.

"Yes, that's a good idea," said the manager, pressing a button on his phone, "Mrs. Dennison, would you please bring us some water."

"Mr. Fredericks," continued Sam, "do you have written reports of these incidents?"

"Uh, yes, I do. Company policy requires it for justification of a firing."

"I'd like to see those, please," said Sam.

Mr. Fredericks looked even more nervous and irritated, but rose from his chair and went to a filing cabinet on the back wall. There were five cabinets side-by-side. While he was there, his secretary returned carrying a tray with a pitcher of iced water and three glasses. She placed it carefully on her boss's desk, which was clear of any papers, and only held a calendar, a computer, a stapler and a tape dispenser. Mr. Fredericks nodded at her in dismissal, handed Sam a file and poured himself a glass of water, drinking it immediately. Sam took his time reading the reports, and handed the file to Jeff, who read them carefully as well.

"I noticed that Mr. Martin only accepted partial responsibility for the broken glass, because he claims his co-worker dropped his end first, which story the co-worker supports," said Sam, "And both men offered to make restitution."

"Well, yes, but we have insurance, so the company covered it," said Mr. Fredericks.

"And on all of these other reports," continued Sam, "Mr. Martin wrote above his signature that he respectfully disagrees with your written version of events. For example, he states that he should have been allowed a personal day to stay with his sick daughter, because his wife had all ready taken a day off work to stay home with her. He writes that you required that he come in or he would lose his job. He was late, because it took him awhile to get hold of his mother to care for the child. Wouldn't that be an excused absence?"

"Strictly speaking, it might have been," Preston Fredericks replied stiffly, "But he was a relatively new employee and I felt it was awfully soon for him to be missing work. We were very busy and needed him."

"I didn't see any reports referring to him not getting along with other employees," said Jeff.

"The employees in question declined to file a grievance. But they didn't like him," stated Mr. Fredericks.

"We'll need the names of any employees who worked with Mr. Martin on a regular basis and their phone numbers," said Sam, " I noticed there are two incidents reported in which you felt Mr. Martin was being disrespectful, but he wrote that it was simply a difference of opinion. You have no quotes from him, but you wrote that he used a disrespectful tone."

"He did use a disrespectful tone and he was in no position to disagree with his boss," Mr. Fredericks was getting worked up again, "That's insubordination."

Sam and Jeff both stared at the manager, until he lowered his eyes.

"We will need copies of these reports, as well," said Jeff.

"Is that all?" asked Mr. Fredericks, who was visibly trembling with anger.

"For now," said Sam.

When Sam and Jeff walked into the parking lot, Jeff shook his head and said, "What a prick."

"He's a sorry excuse for a human being," agreed Sam, "Maybe we should interview his boss, as well."

Jeff grinned for the first time that day.

"Maybe," he said, "That can be arranged."

Chapter 31

Sam called Mac as he drove back to Versailles.

"Sorry for the short notice, but is it OK if I come out tonight?"

"Yes," said Mac, "I have the feeling this is pretty standard for a deputy sheriff."

"What's pretty standard?"

"Short notice. Dates interrupted. Too busy to call," she mused.

"Actually, this is not the norm for my work life. I guess you'll have to wait and see. Seven o'clock all right?"

"You'll miss supper. I'll save you a plate. We can play cards with Sarah and Connor."

"Sounds good. See you then."

Freshly showered and wearing jeans and a plaid flannel shirt, Sam arrived at 6:55 to find they'd waited for him before having dinner. He was a little embarrassed and apologized for holding them up.

"I'm fainting from hunger. Never again, Sam," said Sarah.

"Yeah, I had to finish chores before eating. I'm worn out," Gabe grinned at him, "but Mac wouldn't have it any other way."

"Dad, that's not true! It was Connor's idea," Mac objected.

"It was my idea," admitted Connor, "I wanted the men to outnumber the women!"

"Three to two's not a problem," stated Sarah, "Mac and I easily equal four or five men in intelligence!"

Connor shook his head, smiling.

"It was an easy meal to hold, Sam. I'll put the corn in to boil. Beans are ready. Hot dogs on the grill."

"And I made the salad," announced Mac.

"About the only thing she can cook," muttered Connor, who was promptly slugged in the arm.

Soon they were seated around the oval kitchen table, chowing down. Afterward, Mac and Sam insisted on cleaning up, while Gabe got the cards out.

"What's your game?" Sam asked.

"Hearts. Know how to play?" answered Mac.

"Yep. One of my favorites."

After a few hands, Sam was losing heavily and Gabe was winning.

"You guys are cutthroat!" Sam complained.

"Yeah, we kinda are," said Mac, dealing a new hand, "Dad is usually the winner. You should have seen it when Mom played. She was so sweet and innocent, then, bang! She'd shoot the moon or give you the Queen."

"When did you start playing?" asked Sam.

"I was twelve or thirteen, so Mac was nine or ten," said Connor, "Mom and Dad tried to be gentle with us at first, but that didn't last long."

"No tears over losing games in this family," smiled Mac, "I learned that with Go Fish and checkers. Mom and Dad would not 'let' us win. We had to win on our own merits."

"Real life lessons," said Gabe, putting the Queen of spades on the hand that Connor had to pick up.

"Looks like they continue," said Conner, "I'll take the rest, thank you. Sam, you still have a chance."

"You know who else loves cards?" cried Mac, "Aunt Tina!"

"We should have her out," said Gabe, "Haven't seen her since the Fourth of July."

"Want to come back tomorrow, Sam?" asked Mac, "I'll call her right now and see if she can come."

Mac jumped up from the table and went to find her cell phone.

"Is she your sister, Gabe?" Sam asked Mac's father.

"No, she's Meg's sister, Mac and Connor's mom," Gabe answered, "Mac lived with her most of the summer that Meg was sick. She'd always gone to Tina's house after school and Meg would pick her up after work. She was a librarian, the Belleriver head librarian."

Gabe suddenly looked tired, then stood up.

"I'll be right back," he said. He returned in just a minute, carrying a photograph in a wooden frame. He handed it to Sam.

"That's Meg and Tina," he smiled fondly, "Meg is the redhead, like Mac, and Tina is the strawberry blonde. They were in their early twenties there. She was about four years older than Meg. Married to Rod McCormick, a fireman. He died in a car accident only a few years after they were married. No children, so she kind of adopted ours."

Sam looked at the photograph, while Gabe talked. The sisters looked very different, but he could see some of each of them in Mac. Tina was fair-skinned and freckled, and even thinner than Meg, who was taller, curvier with darker hair and skin. They were grinning mischievously, Tina glancing sideways at Meg, who looked at the camera daringly.

"They're both beautiful," said Sam.

Mac came back to the table, smiling.

"She can come. Connor, you'll fix her favorite for supper, right? Oh, I love that picture," Mac looked at the photo over Sam's shoulder as she sat down.

"Where's the house in the background?" asked Sam.

"That's Aunt Tina's house in Belleriver," answered Connor, "where she and Uncle Rod lived. She still lives there, on Fifth Street, 402 S. Fifth."

They continued the game for an hour with Gabe triumphant and Sam second to last. Gabe headed up to bed, Sarah and Connor went to the living room to watch a movie, and Mac and Sam sat on the porch swing.

"You'll like Aunt Tina," said Mac, "She's a lot of fun, now that she doesn't have to discipline us."

"You're close to her," Sam said.

"Yes. She took care of me after school for years, until I went to Woodford High School. I also lived with her the summer that Mom was sick. We went through a lot together. She and my mother were best friends, as well as sisters. They were very different, but hysterical when they got together. Aunt Tina was the responsible big sister who took care of Mom and tried to keep her out of trouble. I guess Mom was a handful as a kid, curious and mischievous. I'll let Aunt Tina tell you the stories. I don't think she relaxed until Mom and Dad got married. Four years apart, and they were married the same year. Mom and Dad in May and Aunt Tina and Uncle Rod in September. Uncle Rod said he'd waited long enough!"

Mac paused and Sam waited for her to continue.

"I only realized a few years ago that Aunt Tina held it together for me. I only saw her cry once, at Mom's funeral. She was quiet, tears just rolling down her face. She was the one who held me, when I finally cried. And she'd already lost Uncle Rod a few years before. She's had a hard life, but she keeps going. She took in ironing and cleaned houses for years, because she could adjust her schedule to be home for me. She had Uncle Rod's pension, but she wanted to be active. After I went to high school, she volunteered at an animal shelter in Versailles. Now she runs it! She fosters puppies and kittens at home sometimes, so they get more socialization and some training."

"She sounds great. I can't wait to meet her," said Sam, "I might be late again. I'll try to call you. Don't hold dinner for me this time."

Sam put his arm around Mac's shoulders and pulled her into him. They sat that way, until Sarah and Conner walked out the door and sat in his truck, signaling time for Sam to leave. He kissed Mac tenderly, but some beeps from Conner's horn broke it up. Sam laughed and said, "Big brothers are a pain." He walked out to his car with Mac, kissed her again, and followed Conner's truck down the lane. Mac watched them until they went around the first curve, out of sight. She walked slowly back to the house, looking up at the stars, and feeling happier than she had in years.

Chapter 32

"It's hot enough for the baby pool," said Mrs. Wade, "Would you mind filling it?
Then we can have lunch and let it warm up a bit."

Lucy Wade liked to have twelve-year-old Mac come down and help her with two-
year-old Riley and baby Clara. Riley was a handful, all energy and noise, until he
collapsed for a nap. Mac had been coming down a couple of mornings a week since
school let out. She was good at playing games with Riley that helped wear him out. He
loved the small plastic pool, especially going down the three-foot slide into the water. He
was now trapped in a high chair, eating some Cheerios and throwing others, while he
waited for his lunch. Six-month old Clara was in her baby seat on the kitchen table,
watching her brother with large blue eyes.

Mac hurried out the back door, uncoiled the hose beside the porch and turned on the
faucet. When she reached the pool, she started to lift the slide out of it, then dropped both
the slide and the hose. Lying in the three inches of water left in the pool were four tiny
kittens, hopelessly limp. Mac lifted them out, crying, and laid them on the grass. She
dried her hands on her jeans, wiped her cheeks on her arm, and turned off the hose. Then
she ran back into the house.

"Mrs. Wade, could you go out and look by the pool, please? I'll stay with Riley and
Clara while you do. Maybe take a plastic bag with you."

Lucy knew that Mac was upset and didn't want Riley to know. She took a trash bag out of a drawer and walked outside. Mac picked Cheerios up off the floor while she waited. She heard the back screen door close quietly and Lucy beckoned her into the mudroom. Lucy looked very sad as she gently put her hands on Mac's shoulders.

"Mac, I'm so sorry you had to find them," she said.

"It's OK. Better than going out there with Riley and Clara."

"I've put them out in the garage and Matt will bury them tonight."

"Who would do that?" Mac's voice cracked with anguish.

"I don't know, honey," said Lucy, pulling Mac into a hug, "Someone sick and mean. I'm so sorry."

There had been other animal deaths that spring. Aunt Rita and her neighbors had been talking about it, sometimes within Mac's earshot. There had been two squirrels, a possum, and lots of baby birds, not killed by cats or hit by cars, but smashed, like a big rock had fallen on them. They had all been found in back yards or the alley. School bully Jed Parker found a stray dog with its head crushed and showed as many of the kids in the neighborhood that he could find. Mac missed that, but heard about it, of course. At first Mac though Jed might've done it, but decided he would have bragged about it to the other boys. After finding the kittens, she decided she would catch who was doing this.

This was the summer Mac was staying with Aunt Rita. She'd had to come in May when her mother was taken to the hospital in Lexington. She talked to Bud about it and they came up with a list of suspects. It was short. They'd known almost everyone in the neighborhood all of their lives. Oddities about people were well known and accepted. The Harley brothers often kept their hunting dogs locked up in kennels and runs in their back yard, but they didn't otherwise mistreat them. Aggie Putnam lived alone, except for about a million cats. She was not friendly to people, but she was ancient, and Mac didn't think she could drown kittens or lift a rock to smash a dog's head.

Mac and Bud both suspected Sherman Ames for about a week. He was a lanky, grey-haired and bearded man who wandered the town of Belleriver. Aunt Rita and her mother had already told Mac that he was harmless, but not to talk to him. He lived with his mother about two blocks away, closer to Bud's family. Mac had overheard old Mr. Pendergast call them "trash pickers". She had seen Mrs. Ames digging through someone's garbage one evening. Sherman wandered every day. If he found any kind of work crew out, he wanted to help. Most of the men tried to give him simple jobs, like picking up fallen branches, sweeping along the curb, raking leaves or shoveling snow. Mac and Bud followed Sherman for a few days, but didn't see him do anything unusual. He shuffled away from barking dogs, but petted friendly ones. They had pretty much decided that if he did anything bad, it was after they had to be in for the night. One afternoon on the Field's porch, they were discussing a plan to sneak out after midnight, when Mrs. Field came to the screen door and called them inside.

"I just got a call that people have been seeing you two following Sherman around town," she said, "Bud, is that right?"

"Yes, ma'am."

"Why in heaven's name are you bothering that poor man?" Alma Field looked as cute as a button, but she was still intimidating to her youngest son.

"We aren't bothering him, just watching him," answered Bud.

"He might be the one killing the animals," blurted Mac, trying to defend her friend.

"Ooooh," Mrs. Field drew out the word, then continued, "Listen you two, Sherman is a sad man. He came back from the Vietnam War different than when he left. He couldn't hold a job. His mother is in her eighties, but still gets around. They live on his disability payments and some help from the churches and neighbors. Anyway, he's never been known to hurt anyone or anything, so I want you to leave him alone. Understood?"

"Yes, ma'am," they said in unison.

Two days later, Mac and Bud were playing softball in the empty lot next to Mr. Hopps' house. The kids all called it Hopps Field; it was the perfect size for baseball or softball or kickball. Mr. Hopps was not a friendly old man, especially since Mrs. Hopps died, but he never objected to the neighborhood kids playing on his lot. Sometimes they even caught a glimpse of him watching them out a window or from the front porch, hiding behind his newspaper.

Mac was in left field, nearest the trees lining that edge of the property. When running to field a grounder, she noticed a face peeking out from behind one of the trees. She waited until her team was headed in to bat and called to whoever was watching them.

"Hey! Hey, come on out. You wanna play?"

The pale face and blond hair disappeared behind the tree.

"Hey," she tried again, "You. Behind the tree. Do you want to play with us?"

The kid took off running this time. She could only see his small frame, pumping legs and long blond hair blowing behind him. As she joined her teammates, Bud asked, "Who was that?"

"I don't know. Must be a new kid. I didn't get a good look at him."

"That's Randy Bayard," spoke up Jack Frazier, one of the youngest boys playing with them, "He's new on my block. Family moved from Lexington. They live in that big, old house down at the end. He's going to be in my grade in the fall. Mom took a casserole and pie when they first moved in. "

"Not very friendly is he?" commented Red Peak, knocking dirt off his cleats with a bat.

"His mom told mine that he's shy," said Jack, "I've yelled "hi" at him a couple times, but he always runs away."

Mac and Bud looked at each other, both thinking they had a new suspect. Fair or not, none of the animal killings had happened until the new kid moved to their neighborhood.

Mac tried to find and follow the kid, but if he saw her, he ran away. She walked by his house, but there wasn't any place to hide and watch. It was also three blocks away from Aunt Rita's, and the opposite direction from Bud's house. Bud walked with her sometimes and they rode by on their bikes, but that was definitely not good for surveillance. Once Mac thought she saw someone watching back from a second story window, but the sunlight's reflection was too bright for her to be sure. All she knew was that she hated whoever killed those kittens. That person was evil, even if he was a little boy.

One afternoon in late July, her dad picked her up and they drove to Lexington to visit her mom. On the way he told her that Mom had been moved to a new building with a pretty room. He called the place "hospice". His face looked unbearably sad and Mac could see tears brimming in his eyes. When she saw Mom, she could tell that her mother wasn't getting better. Mom smiled, wearing a Keeneland baseball cap to cover her bare head, and hugged Mac hard and made a fuss over all the drawings she'd brought. Mac and her dad hung them up around the room. They were all animals from the ranch and

Mom said it made her feel at home. That afternoon Mac knew Mom would never come home. She forgot about the new boy and just drew and painted as many pictures as she could for her mother. Mom died in early August and something inside Mac died too.

Chapter 33

Mac woke up, sobbing from the dream. She wasn't crying tears, but her breath came in shudders. The dream had seemed so real, as if she were living it again. She sat up and swung her legs over the side of the bed. She looked at her alarm clock and saw that it was 6:15, time to get up anyway. She drew a deep, shaky breath, then stood up and padded barefoot down the hall. As she splashed warm water on her face, she realized that she hadn't dreamed about her mother's death in years. Then she remembered the rest of the dream. The kittens. The little boy. Randy Bayard.

"What the hell!" she said out loud. Toweling off her face, and getting dressed, she went over and over the dream, which had awakened memories. That little boy was Randy Bayard and if he did kill those animals, then he was now a seriously screwed up adult. She had to tell Sam. It wasn't evidence, and everyone thought the sniper was Heck Martin, but what if he wasn't? No wonder she'd felt uncomfortable with Randy. And he'd remembered her. He said they were in grade school together. He hadn't been in her class. Probably younger. And she hadn't paid much attention to anyone else the year after Mom died. Wait. She was in 7th grade that year, and had transferred to Woodford County Middle School. So she wouldn't have seen him at all. She didn't remember him in high school either. What happened to that kid? She was going to find out.

When she went downstairs for breakfast, Connor was already flipping pancakes. Before she could ask, he announced, "Blueberry. Have a seat."

Her dad was at the table, reading the paper and sipping coffee. Mac decided to make herself some tea. As she boiled her water in the microwave, she thought back to grade school, trying to remember the teachers.

"Dad," she said, "what teacher has been at Belleriver Elementary the longest? Someone who was there around when I was there, 5th or 6th grade."

"Miss Tippet was there. She's retired, I'd guess," he answered, "and Mrs. Englewood still teaches and lives in town."

"Wow," Connor chuckled, "I remember Miss Tippet. All of the boys loved her, but she was strict. Some of the guys got in trouble just to get smacked with that ruler!"

"She taught 6th grade, didn't she?" asked Mac, "Boys that age needed a tough teacher. I wonder why she never married. She was so beautiful. And a good person."

Gabe cleared his throat, "I know the reason. Her fiancé was killed in Vietnam. They were high school sweethearts, like you and Bud. She is a very gracious, private person. Apparently, she never met anyone else she could love as much."

"I don't remember anything ever being said about it," said Connor, "She would have been in her thirties when she taught me, but none of us thought she was that old."

"Mrs. Englewood taught 4th grade, I think," continued Mac, sitting at the table across from her dad, "She was strict too, but very loving. At first you'd be scared of her, because she looked mean and she was older. She wore her hair up in a bun and looked like a crotchety old maid, but after a few days, you'd find out she was fun and a great teacher."

"She and her husband Larry have six kids," said Gabe, "So much for appearances."

Mac smiled at him, then at Connor, when he handed her a plate of blueberry pancakes and bacon. While she was eating, Sarah called.

"Sure you have the right number?" Mac answered her phone, "Did you want to speak to Connor?"

Connor looked over at her and smiled.

"Yes and no, I want to talk to you," said Sarah, "Any chance we can ride this afternoon? Desensitize Gus some more?"

"Sure. What time's good for you?" answered Mac.

"About 2:00. I have papers to grade first."

"Have time for a trail ride too? Bring a change of clothes. You can clean up here for supper. Remember Aunt Tina's coming."

Well, thought Mac, that gives me time for a little investigating. She finished her pancakes, rinsed her dishes, and took the phonebook up to her room. She found both the Englewoods and Miss Tippet listed, so she copied their phone numbers and addresses. She called Miss Tippet first, who seemed happy to hear from her, and made an appointment for 8:30 that morning. Next she called Mrs. Englewood, whose answering machine stated that her call would be returned.

Miss Tippet's home in Belleriver was a small, brick two-story that looked like half of a duplex, but the other side was missing. The yard was neat with a few old trees and spirea bushes surrounded the house. Mac knocked and the door opened immediately. Miss Tippet looked closer to fifty than sixty, although her hazel eyes were surrounded by wrinkles. Her hair was chestnut streaked with blond and some white. She was a slight woman, much smaller than Mac, but did not seem frail. She smiled at Mac and held the screen door open.

"Welcome, Mackenzie," she said, "It's so nice to see you."

"It's nice to see you too," Mac smiled back at her former teacher.

Miss Tippet led her into a sunny living room with flowered furniture in greens and pinks on a cream background. The walls were a soft yellow and the curtains were light green. A couch and two armchairs faced a wood-mantled fireplace. The walls and mantles were covered with photographs of children surrounding a few larger paintings of fields and gardens. Miss Tippet saw Mac staring at them.

"Those are my nieces and nephews and many of my students. I tried to take candids of the children, when we were on field trips. I update them every few years, because there are so many. I'm afraid I have favorites, which I shouldn't admit. Some of these go back to my first years teaching. You're up here, Mackenzie."

She pointed to a photo of a group of children surrounding a large, white draft horse. Mac was reaching up to pet the big head, while the horse sniffed her.

"I remember her," she said breathlessly, "She was the biggest horse I'd ever seen. A Percheron, right?"

"Yes," smiled Miss Tippet, "We went on a tour of the breeding farms around here. That farm bred Thoroughbreds, of course, but she was the owner's pet, raised from a filly. You all loved her the most. The owner even let you take turns sitting on her, but those photos are somewhere else. In an album, probably."

Mac looked around the room at the photos, feeling a little overwhelmed. As she turned, she noticed a small, framed drawing of a horse behind her.

"That's one of mine," she looked at Miss Tippet in surprise.

"Yes, you gave it to me at the end of the year. I could tell you had talent even then."

Mac blushed a little and smiled, touched that one of her childhood drawings was so treasured.

"Would you like some hot tea?" asked Miss Tippet, motioning to the teapot and mugs on the coffee table. There was a plate of Oreos as well.

They both sat on the couch, and Miss Tippet poured tea into two mugs, both likenesses of animals with their tails as the mug handles. She held a spoonful of sugar over the fox mug, and glanced at Mac, who nodded. They both sipped some tea, then Miss Tippet spoke.

"Go ahead and tell me why you came, Mackenzie. I know it's not to reminisce."

"I need to ask you about a student you may have had a year or two after me. His name was Randy Bayard. I hope you'll trust me that it isn't just nosiness. It may be important."

"I trust you, Mackenzie. Maybe you can explain more to me later," Miss Tippet looked thoughtful, "I had Randy in my class briefly, but only for two or three months. He was withdrawn before the holidays that year."

"Why?" asked Mac.

"First let me tell you my impressions of him," Miss Tippet paused and answered quietly, "Randy was a quiet little boy. He started our school in fourth grade, but still had no friends by sixth grade. He never volunteered in class, but when I called on him, he knew the correct answer. His work was accurate and very neat. He was a straight A student. I met his mother at an Open House we had at the beginning of the year. She was polite, but didn't want to talk about her child the way most parents do."

"You seem to remember a lot about him," said Mac, "You had so many students." She ate an Oreo, even though she wasn't hungry.

Miss Tippet laughed, "I don't have a photographic or eidetic memory, but I seem to remember most of my students. Certain ones are more memorable than others, and if they still live in Belleriver, that helps. Randy I remember for sad reasons. First of all, the teachers were concerned about him. As I said, he was smart, but not a show-off about it, and he wasn't geeky, if you know what I mean. He was good-looking, which is usually attractive to other kids, but that didn't seem to be the case with him. He had good physical skills, good enough to do well in PE, but he wouldn't play on the playground, and he wasn't in any organized sports. He was in a world of his own, but observed ours at the same time. At recess, he would sit by himself, and watch the other kids. At first we thought he might be borderline autistic, but his parents wouldn't allow testing. Besides, he didn't fit all of the criteria. Then he was withdrawn from school, no reasons given. Just that he was going to a private school. When we received a request for his records, it was from a private sanitarium in Ohio, a mental health hospital."

Mac stared at her former teacher, enthralled. Without realizing it, she reached for another cookie.

"Of course rumors spread around town," continued Miss Tippet, "The family had moved to Belleriver about two years before. Mr. Bayard was some kind of broker or financier and commuted to Lexington to work. Before that, they had supposedly lived in Cincinnati. They bought that big Victorian mansion on Willow Street, but they were not social. Their neighbors all had big homes and lots, too, and wanted privacy. People did say they rarely saw anyone in the front yard and the back was fenced in. No dog though. Apparently the yard work was hired out, but not someone local."

Miss Tippet paused, and sipped her tea.

"Then one night, a neighbor walking his dog in front of the Bayard house, heard screams. He called the police, who were there in about twenty minutes. The neighbor waited for them, although the screaming had stopped. He said the police were inside for about an hour, and during that time, an ambulance arrived. He and a few other neighbors watched Mrs. Bayard being taken away in an ambulance. The police left shortly afterward. None of the people gathered saw anything else that night. The same neighbor, who was retired and nosy, and a good friend of mine, saw Mr. Bayard put Randy in a black limo the following day. Two large men in uniforms and a female nurse accompanied the boy. This neighbor could not see Randy's face, but he appeared to go quietly. I have not talked with anyone about that since my friend told me. The rumor mill spread stories that Randy stabbed his mother. She returned to the house after Randy was taken away. The stories vary in motive and the weapon. It was not reported in any paper at the time. I don't know how Mr. Bloom managed that."

"Oh my gosh!" exclaimed Mac, "I had no idea. He is back in town. Do you know when he came back?"

"You had enough on your plate without listening to rumors," Miss Tippet replied, "I think he came back seven or eight years ago. His father had died that year. Randy moved back in with his mother. I've seen him a few times, always carrying his camera or the case. He is a handsome young man, and still polite. I was only close enough to say hello once, and he was cordial. He remembered me; in fact, he spoke first. He seemed pleasantly surprised that I remembered him. After the first excitement of his return, people didn't talk about him much. I gather he works as a free-lance photographer, but doesn't have to. His father left investments that Randy and Mrs. Bayard can live on. The house is still kept up. Can you tell me now why you wanted to know about him?"

"I've run into him a few times recently. I had no idea who he was. He introduced himself, and said we went to grade school together. I still couldn't place him," Mac frowned.

"I think you have remembered him, though, before you came to see me today. Something is troubling you about him, and what I've told you has confirmed your worries."

"True," said Mac, "but there's not much I can do, except avoid him. He just seems to appear at the most unexpected times."

Mac thanked Miss Tippet for the tea and conversation. Miss Tippet thanked her for visiting.

"Do come again, Mackenzie," the older woman said, "And for now, try not to be alone. Randy Bayard may just have very bad social skills, but I think you should be careful."

As Mac settled in her Jeep, her cell phone rang. It was Mrs. Englewood, who was home and agreed to see her for a little while.

Chapter 34

Sam had still not heard from the State Police about Randy Bayard, and he was getting impatient. He decided the grade school might be a good source, but it was closed on Saturday, of course. He was meeting Mac's Aunt Tina tonight, so he could ask her about teachers who were at the school back then. Maybe Tina even knew something about Randy. When he consulted a map of Belleriver, he saw that Randy's house was only a couple of blocks from Aunt Tina's. (Whoa, he thought, she's not my aunt. I'd better use Mrs. McCormick.)

Sam thought about his fellow deputies and people who worked in the Sheriff's office. No one was from Belleriver, but surely someone had a relative or friend from there. Todd Lakewood and the Sheriff had been with the office the longest, and were the oldest members of the staff. Sam decided to call Todd first.

"You caught me heading out the door, Sam. What can I can I do for you?"

"Do you know anyone from Belleriver, particularly someone who works at the school there?'

"I don't, but Mary Jane might. Hang on a minute."

Sam could hear muffled footsteps, then Todd's voice calling, "Mary Jane!" For a few minutes, he heard muffled noises, including male and female voices, but not what was said. Then Todd returned.

"Mary Jane has a cousin who has worked in the grade school office for years. Estelle Forrest. Mrs. You got a pen? Here's her number."

Sam thanked Todd, and immediately dialed the number. A little girl answered, but promptly brought her mother to the phone. Sam introduced himself, explained how he got her number, and apologized for calling on a Saturday. Then he asked if she knew a teacher who had been at the school for at least fifteen years.

"Well, yes," Mrs. Forrest hesitated, "but how do I know you are who you say you are? Can't this wait until Monday, when you could come into the school?"

"You could call Todd and Mary Jane Lakewood, and verify who I am," suggested Sam, "To be doubly sure, you can call me back at the Sheriff's office. I wouldn't ask if I didn't think it was important."

Sam waited as patiently as he could, sending another email to the state police. About five minutes later, his cell rang. It was Jeff Parker.

"Hey, Sam, I've got another interview set up with Lynette Martin for 1:00 this afternoon. I asked her if her mother could bring her and Heck's work schedules for the last month, and she said 'yes'. That OK with you?'

"Yes," said Sam, as the phone on his desk began to ring, "I'll see you there, Jeff."

Sam answered the landline, and was relieved to hear Estelle Forrest's voice.

"I have two names for you, Officer Kincaid, and their phone numbers, as well. Miss Lorraine Tippet is retired, but taught 6th grade for many years. She's quite brilliant, and in good health. She might even enjoy a visit. Mrs. Meredith Englewood still teaches 4th grade at Belleriver Elementary, and has been with us for at least twenty years. She has a growing family, so she may be busy today."

Sam thanked Mrs. Forrest for her help, and dialed Miss Tippet's number. The woman who answered the phone did not sound old, and seemed curiously delighted to have him come to her home. He arrived at her home about 10:15. A small, thin, but lovely woman with bright hazel eyes opened the door. Sam couldn't believe she was old enough to be retired. She asked to see his ID, and read it carefully, even though he wore his uniform. Then Miss Tippet invited him in, and asked if he would like something to drink.

"No, thank you," said Sam, following her into a pretty living room. The colors were bright and spring like, and the walls were covered with photographs of children. Sam smiled.

"I guess you loved your job," he said.

"Didn't your teachers love teaching?" Miss Tippet asked.

"Some of them did, I'm sure. I was a handful back then. I probably gave them more headaches than inspiration."

Lorraine Tippet smiled, "Sometimes those headaches are inspiration. Besides, the rebellious child is often better able to handle life. How can I help you today, Deputy?"

"I need some information about someone who may have been a former student of yours. It's partly police business, and partly personal, but what you tell me will be confidential. I can contact you, if it becomes public," said Sam.

Miss Tippet was looking at him intently and expectantly, so he went on, "What can you tell me about Randy Bayard?"

Miss Tippet closed her eyes, and leaned back into the couch.

"You are the second person today to ask me about him," she stated, "so I'm afraid this is more serious than I would like."

"Who was the first?" asked Sam.

"Another former student of mine. I don't know that I should reveal her name, but I will tell you what I remember about Randy."

"Mackenzie Field," said Sam. He tried to keep a poker face, but doubted his success.

"Well, I wish one of you would tell be what this is about," said Miss Tippet forcefully.

"I'm dating Ms. Field, and Randy seems to be following her," Sam admitted, "I need to talk with him on police business, as well, but I'd like some background before I do. He has made Mac feel uncomfortable on a few occasions. He seems to be a little weird. I'm sorry. I know that's not a professional term."

"I have to agree with you," said Miss Tippet, "He may just be socially immature, but I don't think so. I'll tell you what I told Mackenzie."

She proceeded to do so. When she finished, Sam had one question.

"Do you know the name of the institution where he was sent?"

"I can find out. You might want to talk to Meredith Englewood first. I doubt that the mental health facility will give you any information without a subpoena."

"You're right," said Sam, "Thank you for your help."

"You're welcome. It's been a most unusual morning," said Lorraine Tippet.

* * *

Sam sat in his car, debating whether to try to visit Mrs. Englewood now or another day. He didn't want to be late to his interview with Jeff Parker and Lynette Martin. It was almost 11:00 a.m. He finally decided to give her a call. A child answered, but soon Mrs. Englewood was on the line. Sam introduced himself, and made his request.

Mrs. Englewood immediately said, "Is this about Randy Bayard?"

"Yes," said Sam hesitantly, thinking that Miss Tippet hadn't had time to call her fellow teacher.

"Perhaps you should come over right now, Deputy," responded Mrs. Englewood.

When Sam pulled in front of the purple, green and soft yellow Victorian house and saw Mac's Jeep, he guessed why he'd been summoned. The woman who answered the door did not fit Connor's description. She was tall and big-boned with a sculptured face and short, curly brown and gray hair. She held out her hand, as she held the door open.

"I'm Meredith Englewood, Deputy Kincaid. Would you please come in?"

Sam shook her hand, and followed her down a long hallway to a bright cornflower blue and yellow kitchen with white cabinets. Mac sat at a white, wooden table, and smiled at him.

"Hi," she said.

"Hi," Sam answered, still not sure what he thought about her being there.

"Have you already talked with Lorraine Tippet?" asked Mrs. Englewood.

"Yes, I have," said Sam.

"That will save us some time," Mrs. Englewood continued, "Everything she told you, based on what Mackenzie has said, is true. Randy did attack his mother in some way during his 6th grade year, and was institutionalized, until his father died. None of the teachers truthfully knows what her injuries were, or why he attacked her. He was under psychiatric care for seven years. I can probably get you the name of the institution, when I go to school on Monday. His father left Mrs. Bayard enough money to care for herself and for Randy's care for both of their natural lives. At least that is the supposition. There may have been a way for Randy to inherit, if he was released from the sanitarium or hospital. He did come home to live with his mother about six months after his father died. He has only worked as a free-lance photographer since then, as far as anyone knows."

Just then a girl of about ten years old tore into the kitchen, threw open the refrigerator door, grabbed a juice box, slammed the door, yelled "Excuse me!" and fled.

"Would you like something to drink, Deputy Kincaid? Mackenzie, have you changed your mind?" Mrs. Englewood asked, as though her daughter's interruption was a cue.

Sam and Mac were smiling at the whirlwind of a girl.

"No, thank you," they answered together.

"I taught Randy in 4th grade," Mrs. Englewood continued, "He was new to the school that fall. His family moved to Belleriver during the summer. Mr. Bayard was a stockbroker, and commuted to Lexington. He came to Randy's teacher conferences, but didn't contribute much. Randy was very shy. He handled schoolwork well, but did not participate verbally in class, unless I called on him directly. He did not get along with the other children. He isolated himself. A few of them tried to be friendly. A few others teased him, but he ignored all approaches. We wanted to have him tested for Asperger syndrome, but his father said he had been tested and was fine. I remember when he said that Mrs. Bayard looked surprised, but didn't object or add anything. There was one odd incident with Randy that year. We had a class guinea pig that we kept in a big cage. The children took turns feeding it and cleaning the cage. Each weekend, a child was allowed to take the guinea pig home to care for it. Randy got to take it home over Christmas vacation, which he won by a random drawing. On the 27th of December, I received a call from Mr. Bayard. He said that the guinea pig had died, even though they had followed all of the directions carefully. He offered to replace the animal, even get the same color, so that the other children wouldn't have to know. I debated, but decided that I would be honest with the children, and let them decide whether we would get a new pet. Mr. Bayard also said he would take care of the burial. The children were quite sad, but understood. Randy apologized to me, but didn't say a word otherwise. We had a memorial service. Randy did not speak at it. The class also decided that they would like an aquarium instead, if I would take it home over vacations. At any rate, I've always wondered what happened to that guinea pig, and I felt guilty for suspecting Randy. I'd never seen him be intentionally cruel. It was just a feeling I had about him."

Mrs. Englewood sighed, and looked at Mac and Sam steadily.

"Do you have any other questions?" she asked.

Mac felt sick about the guinea pig story. An image of the drowned kittens flashed through her mind, and she felt worse. Then Sam was standing and thanking Mrs. Englewood. Mac thanked her too, as she walked them to the front door.

Sam and Mac were halfway down the walk, when they both spoke at the same time. Mac could barely contain herself.

"Sam, I remember…"

"Mac, what are you doing," Sam talked over her, "Why are you investigating Randy Bayard?"

"I just wanted to get some background on him," Mac was starting to feel angry, "I'm trying to figure out why he's bothering me."

"Mac, I want you to leave it alone," said Sam sternly, "You're not a police officer."

"What does that have to do with anything?" she shot back, "He's following me. That's not police business. Why are you trying to find out about him? He hasn't committed a crime!"

"Look, I don't want to talk about it now. I have another appointment. Just do me a favor and stop asking questions about him. OK?"

Mac looked at him furiously. She wanted to yell at him, but couldn't think of a good comeback. She whirled and strode to her car, yanked the door open, and then slammed it, starting the engine. Sam's annoyance was dissipating rapidly, knowing he hadn't handled that well. He watched helplessly, as she peeled away from the curb, but slowed down for the yield sign at the corner.

Chapter 35

"Hello, Lynette, Mrs. James," began Jeff, "Thank you for letting us see you again. How are you doing?" That question was directed at Lynette, who looked about the same, very pale, and her hair needed washing. Jeff pulled up a chair next to her bed, while Sam leaned against the wall. Mrs. James was seated on the other side of the bed.

"I'm better, thank you," said Lynette, "The doctor says I can probably go home tomorrow." Her lips trembled and her eyes filled.

"Sorry," she continued, "Not home. I'll be going to Mom and Dad's. So will Colette. She's with Grandma Martin right now."

"Do you have a copy of your and Heck's work schedule for the last two weeks or so?" asked Jeff.

Mrs. James passed him a sheet of paper.

"Heck's hours were fairly regular, but Lynette's changed sometimes, so they wrote it on a calendar in the desk," she said, "Lynette always gave me a copy of the calendar, or just wrote out a simple schedule, if that was easier. That way I would know where to reach her."

"We have to ask you about certain dates," said Jeff, looking at Lynette. She nodded.

"Here. Wednesday, Sept. 10th. It looks like Heck was off," Jeff continued, "Did he stay home with Colette?"

"No," Lynette answered slowly, drawing out the word, "He took a sick day, with a migraine, so his mother still had Colette. I worked 7:00 to 3:30, picked up Coley and came home. He was better by then. He rarely missed work."

"Did he go out that night?" asked Sam.

"No. No. I'm sure he didn't," said Lynette. She didn't sound sure.

"Could he have gone out that night without your knowing?" Sam rephrased the question. Lynette looked down at her hands on the covers. Mrs. James leaned forward, as if to speak, but Sam caught her eye, and she remained silent.

"Maybe," Lynette finally said, "I was so tired. We put Coley to bed about 8:30 and I took a bath and was in bed by about 9:00 or so. Heck kissed me good-night, and went downstairs to watch TV. I slept solidly all night. I don't even remember waking up when he came to bed. He was asleep, when I got up in the morning. I stayed home that day, and Heck went to work. I just can't believe he would kill anyone else! He always walked away from arguments, if he felt himself getting too angry. And why would he kill complete strangers?"

She was crying now, her hands covering her face. Her mother climbed on to the bed next to her, and wrapped her arms around Lynette. After a few moments, the young woman got control of herself. Mrs. James handed her a wad of tissues, and Lynette wiped her face, and blew her nose.

With a shaky sigh, she said, "I'm sorry. Let's go on. What are the other dates?"

"The following Saturday evening, Sept. 13th," said Jeff, "Actually, it was late evening, around 10:00."

"Again, I can't be sure. I worked until 5:00 that day. We ordered pizza, which was a big splurge. We played card games with Colette – Go Fish and that matching game. She was in bed by 8:30 and I was asleep about 9:00 or so. I did wake up during the night, and Heck wasn't in bed. It was around 1:00. I went downstairs, and he was asleep in front of the television. I woke him up, and he came to bed."

"Any other dates?" asked Mrs. James, "Or questions?"

"Have either of you seen Heck get his guns out in the last few weeks?" asked Jeff, "To clean them, or for any reason?"

Both women shook their heads.

Jeff looked at Sam, and cocked an eyebrow, as though asking if there was anything else. Sam shook his head.

"I'm sorry we had to interview you now," said Jeff, "I'm very sorry about all of this. I'll be in touch."

Sam nodded at the two women, and he and Jeff left the room. Both men were silent, until they reached the parking lot.

"Well, that still leaves Heck a possible," said Jeff, "We haven't received any calls that someone saw Heck either night, or Wednesday morning when the horse was shot."

"Any word on ballistics?" asked Sam.

"We're hoping for early next week, but that would be a first," answered Jeff, "Do you have any leads? What about Bobby Lee?"

"He's still in the running," said Sam, "No alibis for any shooting, except the horse. He was at work that day. You guys have his rifle. I don't think he's the one, but I'm not sure about Heck either. We really need the ballistics report."

"What now?" asked Jeff.

"Office," said Sam, "Read everything again."

"Yep," responded Jeff, "What are we missing?"

"Something," said Sam, "Something. Keep in touch."

Chapter 36

While Sam was driving back from Lexington, Mac and Sarah were saddling their horses.

"How do you think Gus is doing?" Sarah asked, as she tightened his girth.

"Great," answered Mac, "We'll do some more desensitizing before we go out on the trail."

The women soon led the geldings out to the round pen. Mac pulled a wadded up plastic bag from her pocket, and handed it to Sarah.

"First, just rub him all over with that. No, don't unfold it. Keep it small at first."

Sarah began rubbing Gus's neck, front let, barrel, back hind leg, hip and around to the other side. As she rubbed, Mac continued talking.

"Horses are naturally afraid of anything that moves or makes noise. Also anything new in their environment. Plastic bags terrify a lot of horses, especially when they blow in the wind. OK, now open the bag a little bigger, and rub him again."

Mac watched Sarah and Gus, as she stroked Sprint's neck. Sprint lowered his head and looked like he was going to sleep.

"You can open the bag all the way now. Rub him again. As long as he holds still, he's learning not to be afraid of it, and to trust you."

"He's doing great, isn't he?" Sarah looked at her friend and smiled.

"Well, to be honest, Dad does a lot of desensitizing when he trains horses, so Gus has been through this. Still, it's been awhile… OK, now stand in front of him. Loosely hold the reins in one hand, and wave the bag to the side of his head. Good."

"Doesn't phase him," said Sarah.

"Now the other side. Wave it five to seven times, then switch sides and wave it harder. Make it noisy."

The bag cracked, and Gus threw up his head, but stood still. Sarah stopped.

"Keep going," said Mac, "As long as he stands still. Just increase the motion. Wave it over your head. Flip it at his legs."

After a few more minutes with Gus standing stock still, Mac was satisfied. They mounted their horses, and warmed up at the trot in the corral. Then Mac and Sprint did a nice side pass and opened the gate.

"I want to teach that to Gus too," said Sarah, "Where are we going?"

"You know that row of trees where you and Connor were, when the gunshot spooked Gus? If we go past that and down the road a mile, there's a place with a few acres of woods. It's not big, not a lot of trails, but it's a nice change. Mr. Mowery owns it, right on the edge of his pastures, and he's always let us ride there. He has thoroughbreds that he sells for racing, but he likes to give them lots of experiences, not just the track. Everyone calls it Little Woods."

"Sounds great!" grinned Sarah.

The two women rode side by side for most of the mile and a half, which made conversation easy.

"You and Connor seem happy," commented Mac, looking at her friend with a smile. Sarah's face lit up.

"We are. He's so much fun and sweet to me. Well, you should know."

"Because he's my brother? Ha!" replied Mac, "Not exactly the same kind of relationship. He is sweet to you and you both seem to be having a lot of fun. Took long enough!"

"Yeah. Thanks for pushing," said Sarah, "What about you and Sam?"

"What about us?"

"He's hot. He's smart. He obviously likes you. And, oh yeah, he's hot!"

Sarah was laughing, and Mac smiled at her, and then grew serious.

"I don't know. He is gorgeous and sweet and funny. But he can be overprotective and kind of macho too."

"Well, he is a cop. Deputy sheriff, I mean."

"Yeah, maybe it goes with the territory. I just don't need that in a man."

"How is he overprotecting you?"

"You know how Randy Bayard has been bothering me? I think I remember how I knew him," Mac went on to tell Sarah about her dream, and her talks with Miss Tippet and Mrs. Englewood.

"Wow," said Sarah, "Sounds like he's had problems."

"Yes, it does. I don't know what to do next, but Sam ordered me to stop investigating Randy!"

"What?" cried Sarah.

"Yes. He didn't even let me tell him about the dream or what I remembered. He just rushed off."

"Wait until you can talk to him again. He's coming tonight, right?"

"As far as I know. I'm not sure how we can fit in the conversation with Aunt Tina here."

"Include her. Bring her up to speed. Randy lived in your old neighborhood, right? Maybe Tina knows something."

"His house is a couple of blocks away. I remember walking up and down the sidewalk in front, wishing he'd come out, so I could confront him."

"That's probably why he remembers you. I'm not sure that's good."

"I'm not either."

They rode in silence for a few minutes.

"Hey," said Mac, "let's lope, until we reach the trees."

"OK, but no galloping yet," answered Sarah.

She waited for Sarah to cue Gus, and then she barely touched Sprint's side. He responded in the gentle, rolling gait that Mac loved. She could feel him wanting to take off, but he willingly stayed at Gus's side. Mac looked over at Sarah, who was relaxed and smiling back at her. After a half mile, they could see the woods, and the horses slowed to a walk.

"I love that so much," said Sarah, "I will gallop with you sometime, but I'm not ready yet."

"You don't ever have to be ready," said Mac, "Not everyone likes it. I do once in awhile. I like going fast around barrels. But I like that lope we just did the best. And I like having a horse that's relaxed and can enjoy the lope. Some barrel racers won't do anything but go. Of course, it depends on the horse, the rider and the training."

"I think loping is pretty exhilarating!" smiled Sarah, "And Gus does too." She patted her horse's dark brown neck.

"We'll have to go single file through most of the woods," said Mac, "Do you want me to lead or you?"

"I'll start," said Sarah, "but maybe we can take turns. I read it's good to do that."

"Yeah, it is. Keeps your horse from fighting about being the leader or follower."

Sarah took Gus into the trees with Mac and Sprint following a few feet behind. In a few minutes, the forest surrounded them.

"It's hard to believe we're in the middle of thoroughbred country," Sarah turned in her saddle to be sure Mac heard her.

Mac nodded.

"It's nice," she said, "and since it's not a public park, we won't run into a lot of other people. I don't think he lets motorcycle riders in here."

The trail twisted through the trees, sometimes forking in two directions. When they had enough room, Mac would pass Sarah and Gus to take the lead. Sprint wanted to stay in the lead, but he complied, when Mac took him back behind Gus.

"Could we get lost?" asked Sarah.

"No. I used to ride here a lot. Besides, the horses will always take us home."

Suddenly Sarah began to sing "Cowboy, Take Me Away", an old Dixie Chicks song. She had a beautiful alto voice. Mac didn't think her own voice was very good, but she joined in on the chorus.

"Cowboy, take me away,

Fly this girl high as you can into the wild blue,

Set me free, oh, I pray,

Closer to heaven above…"

A shot cracked through the forest quiet. Mac watched in horror as Gus took off, a bright red gash on his hindquarters. Sarah's body flew back, then forward, as she tried to balance and stay on. Mac leaned forward, but Sprint was already flying after Gus. Mac lost sight of Sarah, as the trail serpentined. She couldn't believe Gus could move that fast. Another shot split a branch behind her. What the hell! She and Sprint rounded a sharp turn, and she saw Sarah lying beside the trail. Gus was gone. She pulled Sprint to a sliding stop, and jumped off. He was trembling, but stood still, while Mac knelt next to Sarah. A red scratch ran down Sarah's cheek to her neck; her helmet was cracked. Mac heard an engine, and turned to look behind her, just as Sprint yanked the reins free from her hand, and barreled down the trail. She turned back, helplessly watching him. She heard tires spinning and braking behind her, and before she could turn again, she felt a sharp pain in her head. Mac fell unconscious on the trail beside her friend.

Chapter 37

Sam leaned back in his desk chair, his feet up on the desk, rereading the working case files on the sniper murders and Heck Martin's suicide. There was so much material after eleven days, but it wasn't looking good for proving a case against either suspect. He was trying to clear his mind and focus on each interview and report, not jump ahead to his next step. At 4:07 his cell phone rang. Sam saw Connor's name on the display. He wondered if he needed to bring something for the evening.

"Hello."

"Sam, it's Connor. Can you get out here right now? Sarah's hurt and Mac is missing!"

Sam was on his feet and headed for the door, as they talked.

"On my way. What happened?"

"They went for a ride down to Little Woods. About an hour ago, Gus came tearing back to the barn with a flesh wound on his butt. Sprint was just a few seconds behind him, not hurt. Dad and I put them in the corral, and took the Gator to the woods. We found Sarah unconscious, but no sign of Mac. An ambulance is on the way. I'm going with Sarah to the hospital. Dad will wait for you and you can decide what to do."

"I'll get any free deputies to search. Can Gabe round up some other people to help?"

"He is. They'll be here."

"You said 'flesh wound'? From a branch or a gun or what?"

"As far as we can tell, it's from a bullet. Definitely not a knife or arrow."

"Has Sarah come to yet?"

"Yeah, she is, but kind of woozy. I'll call you if she knows anything."

"Take care of her."

"I will. Good luck, Sam."

Sam threw his phone on the passenger seat, and radioed dispatch, requesting help for a search. Then he turned on his siren and lights and flew down the streets and roads. He was at the ranch in eight minutes. Gabe was waiting anxiously, pacing in front of the house. Sam jumped out of his cruiser, and hurried to Gabe.

"How many have you called?" asked Sam.

"There will be ten or more here soon. I called people with four wheelers and Gators, so they can get into the woods. The trails are too narrow for cars and trucks."

"Can I see the horses?"

"Sure."

They strode to the corral. They were still saddled, but their bridles hung on posts. Both were shiny with sweat. First Sam looked at Gus's wound, which had a drip of blood running down his hindquarter.

"It's not bad, just a graze," said Gabe.

"Yeah, but it's a gunshot. Someone shot him to spook him," said Sam.

"That's what we thought," answered Gabe, "He ran, and Sarah fell off. Hit her head."

"You've looked them both over, right? See anything unusual?"

"We checked right away. They're OK, except for Gus's wound. Nothing else odd. Help me take the saddles off."

As the two men took off the saddles, a second sheriff's car drove up the lane, followed by a small blue car, and two four wheelers. Sam and Gabe hurried back to meet them.

Sheriff Dade and Mary Preston got out of the sheriff's car. A thin woman with a long, light grey braid down her back stepped out of the blue car, while two men in baseball caps climbed off the ATV's. The woman reached Sam and Gabe first.

"Sam, this is Tina McCormick, Mac's aunt," said Gabe, "Fred, Mark, thanks for coming. You, too, Sheriff and Deputy."

Sam shook Aunt Tina's hand and said, "Good to meet you."

"You, too. Now, let's go find Mac," she answered.

Gabe repeated what he knew, and looked at Sam and the Sheriff.

"Gabe, I assume you know the layout of the woods. Are there multiple entries and trails?" asked Sam.

"There are four entrances, and the trails crisscross."

"OK. We need someone at each trailhead. You and I will start where Mac and Sarah rode in. Anyone know where the other entrances are?"

Fred and Mark both raised their hands.

"There are two entrances about a mile apart off Powell Road. We can each come in one of those."

"Good. Go slow. What was Mac wearing?"

"Jeans. Turquoise long-sleeve tee. No, a short-sleeve tee with a green long-sleeve shirt under it. The short-sleeve was for some horse rescue," answered Gabe.

"Good. The turquoise should be easy to spot."

Three more four-wheelers pulled into the yard. A fortyish woman and a teen-aged boy and girl joined the group.

"Thanks for coming, Lisa, and kids," said Gabe, "Could you talk to Fred and Mark and divide up the other three trailheads? Now, Tina, could you please stay here and direct anyone else to the woods? Do you have your cell phone?"

When she nodded, Gabe continued, "Bring the cordless out on the porch. Or you can forward calls from it to your cell. I'll call you the instant we find her."

Sam spoke quietly to the Sheriff and Mary, "Could you come with us to the trailhead? We'll go down the trail. As soon as more people get there, you can organize a ground search on either side of the trail. Sound right?"

Sheriff Dade and Mary Preston nodded.

"Can we take the car there?" asked Mary.

"Sure," said Gabe, "Follow us."

Sam and Gabe climbed in the Gator and pulled out, the Sheriff's car right behind them. Two more Woodford County cruisers and three ATV's drove up the lane, as they left. The Gator felt slow to Sam, but he knew Gabe had it up to its top speed. Neither man spoke. In twelve minutes, they were in the Little Woods. Sam glanced back briefly, seeing the Sheriff's car stop and the edge of the woods, several other vehicles on the road behind him. Then Sam started looking around, even though they hadn't reached the accident site. Twenty minutes later, Gabe slowed and said, "Here we are."

They climbed out of the Gator, and Gabe showed Sam where Sarah had been thrown at the base of a tree. The trail and ground were full of horse, foot, and tire prints.

"I can't tell anything," Sam said in disgust.

"We weren't careful," answered Gabe, "We just wanted to get to Sarah. Maybe you can find something later. Right now we have to look for Mac. I'll take the left side of the trail. You take the right. I'll drive a lot slower."

Without another word, they took off in the Gator again. Sam tried to look systematically from the edge of the trail to further out in the woods, then back to the edge. The woods were fairly young and open, with thin trees spaced far apart. Once in awhile a pine tree blocked some of the view, but most of the area had room for a horse and possibly an ATV to go off the trail, and it was fairly easy to see for about twenty yards. Whenever they came to a fork in the trail, they would get out, look at the ground, and try to determine which way to go. Sam thought he recognized some tire prints from back at the accident site, and asked Gabe to follow those. The tracks seemed to stay on the main trail anyway. After half-an-hour of searching, Sam heard an engine. Gabe stopped and listened too. The man Gabe had called Fred pulled up.

"Anything?" he asked.

"No," said Gabe, "Not yet."

"Me neither," Fred answered, "Sorry."

"Gabe, can you take me back to where you found Sarah?" asked Sam, "I want to look around more and secure the crime scene before it's completely destroyed."

Sam pulled out his cell phone and was relieved to have a signal. He called the Sheriff and asked if Gabe could pick up Mary with a crime scene kit.

"As soon as I get Mary started, you and I can go back out on the trail. For now, could we stay on one side of the trail?"

"OK, Sam," Gabe seemed reluctant, "Fred, you got any side trails you could go back and check?"

"You bet," Fred u-turned his ATV, and headed back up the trail he'd been searching.

Gabe returned quickly down the trail, he and Sam still searching the woods for a splash of color. When they reached the accident site again, Sam looked at Gabe. The older man's jaw was clenched.

"I know you want to keep looking," said Sam, "but I don't think she's here. If there are any clues as to where she..."

"What do you mean, 'not here'? Where else would she be?"

"Gabe, I think someone took her. I know it sounds crazy, but that's what I think. I want to look for clues as to who might have taken her, and how, and they would have to be here, where Sarah fell. I'd like Mary to take pictures, and maybe tire casts, and cordon this area off. I'll start while you get Mary. You and I can continue searching, when you bring Mary here."

Gabe nodded, "Yeah, that's possible. I don't think Sprint would have left her. Something else scared him off. I'll be right back."

Sam began going over the area immediately, concentrating on the tire tracks first. The tread he had been following was easy to see, in spite of the Gator's worn tracks partially covering it. In one spot off the trail, a ten-inch square of the track was untouched by footprints. Sam photographed as many as he could find. When Gabe returned with Mary, Sam showed them that track first.

"I want to focus on this, Gabe. Can you tell anything from it?"

"It's a pretty standard tire tread for an ATV. You know, for regular usage, not special for mud or anything. But it looks new. The tread is deep. Edges are sharp. I doubt any of the 4-wheelers out here today have that clean a print."

"Good. That's something. Let's see how far we can follow it."

Leaving Mary to process the scene, Sam and Gabe took off in the Gator again. Gabe stayed to the side of the trail, so that Sam could look for the distinctive prints. The ground was soft enough and damp where tree cover was heavier, so he found it every few feet. Then it veered noticeably off into the trees. They had to slow down considerably to look for signs.

"Maybe we should walk," said Sam, "Or I can walk, and you can head back to the trail."

"I'll park here and help you," responded Gabe.

It was slow going, but Gabe was a big help. Gradually Sam became adept at following pushed down leaves, broken sticks, and glimpses of tread marks. They finally came out on a paved road, not far from one of the other trail entrances to the woods. They walked up and down both sides of the road without finding any more of the ATV tracks.

"If he carried her out on a four-wheeler," said Gabe, "he'd need a place close by to hide it and get Mac in a car. Or else he'd need a place to hide her."

"My thoughts exactly," Sam answered, pulling out his phone. He spoke to Sheriff Dade, requesting a five-mile search in the area surrounding the woods, for a new ATV or one with new tires.

"OK, let's follow the prints back to your Gator, then see if Mary is finished."

Sam had left markers as they went, so the trail was easier to follow back to the Gator. Mary said she wanted to stay at the scene, waiting for more techs to help her, so Sam and Gabe drove back to the starting point. When they reached the trailhead, Sam briefed the Sheriff on what they'd found, and what he suspected. A small crowd was gathering at the edge of the woods with another deputy directing them to spread out in a line about five feet apart. Sam walked over to the deputy, Dave Mills.

"A foot search is a good idea, Dave," said Sam, "but tell them to watch out for the red flags I left as markers. We don't want them walking over the tire tread prints."

He glanced at some of the people lining up to search, nodding at a few familiar faces. He started to thank them for coming; then he saw a face he didn't expect. Near the furthest end of the line stood Randy Bayard, talking to a young woman next to him.

Chapter 38

Sam stared at Bayard, feeling heat rise in his face and chest. He turned to walk down the line, when a hand landed on his arm, none too gently.

"Sam, are you OK? I came as soon as I heard."

It was Jeff Parker. When Sam turned to face him, Jeff let go of his arm.

"See that tall guy at the end of the line?" asked Sam.

"Yeah," Jeff dragged out the word, not sure what to think.

"That's Randy Bayard."

"What's he doing here? How did he find out so fast?"

"That's what I want to know. I'm going to talk to him."

"Hold on, Sam," Jeff grabbed his arm again, "Calm down first. Do you have any reason to suspect him in this?"

Sam took a deep breath.

"Not logically. It's a gut feeling. He's never seemed normal when it comes to Mac. Besides, the only other civilians here are neighbors and friends of the Quinn family, people Gabe called, and they called someone else. Like you said, how did he find out so fast?"

"OK. Why don't you just keep going down the line thanking people. When you get to him, you can ask some questions. I'll tag along."

"Yeah. Sounds good."

Glancing back at Dave Mills, Sam saw that Todd Lakewood had joined him. The two deputies were talking. Todd looked over Dave's shoulder, and nodded at Sam, who gave a slight nod back. Sam and Jeff walked down the line, thanking the people lined up to help, shaking hands with a few. Then they reached Randy Bayard. The young woman next to him took the opportunity to move back up the line, and slipped in next to a young man, whispering to him briefly. Sam noted this, and then looked directly into Randy's eyes.

" It was nice of you to come help," Sam said, but didn't offer his hand.

"Not a problem," answered Randy, looking down, around, and at Jeff.

"This is my friend, Officer Jeff Parker," said Sam, " He came to help too. How did you hear about this?"

"I was a couple miles away, taking pictures. I saw two or three sheriff's cars go by, and decided to follow. Thought it might be better photos than horses and landscapes. Then I saw them pulling into Mac's place, and got worried. A nice lady at the house directed me here," Randy seemed more confident now, and looked back at Sam steadily.

"How did you know that was Mac's place?" asked Jeff.

"We're friends," Randy answered, glancing at Jeff, then back at Sam, "from way back."

"Well, thanks again for coming," Sam made his voice a little warmer, "Be careful in the woods. And if you find anything, tell the deputies. Leave the picture-taking to them."

"I don't even have my camera with me," Randy said coldly.

This time Sam took Jeff's arm and led him back up the line. As they headed toward Sheriff Dade, Jeff asked, "Why didn't you ask him more?"

"Not yet. He put himself in the area, and that's enough for now. Let's help with the search."

* * *

It was after dark when the Sheriff called off the search. Over fifty people had joined the search and they had gone through at least half of the woods by then. Sheriff Dade asked Deputies Mills and Lakewood to organize another sweep the next morning at sunrise. The woods were under a mile square, and the Sheriff felt there would be enough volunteers to cover it thoroughly the next day.

Sam had thought about following Randy Bayard after the search, but Randy wasn't in sight when searchers walked past the deputies and policemen at the trailhead. They agreed to meet there in the morning about 5:00. Gabe invited Jeff back to the house, but he said he had to get home and let his wife know what had happened.

While Sam and Gabe rode back to the house, Sam's phone rang. It was Connor.

"Hey, Sam, sorry, but Sarah doesn't remember much at all," he began.

"How is she?"

"Pretty good. She's awake, but has a terrible headache. I guess the Tylenol hasn't kicked in yet. Doc says she can go home, but has to rest and have someone with her. She wants to come out there, and I don't know if we can keep her down."

"I'll bet Aunt Tina can. What does she remember?"

"Just the shot and Gus running. She tried the one-rein stop, and that's when he dumped her. He didn't buck, just lost his balance, and she lost hers, and went off."

"Bring her out. I'm pretty sure we'll be in the kitchen for awhile."

When they reached the house, they found Aunt Tina had fixed vegetable soup and sandwiches. They ate quietly, filling in Tina on what had been done. Then Connor and Sarah came in, Connor's arm around Sarah's waist. Everyone asked how she was, and Sarah gave a small smile, and said, "Fine."

"Oh, that soup smells good," she added. Aunt Tina was already filling a bowl. Gabe pushed the plate of sandwiches over to his son. Gabe and Sam told Sarah and Connor about the search and the ATV prints.

"The fact that the tread looks new means either new tires or a new vehicle," said Sam.

"Or someone doesn't use their 4-wheeler very often," said Connor.

"At least we can contact area dealers, and check on recent purchases," Sam continued, "It's about our only lead."

"What I don't get is why," Sarah spoke, "Why would anyone take Mac?"

"I have two possibles," said Sam, "but this has to stay here." He looked at each person, and everyone nodded.

"You all know how Randy Bayard has been following her. He's number one. I don't get why, but he made Mac nervous, and I think we all agree he's been over the top. He was even out there searching today."

"Doesn't that eliminate him?" asked Connor.

"No. It was at least two hours after the incident, probably more. Also, I'm wondering about Bobby Lee. He's still on the list for the sniper shootings, and he came out here to talk to Mac."

"Yeah, he did," said Connor, "He said he knew Bud in Afghanistan. After he left, Mac said she wasn't sure why he came. But she didn't seem bothered by him."

"I remember the Bayard boy from when Mac was twelve," Aunt Tina broke in, "She doesn't know that I knew she was watching him. Many adults in the neighborhood were upset about the animals that had been killed. His family was new in town, and he was an odd little boy. People saw him sneaking through their yards, hiding behind bushes."

"What are you talking about?" Sam asked a little harshly.

Tina looked at him in surprise, "She didn't tell you?"

"Tell me what? Randy Bayard tortured animals as a kid?"

"She may not have remembered that it was him," began Tina.

"Her mother died that summer," said Gabe softly.

"I put it together later, when Randy attacked his mother and was sent away," continued Tina, "I hadn't thought of anything but Meg's family all that autumn. The Bayard family was gossip fodder for months after Mrs. Bayard went to the hospital, and then Randy was sent to a mental hospital. If he was disturbed enough to stab his own mother, then he probably was disturbed enough to hurt animals. That's one of the early signs of a psychotic personality, I believe."

"What do you know about Randy that is factual?" asked Sam.

"What I said about his strange behavior," replied Tina, "I saw him sneaking through some yards, including mine. I also saw him watching Mac and Bud one day, but he disappeared when I came out. And somehow Mrs. Bayard was hurt, and was in the hospital overnight. What became accepted as fact was that Randy stabbed his mother in the torso with a knife. It must not have been too serious, because she was back home the next day. Randy was gone by then, taken away in a black limousine. He's been back in town for about eight years now with no signs of trouble, as far as I know. Gabe told me about Randy bothering Mac, but why would he kidnap her? Maybe that's not even the right word. We've had no call for a ransom."

"That's partly why I suspect him," said Sam, "He seems fixated on Mac. At the search, he told me they were friends, which is a bald-faced lie."

They talked for a while, and then Tina said that Sarah needed to be in bed. Connor helped Sarah up the stairs. Tina started to wash the dishes and Gabe said he would dry. As he stood, he looked at Sam and said, "You'd better get some rest."

"Yeah," was all Sam could manage. Gabe looked older and tired, but still stood tall. He walked Sam to the door. Suddenly Gabe gripped Sam's upper arm, hard. Sam put his other hand on top of Gabe's and looked into the older man's dark grey eyes. Neither spoke, until Gabe's grip relaxed.

"See you tomorrow, Sam."

"Tomorrow."

Chapter 39

Mac's head hurt like never before. The slightest movement made it worse. Then she realized she could barely move anyway. She was lying on her back, her wrists bound in front of her, her legs bent, and crossed and tied at the ankle. Her mouth was taped shut. She didn't want to open her eyes, because she could tell it was dark beyond her eyelids. She was lying on something soft, like a bed or couch, but it was short; she couldn't stretch her legs out all the way. Finally she opened her eyes, and let them become accustomed to the dark room. Soon she could distinguish the slightly lighter grey of three windows across the room from her under a pitched roof. She could move her head from side to side, even though it sent bolts of pain shooting through it. She lay still, closing her eyes, until the pain subsided to a throbbing ache. Opening her eyes again, she saw that she was on a wooden bench with a cushion underneath her. A broad strip of cloth or tape went across her chest, and it was somehow fastened to the slats of the back of the bench. Another went across her hips, and whatever tied her feet was tied to the bench as well.

"Damn," she thought, "What the hell?" Mac decided to work at each bond individually. She began with her mouth, stretching her cheek and jaw muscles repetitively. That made her headache worse, so she switched to her wrists, tensing, twisting, relaxing, and tensing again. Her arm muscles ached, but she didn't feel any loosening. Next she tried her ankles with no success. She kept repeating the process, until she hurt all over. Frustrated, angry tears ran down her cheeks. She told herself to stop. She didn't want her captor to see her crying. She lay still, breathing slowly and deeply, until she was calm and her tears had dried. Exhausted, she didn't feel herself fall asleep.

When Mac woke up again, she felt someone near her. She could hear soft breathing. Then she felt it on her face. Her eyes flew open, and she tried to jerk away. Randy Bayard jumped back in his chair. The room was lighter, but not bright. Randy leaned forward again, his elbows on his thighs.

"Hello, Mac," he said, "Surprised?"

She slowly turned her head from side to side, but stopped as the headache flared.

"I bet you'd like to know what you're doing here," Randy continued, "Can't talk? Cat got your tongue?"

He laughed softly.

"Sorry. Bad joke. I'm a little nervous. I'd like for us to talk, but I think you'd try to yell. Pointless really. This room is soundproofed. Besides, there's no one to hear who would help you. Now here's how we stand. You are tied with belts made from duct tape and surgical tape, so you cannot work your way loose. You are wearing an adult diaper, which I will change as needed. I couldn't get your jeans back on, so you're wearing a pair of my warm-ups. I will remove the tape from your mouth, so that you can eat and drink, but if you make the slightest noise, I will cut you."

He slowly reached back, and pulled an x-acto knife from behind him, "You are here to be my witness, among other things. I have a story to tell you. For now, you might as well rest some more. I'll be back in a few hours."

He stood, moved the chair away from the bench, and turned away, out of her line of sight. She heard a door open and close softly. Mac's heart was beating wildly, so she returned to deep breathing. She had a chance. He didn't want her dead, at least not yet. In spite of Randy's warnings, she went back to her tensing and relaxing exercises, hoping to weaken the tape. When she got too tired, she would doze. She also thought about Sam and her dad, Connor and Sarah, and Aunt Tina. She knew they would be frantic. They would be looking for her, but she didn't think there were any clues to bring them here, wherever "here" was. At least Sam had talked with Miss Tippet and Mrs. Englewood, and he already didn't like Randy. Mac had to stop thinking about them, because it brought the tears back. When she woke for about the fourth time, the room seemed brighter.

She could turn her head to the right, where she could see the three small windows, sunlight leaking around the edges of shades. Boxes were piled under the windows. A wooden rocking horse stood forlornly to one side. If she looked down past her feet, she could see that the room extended around a corner. She could see part of the woodwork of a larger window with some kind of light blue patterned curtain pulled back with a tieback. She could see some white painted bars from a piece of furniture. She closed her eyes, when staring downward made her vision blur. I'm in an attic, she thought. Maybe it's Randy's house. She remembered standing across the street, looking at the big Victorian style home, when she was a kid, half-wishing Randy would come out, and she could confront him. She could visualize the three small windows under the peak of the roof, remembering that she once thought she saw the boy, or someone, looking out the window at her.

Just then, she heard the door open and close. Randy appeared, carrying a plastic cup with a lid and a straw.

"Hello, Mac. I brought you some nourishment."

He pulled the wooden chair up next to the bench, and sat down, putting the cup on the floor. He leaned over her and did something to the band across her chest, loosening it. He let it fall under the bench. He pulled a pillow from below, and put it behind her, lifting her up, and then letting her lean back against it. The change in position was an enormous relief.

"I'm going to take the tape off your mouth now, so you can drink. It's a fruit smoothie, very healthy. Please don't make a sound, unless I ask you a question. I don't want to hurt you. I'd like to loosen your other bindings, but I'm quite sure that I can't trust you yet. Just nod, if you'll be quiet and drink."

Mac nodded. Randy ripped the tape off her mouth, and she smothered a cry of pain. He held the mug and straw up to her mouth. She took a small sip. It was delicious, strawberry flavored and cold. She drank more. He let her have about half the cup, but then pulled it back.

"Let's take a break, and make sure it agrees with you," he said, "For now, I think we'll stick with smoothies. They are very nutritious. I'll bet you can't even tell I put veggies in this."

She shook her head.

"Good girl," he put the straw back in her mouth, "If you continue to be a good girl, I can unfasten your hands, and bring you more of a variety of food."

Mac finished the smoothie. She was still hungry, but felt better. She hated his patronizing tone, but knew she had to cooperate. Worse, she had to go to the bathroom.

"Thank you, Randy," she whispered.

He looked at her in surprise, frowned, then shook his head, and smiled.

"You spoke without permission, but you're welcome," he said, "I guess I need to give you a signal. If you want to speak, move your eyes up and down three times, or until I notice."

Mac wanted to scream at him, but used the signal as instructed.

"OK. Go ahead," Randy said.

"Could I please use a bathroom?" Mac spoke softly, and allowed a pleading tone in her voice.

"Well, this is your lucky day. I do have a bathroom up here, and I'd rather not have to change your diaper. It has already put the wrong tone on our relationship."

Randy unfastened the wide cloth belt holding her hips to the bench. Then he picked her up and carried her to a tiny bathroom that she couldn't see, when laying on the bench. He leaned her against the small sink, and quickly pulled down the grey warm-up pants and diaper. He gently sat her on the toilet, and left without looking at her. To her surprise, he even closed the door partially.

"Call me when you're finished," he said.

Mac was too angry and relieved to be embarrassed. She peed "like a racehorse" (rolling her eyes to herself at that thought), then called to Randy. He lifted her to a standing position, leaning her against his shoulder, and adroitly pulling up her diaper and pants. She was surprised at his strength. He was fast, too, and she didn't have time to knee him in the groin (with both knees), or try to push him over. As those ideas passed through her mind, she realized that unless she knocked him out completely, she wouldn't have time to work the tape loose from her ankles to get away. It was something to think about, though.

Randy carried her back to the bench, laying her down again, and refastening the belts. She wanted to object, but knew it was useless. As he put a new strip of tape over her mouth, he said, "I'm afraid I put some sleeping medication in your drink. I need to be sure that you're quiet for a few hours. When I come back, I'll bring more food, and tell you my story. Sweet dreams, Mackenzie."

Hoping he would go away, Mac closed her eyes. Before she could open them again to make sure he was gone, she fell asleep.

Chapter 40

On his drive home, Sam parked a couple of doors down the street from Randy Bayard's house. In the hour he sat there, he saw one light on in a front room. A tall, solid wooden fence blocked the back of the house. At about 10:00, the front light went out, and a few minutes later, a light went on in a second floor; then a shade was drawn and that light was barely visible. Sam sighed.

"This is pointless," he thought, "I'm in a Sheriff's car, completely visible. I'd better get some sleep, and come back tomorrow."

The faint upstairs light blinked out, and Sam drove away.

Back at his apartment, he showered, and then lay on his bed. He couldn't sleep. He kept thinking of the shootings. Why would anyone shoot a horse, three people, and then kidnap Mac? Sam couldn't see a pattern, even for a psycho. It sounded like Randy was a troubled child, possibly abused, but they hadn't found any connection with the victims, and his relationship with Mac was tenuous at best. In fact, it went back sixteen years for a couple of months one summer. He went over and over his conversations with Randy's teachers, and remembered how he and Mac had parted. She had wanted to tell him something, but he'd shut her down. In spite of his being protective, he'd lost her anyway. He tried thinking about Bobby Lee, another possible suspect. He just didn't get the same feeling of threat from Bobby that he got from Randy. Bobby seemed up front about his feelings, while Randy was devious. Psychotics could be good actors, though, fool people, even fool him.

His phone rang, a ringtone like an old-fashioned phone ringing. Sam looked at the clock and name on the screen. Five-o-one a.m. Jeff Parker.

"Yeah," Sam answered gruffly, rubbing his eyes.

"Figured you couldn't sleep either," said Jeff, "Here's my suggestion. I take Bobby Lee, and you go see Mr. Randy Bayard. Maybe take someone with you. I'll take another cop, too, although I don't expect trouble from Bobby. Or we can go together to see each of them. What do you think?"

"I like the latter idea. If we go now, we can catch Bobby before he goes to church, if he's going today. Also it'll be easier than finding other backup, and we won't take anyone away from the search."

"OK. I'll pick you up in ten."

Jeff pulled up to the apartment building in his own car, a dark green Chevy Camaro. Sam slipped into the passenger seat without comment.

"Get any sleep?" asked Jeff.

"A little," said Sam.

"Me too. This case is so damn slippery. Nothing to hold onto," Jeff muttered, "I hope the ballistics report comes in this week."

"That would help."

As Jeff drove to Frankfort, they didn't talk much. At one point, Jeff did say that at least they knew Heck Martin hadn't taken Mac. Sam gave him a dirty look, and then went back to staring out the window. Soon they pulled up in front of the light blue house that Bobby Lee shared with his mother. It was shortly after 6:00 a.m. when Jeff knocked on the door. He noticed a doorbell and rang that for good measure. They waited about one minute, and Jeff rang again. Bobby Lee yanked the door open, frowning at them. He was in dark blue pajamas, moccasins, and a red plaid robe. When he realized it was a policeman and a deputy, he stopped frowning, but looked puzzled.

"What can I do for you, officers?" he asked.

"We have a few questions," said Jeff, "May we come in?"

"Sure," Bobby stood out of the way to let them pass, "It's a little early, though, especially on a Sunday."

Jeff and Sam stood in the small living room, which was clean and neat, with only a worn, flower-print couch in blue, pink and green, and a rose-colored armchair beside an end table with a lamp. An old-style television sat on full bookshelves in the opposite wall. Just then an elderly woman bustled into the room, looking worried, but smiling at them anyway.

"Would you gentlemen like to have a seat? I can get you some coffee."

She was dressed in a blue gingham shirtwaist with her grey hair pulled into a twist behind her head. She had on blue plastic glasses, and white tennis shoes.

"This is my mother," said Bobby, "who is always up at the crack of dawn. Mom, this is Officer Parker and Deputy Kincaid."

Both men said "Good morning, Mrs. Lee".

"Maybe I could help you with that coffee," suggested Jeff.

Sam looked at Bobby, and said, "Let's sit in here, OK?"

Bobby sat in the armchair, and Sam sat on the couch facing him.

"Where were you yesterday, Bobby?" Sam began.

"When? All day?" Bobby asked.

"Yes. Just run through your whole day for me."

"I worked. I was at Buffalo Trace from 8:00 to 5:00."

"Can someone vouch for you?"

"Sure, several guys. I ate lunch there too. I bring a lunch usually."

"Did you eat alone?"

"Yes. Well, sort of. There were other people there, taking a lunch break too."

"After work?"

"I came home for supper."

Abruptly, Mrs. Lee walked into the room, carrying a mug of coffee that she handed to Sam. Jeff was right behind her, looking helpless.

"He was here, Deputy," she said, "We had pork chops and sweet potatoes and green beans. Then Bobby went to a meeting."

"A meeting?" Sam looked at Bobby, whose face was turning red.

"I went to an AA meeting," he murmured gruffly, "then I came back here."

"It's at the Grace Baptist Church in the basement," said his mother, "Our pastor found it for him. It was his third meeting. He's also getting together with some other veterans once a week. Only once so far, but he will keep going. Last night he did come back here. We watched Masterpiece Mystery, a Twilight Zone rerun, and the late news."

She looked steadily at Jeff and Sam, who nodded, put down their mugs, and stood up to go. Sam glanced at Bobby, who was bright red.

"Good for you, Bobby," said Sam, "We all need a little help sometimes."

"Yeah, well," Bobby mumbled, "She's got plans to fix me up, too, with some girls from church, as soon as I get my head straight."

"I don't think you have much choice, Bobby," Jeff grinned, "Always listen to your mother."

Chapter 41

Mac woke up feeling groggy and disoriented, but the burning pain around her wrists and ankles soon reminded her where she was. She opened her eyes to see Randy sitting in the wooden chair, smiling at her. The room was faintly grey, and a lamp behind her cast a semicircle of yellow light over him.

"Good. Perfect timing," he said, ripping the tape off her mouth.

She hissed in a breath through her teeth, trying not to scream.

"Very good," Randy beamed at her, "Sorry for the pain, but there will be gain. I brought you another smoothie. No sleeping meds this time, I promise. I need you to stay awake for my story."

He loosened the chest belt, and lifted her into a sitting position again, pushing a pillow behind her back. He held the plastic cup with a straw to her lips, and she drank thirstily. Next he unwrapped a granola bar, and put it in her hands. She lifted it to her mouth, and forced herself to eat slowly. When she finished, he put the cup in her hands.

"While you drink that, I will begin my story. It's a true story. The best ones are. Once upon a time, there was a little boy. That's a switch, isn't it? Usually it's a girl, a princess. This was just an ordinary boy, who lived in a big house with his parents. They were fairly kind parents, buying him toys, and his mother read books to him sometimes. When he was about ten years old, they moved from a big house in a big city to a big house in a small town. He didn't know why they moved, but he didn't mind. He hadn't had any friends at his old school. He hoped he would make friends at the new one. They moved at the end of the school year, so he had the summer to explore his new house and neighborhood. His father was gone to work every day, except Sundays. His mother was very busy unpacking, and arranging furniture in the new house. So the boy kept busy exploring. He had never been allowed in the attic at the old house. Mother said it was just full of junk, but she and Father didn't want him getting into it, making a mess, possibly breaking something. The new house had an attic too, and one morning, the little boy decided to see what was in it. His mother was busy with some men installing the new washer and dryer. The boy left the television on in his room, closed the door, and climbed the stairs to the attic. It was a regular stairway, not the pull down kind. When he reached the door at the top, he wondered if it would be locked, like the attic door at the old house. It wasn't. It would need a lock added, and his parents hadn't done that yet. Slowly he turned the handle and opened the door. BOO!"

Randy jumped out of his chair, arms outspread, and fingers spread like claws. Mac cringed, and let out a yelp. Then she glared at him. Randy fell back in his chair, laughing.

"Sorry," he gasped, "Just a little comic relief."

Mac didn't speak, but watched him, feeling both annoyed and curious. She wished he would continue. Without realizing it, she had been waiting years to hear his story.

"I'm sorry," Randy said again, sighing, "This story is not a happy one, as you may have guessed, and the need to laugh came upon me unawares. I won't startle you again, at least not in that frivolous manner."

"The boy came into an entryway that led to a large room, much like this one. The light was very dim, like here, so he flipped the wall switch. At first, all he saw were piles of boxes, luggage, the usual detritus of attics. He walked forward, and, against a far wall, he saw a baby's crib. He wondered if it had been his. As he walked toward it, he could tell there was something in it, and he assumed it was baby toys or stuffed animals. Then the something moved, and he heard faint, but hoarse, breathing. The boy froze. For an instant he wondered if it was an animal, a puppy for him, a surprise gift. He began to walk again, knowing it was not a puppy or kitten. In a few steps he was beside the crib, looking down between the bars at a child."

Randy had been staring at the wall over Mac's shoulder. Now he turned his pale eyes to look directly at Mac.

"He was the size of a two or three year old in his body, but he had the head of a teen-ager. He had dark hair, and big, brown eyes. His eyes were beautiful, and he looked right at me. He would have been handsome, except that his skull and forehead seemed swollen. He could move his head a little from side to side, and he could move his eyes. His legs and arms were paralyzed. His body was much too small for his head. He couldn't talk, although he made some soft sounds. You would think a young boy would be frightened, but I wasn't. He was mine. When he looked at me, I knew that he loved me, so I loved him too. His name was in blue letters on the headboard of the white crib: Marcus. His name was Marcus, and he was my brother."

Abruptly Randy stood up and rushed to another part of the room. He came back with a photo album. He loosened the hip strap, swung Mac's legs around so that she was sitting upright, and sat next to her on the bench.

"You probably don't believe me," he said, "I can see the doubt in your eyes. I'm very good at reading eyes. So I'll show you photos."

Randy opened the small book. The first photo was of a toy rocking horse. The next one was of their house, then one of a yard. When he turned the next page, a child just as Randy had described looked up from a crib. Randy turned the pages slowly. There were only five pictures in all, two full body shots, and three close-ups of Marcus's face, one through the white bars of the crib. In one of the full body shots, Randy had place a stuffed bear next to his brother. It made the size differential even more shocking. The boy's eyes were beautiful, and alert. Mac wondered how much he had known about his condition and situation.

"He knew exactly what was going on," Randy said, as if reading her mind, "We learned to talk through eye signals. He could blink, and look in different directions, so we developed a code. That's why I'm so good at reading people's eyes. I got to be with him all that year. My mother would come up to care for him three times a day, like clockwork, so I knew when it was safe for me to come up. I even hid and watched her with him a few times. I think she loved him, but he repulsed her too. I heard her call him her "sweet little toad". I saw her cry once, but she never kissed him. I kissed him every time I came, which was every day. My father never came up, unless it was when I was asleep."

"You're probably wondering what was wrong with Marcus. I have done a lot of research, and I believe he suffered from some form of Macrocephaly, possibly Hydranencephaly and/or Neurofibromatosis. Obviously it was a brain disorder. However, his intelligence was first rate, which is quite rare with either of those conditions. Through our code, Marcus told me that he needed life energy to improve. He said that full recovery was possible. He directed me to take the lives of small animals, and taught me a verse to recite as they passed.

'My brother lives; I live,

You die; my brother grows,

You die; my brother lives.'

He said that his brain would absorb their life forces, and gradually, he would heal and grow. I could see small changes every time. He would be able to move a finger or make a new sound. It was phenomenal!"

Mac tried to keep her face calm, but she remembered the tiny, dead kittens in the swimming pool, and her eyes filled with tears. She was also horrified for the helpless boy in the crib that Randy had turned into a selfish monster. Her tears became angry, and she lowered her head, trying to hide them. Randy saw them, and, of course, misunderstood.

"Oh, don't feel sorry for him, Mackenzie. My mother told me that Marcus died while I was gone, but she lied, of course. He's over in his crib, and better than ever. Why did I leave? It wasn't my decision, believe me. My mother finally caught me up here, and she lost it. Totally lost it. She was screaming at me. She told me they would have to take Marcus away. She held me by the arm, and was dragging me out. I saw a pair of scissors, so I grabbed them and stabbed her. She let me go then, and really screamed! My father came. He locked me in my room that night. The next day, some people came and took me to a hospital. I was there for over eleven years. During that time, my father passed away. I was not brought home for his funeral. My mother visited me every month at first, but after Father died, she came every week. I tried to tell my doctors about Marcus, but Mother told them I was fantasizing. For the first seven years, I would not speak to her. She came anyway. When I was 19, she told me Marcus had died. I was devastated. A year later, she said Father had died. I did not care. I blamed him even more than Mother. He was ashamed of Marcus, and insisted on hiding his own son from the world. I also

realized that with Father gone, my mother could get me out of the treatment facility. My
doctors and nurses were easy to fool. I had always been a docile patient. After that one
outburst when I stabbed Mother, I realized that I had to hold my temper in check. They
took me off anti-psychotics years ago. In my final year of incarceration, I followed a plan
that would lead to my release. I began conversing with my mother on her visits. I became
more talkative in general, especially about the classic literature that I read. I participated
in group activities. I began exercising in the gym, and in team sports. In therapy I made
up dreams, and led my doctors to believe that my father had abused me. Gradually, they
decreased the dosage of my anti-depressant medication. I acted more friendly and
cheerful, so they were sure it was working. I finally convinced Mother that I could come
home. Dad had left us set for life, the one good thing he did. So six years ago, I came
back to Belleriver to live with Mother. At first, I believed Mother that Marcus was dead.
Mother showed me a beautiful flower garden, where she said he was buried. The first
time he talked to me was out there. He said to keep looking for him in the attic. I did, and,
sure enough, there he was, back in the crib. Wait, wait! I'll show you!"

Randy put his arm around her waist, and lifted her to a standing position.
Her legs wouldn't hold her, so she sagged. Randy picked her up again, but put her down
after just a few steps. They were standing beside a white, wooden crib. In it lay a dark-
haired doll about three feet long. It had a perky face with dark brown eyes that looked
moveable, pink lips curved in a little smile, and ear-length brown hair. It had on a red
plaid shirt and denim overalls. It looked very old. The cheeks were stained, and the
clothes were worn.

Randy continued to hold Mac up. She was dumbfounded, looking from the doll to
Randy, and back to the doll. Randy was beaming.

"Mackenzie, meet my brother Marcus. Marcus, meet Mackenzie Field."

Chapter 42

Sam looked for a doorbell, but not finding one, he opened the storm door and knocked on the frosted glass window of the wooden front door. He and Jeff stood next to a tall, narrow window that was completely covered with tan-colored shutters. The old Victorian house was painted grey-blue with cranberry and tan trim. Sam knocked again, louder, and then noticed an ornate brass ring centered in the door, and realized it was an old-fashioned turn doorbell. He turned it, hearing the tumbling bell sound reverberate inside. A moment later, the big door eased open an inch or two, and a white-haired woman peered at them through the small space.

"May I help you?" she asked, opening the door wider. Her face looked younger than her hair, which was up in bun. She looked tired and worried. Sam guessed she was in her sixties.

Sam introduced himself and Jeff, and they showed her identification.

"Mrs. Bayard, could we please come in and ask you some questions?" Sam asked.

"Do you wish to speak to me or to my son?" asked Mrs. Bayard.

"I believe they want to talk to me, Mother," stated Randy Bayard, appearing behind her shoulder, "Why don't you go ahead and take your nap?"

"We would like to talk with both of you, if that's all right," said Sam.

"That will be fine," said Randy smoothly, "Come into the living room, please."

He motioned them into a room on their right. Mrs. Bayard led the way, Sam and Jeff following. Mrs. Bayard walked immediately to a high-backed green brocade chair by the fireplace. A matching chair faced hers on the other side of the mantel. Next to that chair was a dark wooden end table with a china-based lamp, and a flowered couch with mahogany trim was on its other side. Beside her chair was a long, narrow bookcase holding a television on top, and a turntable, a receiver, a DVD player and books on its shelves. Sam and Jeff sat on the couch, and Randy walked to the mantel, and leaned one arm on the carved wooden edge. Nothing was displayed on the mantel, except for two silver candlesticks on either end. A large landscape painting of horses in a pasture hung above it.

Suddenly Randy brought his arm down and clapped his hands. His mother jumped.

"Please forgive our lack of manners," he said, "Would you gentlemen like something to drink? Sweet tea? A soft drink? I'm afraid we're not used to visitors, let alone policemen. We are rather taken aback."

"Uh, anything would be fine," answered Jeff, trying not to look at Sam, or laugh.

"Mother, would you do the honors, please?" Randy looked pointedly at his mother.

"Let me help," offered Jeff quickly, following Mrs. Bayard from the room.

Randy moved to the chair opposite his mother's and sat down.

"I have some questions to ask you, Mr. Bayard," said Sam, "mostly about where you were on certain dates."

"Fire away," answered Randy, suddenly putting his hand up to his mouth, "Oh, sorry. I suppose that's not very PC under the circumstances."

"Maybe not," said Sam, "but possibly very appropriate. Where were you the evening of Wednesday, Sept. 10th?"

"Probably here, but I only have my mother to corroborate that, and she goes to bed at 9:00."

"You were at the barn dance on Sat., the 13th. When did you arrive?" asked, Sam.

"Shortly before you did, Deputy Kincaid. You remember I was talking with Mackenzie, when you arrived. I stayed until the questioning was over."

"Yes, I remember," said Sam, "Do you own a gun?"

"What kind?"

"Do you own a handgun?"

"No."

"What about a rifle?"

"No."

"Would you be willing to let us search your house?"

"Hmmmm, I'm not sure. That seems a little drastic. I think it would upset my mother."

Just then, Mrs. Bayard and Jeff returned. Jeff was carrying two iced teas, and he handed one to Sam.

"Mother," said Randy, looking sideways at her, "Mother, these officers want to search our house to see if I have a gun."

Mrs. Bayard looked startled, her eyes widening, but she turned to Sam and said, "My late husband abhorred firearms, and would not allow one in the house. I'm sure my son has continued to respect his wishes."

"So true," Randy said, "Although I will not permit you to search, I would be happy to take you on a tour of our home. If you will follow me…"

Sam placed his tea on the end table, stood, and looked at Jeff.

"Would you keep Mrs. Bayard company? Or do you want to come with us, ma'am?" he asked.

"I will stay here and drink my tea," said Mrs. Bayard, "I do not have to have company, unless Officer Parker wishes to talk."

Jeff smiled at her, sat down on the couch, and drank some tea. Randy led Sam through the smaller parlor across the hall, then into the dining room with a mahogany table that would seat eight, and on into the kitchen. The rooms were all wallpapered with flower motifs, even the kitchen. Everything looked old in style, and a little dusty, but not worn or used. In contrast, the kitchen was clean, and a pot of something that smelled good simmered on the stove.

"Beef vegetable soup for supper," Randy gestured toward the pan, "Mother and I take turns cooking. We both seem to have a knack."

Randy opened a door that led to a walk-in pantry, well stocked with homemade canned goods, as well as store purchased cans and boxes.

"As you can see, we're ready for Armageddon or a blizzard, whichever comes first," Randy smirked.

"Where does that go?" asked Sam, pointing to a door in the corner next to the stove.

"That goes to the second and third floors," said Randy, "I assume it was originally a servants' stairway. And this one goes to the basement."

He opened the door next to him, and flipped on a light switch. The stairs were wooden, disappearing into darkness.

"It's not a finished basement," said Randy, "but we can go down, if you're interested."

Sam nodded, and Randy flipped another switch, then led the way down the stairs. The floor was concrete in the first two rooms. At the base of the stairs were a fairly new washer and dryer. On the far wall was a workbench with many dusty tools hanging on a pegboard behind it. A furnace, water heater and utility sink stood on a third wall. Sam followed Randy into the second room, which held piles of boxes on palettes. A boy's bike leaning between two piles of boxes was the only recognizable item. The floor eventually gave way to dirt, and nothing was stored in those rooms. One held a coal shoot with the dirt stained black beneath it, and an ancient coal-burning furnace. As they walked slowly back upstairs, Sam asked if he could see the rest of the house.

"Well, let's hope Mother made her bed," Randy commented.

The second floor held four old-fashioned bedrooms, all looking like they had been decorated when the house was built. All four doors were closed, and Randy opened each with a flourish. The master bedroom had a canopy bed, but with no curtains, just a simple canopy of dark green taffeta (or some other shiny material) that matched the window curtains. Even with the curtains drawn on the tall windows, the room was dark, and, Sam thought, depressing. There were only two personal photographs in the room on a bedside table: one wedding photo and one family photo in which Randy looked about three or four years old. Sam purposely crossed the room, and picked each one up. He thought that Mr. Bayard looked like a serious, "respectable businessman" married to the pretty girl-next-door. Mrs. Bayard's smile was glowing in the wedding photo, but her eyes were sad in the family pose. The photo reminded Sam of older photos, where no one smiled. The next two bedrooms looked like guest rooms, one in blues, and the other in rose and gold. All of the furniture was covered in white sheets, except the double beds and side tables, which looked very dusty.

"We don't clean these rooms, unless we have company," said Randy, "which is never…until today. But today was unforeseen."

"Could I see the attic?" asked Sam.

"Of course," said Randy, "I have nothing to hide."

He opened a fifth door behind which were stairs to the third floor, and more going down to the kitchen. At the top was a hallway with three doors. Randy opened the first, which was very small and held some luggage.

"This was probably a maid's bedroom," Randy said, closing the door, "I believe the room at the end was also a bedroom for the help at one time. It is now my photography lab. That I cannot show you, because you interrupted work in progress."

"Did you ever develop the photos you took of Mac at the football game?" asked Sam.

"Yes, I did. They came out well. In fact I was going to make posters out of one of them to aid in the search," Randy said, meeting Sam's look seriously.

Sam wanted to hit him, but just said, "That won't be necessary."

Randy threw open the third door, flipped a switch and they walked into an entryway that opened into a large room with three windows that Sam recognized as the front of the house. To Sam's right was a slatted wooden bench with blankets piled on top. To his left was a white, wooden baby crib full of more blankets and small boxes. Ahead of him, the room was large, its walls piled with boxes, a wooden rocking horse, a child's bookcase packed with children's books, the base of a porcelain sink, and other usual attic paraphernalia.

"I'm afraid that's all for now," said Randy, "If you want to open boxes and look under beds, you'll have to come back with a search warrant."

Sam didn't answer; he just turned and headed out of the room and downstairs. As he reached the second floor, his cell phone rang. He saw it was Sheriff Dade on the display.

"Yes, sir," he answered. A minute later, he said, "On my way."

Sam hurried down the stairs, and called, "Jeff, we've got to go now."

"Thanks for the tea, ma'am," Jeff said to Mrs. Bayard, "and your time."

"Sorry you have to rush off," Randy said loudly, but Sam was all ready down the front steps with Jeff close behind.

Chapter 43

Sarah and Aunt Tina sat at the Quinn's kitchen table, drinking iced tea, and staring at the grain of the wood. Connor and Gabe were in the barn, stacking hay. They had been out in Little Woods all morning with no results.

" I want to do something to help," announced Sarah suddenly and loudly, "I feel fine today. I'm perfectly capable of helping."

Aunt Tina looked at her, and said, "I have an idea. Let me make a phone call first."

She pulled the phone book out of a drawer, looked up a name, and dialed on her cell phone. Just then someone knocked on the screen door, so Sarah got up to answer it. Standing outside were two women, one slight, the other tall. Sarah smiled, and opened the door immediately.

"Ms. Tippet, Mrs. Englewood, it's so good of you to come," began Sarah.

"We conferred, and we think we may be able to help," stated Ms. Tippet.

"Come out in the kitchen, please. Mac's Aunt Tina is here, so we can all talk."

"Oh, we know Tina McCormick," said Mrs. Englewood, "She has a good head on her shoulders."

Sarah led the way to the kitchen. Ms. Tippet and Mrs. Englewood sat down, and listened quietly while Aunt Tina finished her phone call.

"Is there a way we can get in without being seen from the street?" Tina was asking, "All right. We have some new volunteers. I'll text you when we'll be arriving."

Aunt Tina clicked off her phone, and smiled at the visitors.

"Good to see you, Lorraine and Meredith. I was just talking with Vivian Mitchell."

"Sounds promising," said Ms. Tippet, "She lives in your neighborhood in town, right?"

"Yes," said Tina.

Sarah looked from one woman to the other, baffled.

Ms. Tippet smiled at her, and said, "Sarah, why don't you call me Lorraine?"

"And call me Meredith," said Mrs. Englewood.

Sarah nodded and smiled at them.

"We came," began Lorraine, "because we were just talking with Mac yesterday morning. We also spoke with her friend, that handsome deputy. They came to us individually to ask about one of our former students, Randy Bayard. Both were concerned about his intentions in following Mackenzie around town lately. We were not able to allay their fears. We have no proof of wrongdoing, but he may be mentally unstable."

"Yes," said Tina, "We were all talking about him last night. I know Sam was going to interview two suspects today, and Randy was one of them. We haven't heard anything yet. Sarah and I have been frustrated all day, just sitting here, but I've had an idea."

"Thus the call to Vivian," said Lorraine.

"Yes," said Tina, looking at Sarah, "Vivian lives next door to the Bayard's. I called her to ask if we could use her home to keep an eye on Randy."

"That's a great idea," Sarah leaned forward eagerly, "Can we get in without him seeing us?"

"Can I help?" asked Lorraine.

"And me?" said Meredith, "We'll need to do shifts."

"Yes to everyone," answered Tina, "Vivian has side and back entrances that we can use. She wants to help too, and she said her husband Dave probably would as well. I think we should go over there now, and decide who can watch where and when."

"We'd better take separate cars, and park a block or so away," suggested Sarah.

Half an hour later, the four women were seated in Vivian Mitchell's kitchen, and Sarah had been introduced. Vivian had taken them to the best vantage points in the house, one on each floor.

"Remember, no lights," said Tina, "except normal use by Vivian and Dave."

"I think Dave and I will have the first floor covered for the evening, mainly to see if Randy goes anywhere," said Vivian.

"If he does, I'll call Connor. He can talk to Sam and maybe someone can tail him," said Sarah, "I'd like to be the attic lookout for a few hours. I really think that's his best option to hide Mac."

"What about the basement?" asked Meredith.

"Another good possibility," said Vivian, "but the few windows down there have never been covered. We have rarely noticed lights on there. You have to remember that basements in these old houses are rarely finished, so aren't used for much except storage. There are two windows on this side, so we can see what little there is to see from the first floor."

"Tina, Vivian and I are the only ones who don't have to work tomorrow," stated Lorraine, "so I think we should take the night shift, say from 10:00 to 6:00. Sound all right?"

"I think you and I will be enough," agreed Tina, "One of us can be on the first floor, one in the attic. Vivian needs to get some sleep sometime, and we are commandeering her home."

"I think I'll head home and take a nap," said Lorraine, "I'm quite a night owl anyway."

"I'd better tell Gabe and Connor what we're up to," said Tina, "I don't want them to worry."

The two women left by the side French doors. Meredith settled herself with schoolwork in the dining room, and Sarah climbed up to the attic. She arranged a worn arm chair about three feet from the window. The curtains were sheers with a few holes, tears, and gaps between them, just enough for a clear view with the binoculars she'd brought. The only window across from her in the Bayard house was an incongruously large window. It looked like it had white eyelet curtains hung halfway up, then more white eyelet hung from the top. Sarah noticed that it was very wrinkled, and didn't close tightly, as though it had been pulled to the sides previously. When she walked toward the front of the attic, she could see a much smaller window, which seemed to be completely blocked with boxes, no curtains at all. She returned to her chair, and read for a while, looking up at the window at the end of every page. As the light dimmed outside, she had to stop reading, and used the binoculars to study every inch of the window. Suddenly the lighting of the window changed, going black behind the white curtains. A light had been on in the attic, and now it was off.

Chapter 44

Sam saw lights on in the Quinn home, as he drove up the lane a few minutes before midnight. The door swung open before he reached the top step.

"Come in, Sam," said Connor.

They joined Gabe at the kitchen table. Sam shook his head at the offer of a drink.

"I just wanted to let you know the latest," said Sam, "Jake Wade was walking his property about a mile or so from Little Woods, and found a new four-wheeler hidden in a gully."

"Hidden?" said Gabe.

"Yeah. It had a camouflage paint job, and was impossible to see from the road. Mr. Wade was following deer tracks, wanting to build a blind. If the tracks hadn't led to that gully, that thing could've been there for years. It had some leafy branches thrown across it, definitely hidden. Our techs have processed it at the scene. They found a long auburn hair caught in a joint, so we'll need Mac's hairbrush for DNA. I'm sure it's a match; there just aren't any other dark redheads like her in the area. It looks like the tire tracks match the ones in the woods, too. As soon as businesses open, we'll be scouring the county and Lexington for whoever bought that ATV."

"Good," said Gabe, "That's the first lead we've had."

"We've got some news of our own," said Connor, "but I don't know if you'll like it. Aunt Tina and Sarah and those teachers you talked to are set up in the house next door to the Bayard's. Aunt Tina is a friend with the owners, Vivian and Dave Mitchell. They're doing shifts; Aunt Tina and Lorraine Tippet are on tonight, because they don't have to work tomorrow. Sarah called when she got home, and said she saw a light go off in the attic about 7:30 tonight, but that was it."

Sam sat down at the table, and rubbed his hands across his face.

"Good grief," he said with a tired sigh, " How the hell are they getting in and out without being seen? We've got surveillance set up on the street."

"Apparently there are side and back doors," said Connor, "The Bayard's fence and garage block the back entrance, and the whole Mitchell house blocks the side. Randy can't see anything from his house. Depending on where your guy is, he might see the side entrance, but hasn't so far. Sarah promised me they wouldn't do anything stupid. They're supposed to call you, Gabe or me, if they notice anything suspicious."

"I'll talk to them tomorrow. At least we know we can get some men in there unobtrusively, but we're shorthanded. We were going to have everyone on the ATV hunt tomorrow. Actually, give me Aunt Tina's cell number. I'd better talk to her now."

Connor found the number, and handed Sam his phone. Sam dialed and waited.

"Aunt Tina, it's Sam Kincaid. When is the next shift change?" he paused, listening, "OK. I'll have two police or deputies there at the side entrance at 6:00 a.m. You can show them your setup, and let them take over. No arguing. It was a great idea, but it needs to be law enforcement in there."

"Sarah is going to be so disappointed," said Connor.

"Pissed," said Gabe with a rueful smile.

Chapter 45

Mac's head ached and throbbed when she woke up again. The room was dark, and she could tell she was belted to the bench. What the hell happened this time? She lay still, trying to remember. At first the room seemed so quiet, dead-of-the-night Belleriver quiet. Only her breathing broke the stillness. Suddenly she froze. She could hear someone else breathing very softly. Her eyes adjusted to the darkness. Just some faint light from the streetlamps outside allowed her to see dark grey and black shapes. Looking sideways to her right, she could see a man's silhouette between her and the crib.

"Ah, I see you've found me," Randy whispered, "I was hoping you'd wake up soon, so we could talk."

Mac didn't answer, remembering his earlier orders. She was furious, but making him mad wouldn't help.

"I suppose you want to know why I drugged you again," Randy said with a pained expression, "I'm just not sure I can trust you yet. Marcus doesn't. You looked rather incredulous when I introduced you. I decided you needed some sustenance and sleep to help you think things over. I moved you to another place for a while. Do you remember that?"

Mac nodded slowly. She vaguely remembered Randy carrying her and laying her on the floor of a room with only a red light. Darkroom, she thought, from the light and smell.

"Well, I'll show you how honest I'm being," Randy continued, "Drugging you then was perfect timing. We had some company: the police, and that sheriff's deputy you've been seeing. Sam Kincaid. I don't like him, and he doesn't like me. He doesn't believe that you and I are friends. Anyway, I showed him the whole house, including this room. Meanwhile, you were in the darkroom, which I couldn't open for him, since I had photographs developing. It was all rather stimulating for me – exciting! They're gone now, and we're safe. In fact, I'd like a little light, so that I can see your face."

Randy moved away briefly, flipped a switch, and a dim overhead bulb lit up. Mac was stunned with the news that Sam had been there, but she tried to compose her face. She blinked her eyes a few times at Randy.

"You may speak," he said.

"Randy, you know I'm an artist, right? I could do a drawing of Marcus for you. I could even do a painting. I could work from the photographs you have. I can paint him as he would be now, as a man."

Randy looked down at his hands, then over at the crib where the boy doll lay.

"Would you paint him without his illnesses? Whole and beautiful, like he should have been?" asked Randy softly.

"Yes, however you wanted him. You can help me," answered Mac.

"Is this a trick to get your hands untied?" Randy looked at her, frowning.

"You would need to untie my hands, but I assume you would be here the whole time. I want to do this for you, Randy," Mac said, "My mother died when I was twelve, and my husband when I was twenty. I know how much you love Marcus. I know how you felt, watching him in that crib."

"I'll think about it," Randy said, looking from her to the doll, and back to her again, "Go to sleep, Mackenzie. I'll see you tomorrow."

Randy stood, the light flicked off, and Mac heard the door open and close. She closed her eyes, thinking of Sam being there, so close, but leaving. He would be back, she was sure of it. She didn't think she could sleep again, especially with the headache. It was going to be a long night. She began visualizing a man's face on a canvas, a man with big, brown eyes in a normal sized head on normal shoulders.

* * *

Hours later Mac jerked out of sleep, when the door banged open and shut. The light came on, and Randy stood before her, his arms full of bags, and what was obviously a canvas wrapped in brown paper.

"Ta da!" crowed Randy, "I'm sure I have everything you'll need. I went to Lexington. I think someone was trying to follow me, but I lost him. You're not sleepy, are you? It's only 10:00 o'clock. I thought you could get started tonight."

Randy pulled a sketchpad out of one of the bags, then a package of drawing pencils, a set of oil paint tubes, linseed oil and turpentine. Mac blinked furiously, but he didn't notice, so she whispered, "Randy!" He looked at her, and she blinked again.

"Permission to speak," he said with a smile.

"This is great, Randy," Mac said, "Can you sit me up and undo my hands? I need to do a sketch first. You've got to help me get the likeness right before I can paint."

"Sure," he answered, and immediately lifted her to a sitting position, and cut the tape around her wrists. While she massaged her burning wrists, he laid the sketchbook in her lap, and took the drawing pencils out of the package.

"Look, they're already sharpened," Randy said triumphantly, "and I got you a kneaded eraser. The arts and crafts teacher back at the hospital said it was the best."

"That's good, Randy," said Mac, "Can we look at the photos now?"

Randy sat next to her on the bench, and opened the small photo album for her again. When he reached the close-up of Marcus's face, Mac touched it, and said, "Would you take that one out, and lay it on the sketchpad, so I can look at it, while I draw?"

He did, and Mac began sketching an oval very lightly. In the center of the head, she started the eyes.

"Wait," interrupted Randy, "His eyes should be higher. That's too much forehead."

"Don't worry," Mac looked at him, "That will be covered mostly with hair. See, that's the top of the head, not his hairline. Is that right for the shape of his eyes?"

"Yes," Randy's frown relaxed.

"The eyes are the most important part of the face. I always start with the eyes. You do want this to look like Marcus would now, right, as a grown man?"

"Yes," said Randy, "He was four or five years older than me, so he'd still be a young man, about 30 years old."

Mac worked steadily, stopping to ask Randy about each feature. Was that the right length for the nose? (Yes.) Did he want Marcus smiling or serious? (Just a faint smile, one side of his mouth turned up.) How long would his hair be? Would it cover his ears? (Long over his forehead, but trimmed above his ears.) Were his shoulders wide enough? (Almost, just a little broader.) What kind of shirt did he want Marcus wearing? (Button-down collar.) In a little over an hour, Mac finished a portrait of a handsome, dark-haired, dark-eyed young man. His eyes were large, and warm, but a little sad. His nose had a small bump, like Randy's did. His slight smile was engaging, like he was ready to smile bigger, just for you. She handed the pad to Randy. He stared at it for a long time. When he looked at Mac, there were tears in his eyes.

"It's him," he said with a quaver in his voice, "It's my brother, Marcus. Can you paint him? Can you start tonight?"

Chapter 46

Sam spent most of Monday driving to ATV dealerships in the area, showing a photo
of Randy Bayard, courtesy of the Kentucky Department of Motor Vehicles, and asking if
that man had shopped for and/or purchased a Kawasaki Camouflage Teryx in their store.
Other deputies and Versailles police had the same job, and were texting Sam periodically
with updates. At 3:00 p.m. he'd finished his list, and headed over to the Mitchell's to take
a shift. He'd already heard about the failed attempt to follow Randy Sunday evening, and
was very disappointed. Two unmarked cars were on Davis Avenue now. Sam was driving
his own car, and parked around the corner. He walked up the side steps of the Mitchell
home, and knocked on the French doors. Dave Mitchell opened the door for him.

"Hello, Sam," he said, "Sorry, but no news so far."

"I'm the relief," Sam replied, "and I want to check with both officers. I know it's
tough, but you and Vivian should try to do what you normally would, especially if it
involves going outside. We don't want him to get suspicious."

Dave nodded, and motioned Sam toward the dining room. An older Versailles
policeman sat at the dining room table, where he could easily see out the windows with
or without binoculars. The Mitchell's three windows in a row were covered with sheers,
and heavier tiebacks pulled to the sides. The officer had a good view of the Bayard side
windows, which had curtains closed, and he could see the driveway, and part of the front
porch. Sam recognized Walter Jenson, a big man around 40 years old; he said a soft "hey,
Walt", and sat in another dining room chair.

"Nothing, Sam," said Walt, "I haven't seen a curtain move. Actually Mrs. Bayard came out to get the mail around 11:00, but nothing else."

"You can't see the back entrance at all, can you?" Sam leaned forward, looking toward the Bayard's garage, "That's quite a fence."

"Man likes his privacy," commented Walt, "but you can see over it from the attic. You can see if anyone goes out in the yard, or out that back gate over there. Unfortunately, the garage also connects to the house, so no view when he uses the car, unless he leaves down the driveway."

"Good," said Sam, "I'll go upstairs and check. Who's up there?"

"Your new guy, Carver," said Walt, "How's he working out?"

"Good, so far," answered Sam, "He's a hard worker. Your replacement will be here soon. We'll do three shifts as long as we can. Thanks for coming in on your day off."

"No problem, Sam," Walt looked at him seriously, "Mac is good people. We have to find her." Then he turned back to the windows.

Sam walked through the kitchen, where Vivian was making ham sandwiches. Two sheets of cookies cooled on the stove.

"You don't have to feed us," Sam said, "but thank you for letting us use your home."

"It gives me something to do," Vivian smiled at him, "Besides, you can't focus if you're hungry."

She handed him a paper plate with a thick sandwich and two oatmeal cookies.

"That's for your man upstairs," she said, "I'll bring you up something later."

Sam thanked her and headed up the back stairs to the attic. He came up ten feet behind a young black man dressed in jeans, high tops, and a long-sleeve navy tee shirt, sitting in an old stuffed armchair. The young man was turned, waiting to see who appeared. Sam handed him the plate, and pulled a wooden chair up beside the deputy.

"Hey, Mike," Sam said, "Seen anything?"

"I saw Randy Bayard take a plastic bag out behind the garage this morning," said Mike, "He went right back in the house, and hasn't left since. I think there was a light turned off in the attic when I first got here. It's just visible in the crack between the curtains, and around the edges, but it's hard to tell in the daylight. It was dark enough at 6:00 that I thought I could tell a difference in the light. The lady who was here, Mrs.

McCormick, said she thought a light was on all night. I guess that's why I noticed when it went off."

"Good," said Sam, "All we can do is pay attention to the slightest changes. Stakeouts are rare here, but they are long and boring."

"Here's a log that the ladies started," Mike handed a notepad to Sam.

"Ten-fifteen last night," Sam read out loud, "Glimpse of Randy Bayard's Camry pulling into…"

Just then, they heard footsteps on the stairs, and turned to look simultaneously. Sarah's dark wavy hair and worried face appeared over the railing. She was carrying a cloth bag that Sam was sure held schoolwork.

"I'm sorry, Sam," she began, "I had to come. I can't sit around doing nothing. I went crazy at school all day. The kids must think I've lost my mind!"

"You can stay for awhile," Sam responded, "but this has to be handled by us. Mike, I'll take over now. Can you do the same shift tomorrow?"

"Yeah, anytime," said Mike, "Mary's doing the schedule, making sure everyone gets some sleep, and the regular work gets done. Good luck, Sam."

Mike left, eating his sandwich and carrying the cookies. Sarah plopped in the chair Mike had vacated. She leaned forward, looking intently at the window next door. After a few minutes, she sat back in the chair, and sighed.

"Nothing's changed," she said, "I think I have that window memorized, every stain in the woodwork, every wrinkle in the curtains. I'm going to see it in my dreams for the rest of my life."

"Mike said that Tina saw a light on," said Sam.

"I'm not surprised. I saw one go off when I first got here yesterday. Then I saw it go on later, right before Tina took my place. That's suspicious, right?" Sarah looked at Sam eagerly.

"To me it is," he answered, "Especially since it was on all night. I suppose you could argue that someone just forgot to turn it off. Anyway, it's not enough for a warrant."

"Sam, could I stay just for a few hours, please? I can grade papers, until it gets dark. That way, you can take a break, if you need to."

"Sure," he said softly, "Company would be good."

His Brother's Eyes, Travers   206

Chapter 47

Mac stared at the image on the canvas, watched it blur out-of-focus, then clear up
again. She rubbed her eyes and yawned.

"Randy," she whispered. Her captor looked up at her from the book in his lap.

"I have to sleep," Mac said softly, "I've run out of steam. If you want this to be any
good, I have to eat and sleep."

She had painted all night and morning, only breaking to go to the bathroom, which
Randy helped her do, the same embarrassing routine. He brought her bottled water, and
tied her up, when he went to get that. He was obsessed, and stayed with her the whole
time. At least he stopped watching every brushstroke, after she told him he was driving
her crazy, and she couldn't paint with someone watching. Initially he made her a
makeshift easel, using boxes, and leaned the canvas against the crib. He gave her a plastic
palette to mix her paints, which lay on a box. At first, he was overly concerned about the
quality of brushes and paints he bought for her. She told him everything was excellent,
even though it was all just moderate craft store quality. Her legs remained heavily taped.
He sat on the bench she had been tied to at first, but when she asked him not to watch, he
moved an old, wooden rocking chair into the front part of the room, and rocked and read.
At one point, she asked him what he was reading.

"My Brother's Keeper by Marcia Davenport," he answered drily, "Appropriate, don't
you think?"

"I don't know," Mac said, "I've never read it."

"Well, obviously, it's about two brothers," Randy continued, "It isn't like Marcus and
me. It's very sad in a different way, but it's about loyalty between brothers, and that's

what counts. It's my favorite book. I stole it from the hospital library. I'm sure my father paid enough to cover the cost."

Sometime before dawn, Randy slipped quietly out of his chair and into the bathroom. Mac was stunned. He hadn't tied her up. Still, her legs were tied, and she didn't think she could untie them quickly enough to get out the door. Just then she sensed the bathroom door opening. He was testing her. It wasn't hard to pretend to be completely absorbed in the painting. A few seconds later, the door closed. Soon she heard the toilet flush and water running in the sink. He opened the door again, flipped off the light, and returned to his chair. Mac continued to paint, aware that Randy watched her for a few minutes, then returned to reading.

Gradually, he became more impatient. He was irritated when she asked to go to the bathroom a second time. He looked at what she'd finished when he placed her back in the chair, and frowned.

"It doesn't look like anyone," he complained, "It certainly doesn't look like Marcus. Are you trying to trick me?"

"Painting is a lot different than drawing," she explained, "I have to build up layers to get the shadows right. It takes me weeks to finish the paintings I usually do."

"Weeks!" he cried, "I can't wait weeks! Just get to work. I want it finished this week!"

"Randy, calm down," Mac glared at him, "I'll do the best I can. Do you want it to be good or not?"

"Of course I want it to be good," he pouted.

"Then please be patient," Mac kept staring at him, until he met her gaze and nodded. She went back to work, thinking, "This has to be the weirdest kidnapping relationship ever."

By eleven o'clock, she was exhausted. She didn't know it was eleven o'clock, but figured it was close to midday. She made her request.

"You're right," Randy stood and put his book down on the rocker seat, "I'll go fix us something to eat, and you can have a nap. Let's get you back on the bench."

Mac fell asleep almost as soon as she heard the door shut and lock. It seemed like seconds later that Randy was shaking her shoulder.

"Wake up, sleepyhead," he said, cutting the tape on her wrists, "I let you sleep over two hours. When you eat, you'll feel better."

He handed her a napkin with a sandwich that looked like turkey and Swiss cheese. On the bench he sat a plastic cup.

"It's another fruit smoothie," he smiled, "Nutritious and filling."

Mac took a bite and blinked her eyes at him, in case the no talking without permission rule still held.

"Yes, go ahead."

"Can I ask you some questions?"

"You can ask. I may not answer."

She sipped the smoothie, strawberry and banana this time.

"What have you been doing to help Marcus since you came back?"

"Hmmmmmm," he leaned back against the bench, looking at her suspiciously, "Do you mean what have I done to solve the doll problem?"

Mac frowned. He knew it was a doll? What the hell was going on?

"Mackenzie, I'm not stupid. I know it's a doll," Randy continued, "But I also know Marcus is still here, in that doll. Why else would his eyes move and blink? Marcus and I have talked and talked, trying to figure out how to give him a body, the one he should have had. Obviously, the small animals weren't enough. So we decided to go bigger."

Mac gasped, "Zeke?" She couldn't keep the fury out of her voice, "You tried to kill that beautiful horse?"

"It would have been worth it, if it brought Marcus back to life," Randy stated, oblivious to her fury.

Mac realized immediately that she couldn't get angry with him. He might get angry with her in return. She lowered her eyes, and took another bite of her sandwich.

"That's true," she choked out, and sipped her smoothie again, "What happened? You could have shot again, and killed him."

"I saw you," he said, "I was pretty sure who you were, and that was a sign."

"Of what?" Mac asked.

"I didn't know at the time, but after talking to Marcus, I realized that I had to step it up."

"Step it up how?"

Randy looked at her sideways, "Come on, Mackenzie, you know."

"No, I don't," she looked directly at him, "Tell me."

"I don't think I should. You might not approve. After all, you tried to stop me when we were kids, when I hurt those animals."

"Tried to stop you?" Mac tried to sound incredulous, "I was just watching you. I wanted to know who did it. And why. You seemed too young to be that brave, but I'd eliminated the suspicious people I knew. You were new in town."

She trailed off, thinking she sounded ridiculous. He would never buy that.

"Really? You thought I was brave?" Randy's eyes were bright.

"Well, yeah. I think it takes courage to kill," she stopped again.

"Yes, yes, it does," Randy agreed, nodding, staring at her, "You know what takes more courage? Killing people."

Mac sat up straight, trying to look amazed and impressed, "Really?"

"I'm the sniper," he announced triumphantly.

Mac was trembling, so she put her hand holding the sandwich in her lap.

"Wow, Randy, that's incredible," she managed, "Did it help Marcus?"

"He said he felt stronger each time," Randy answered.

Mac tried not to show her fear, and asked, "Is that why you brought me here?"

"Oh, no," Randy leaned forward and put his hand on her arm, "Marcus said to bring you. For company. And you can be my witness. But now, with this painting, who knows? Maybe that will do it. That's why I'm so impatient. I'm sorry I've been irritable. This has been good. I had no idea you were so sympathetic. Finish your sandwich, and get back to painting, OK?"

"I will," Mac said, "but please don't get your hopes up. I don't know if my painting will have that much power."

"Never know until we try," he said.

Chapter 48

Sam's phone rang softly in the open space of the attic. Sarah looked up from her papers expectantly. Sam saw Jeff's name on the display.

"Yeah," Sam answered, "OK. They've all been checked. Then we have to widen the search. What about a private sale? OK. Thanks. Let me know."

"Damn," he said quietly, as he put the phone down, then he looked at Sarah, "That was Jeff Parker. No luck on the ATV search, so far. You're losing light. Don't ruin your eyes."

Sarah nodded, and began stacking her papers in one pile.

" I know it's your job, but have your guys asked around, talked to ATV buffs who might know about private sales, or out of the way dealers," she trailed off, not wanting to offend Sam.

"It's all right, Sarah. Actually, Connor and Gabe are on that, calling around. They gave my office a list of people they thought could help. Also we've got a deputy who's really good on the Internet, and she's been searching too. The title is under a name we can't find anywhere in the state: Seymour Randall Holt. It's got to be an alias, so it could be Bayard."

"The 'Randall' fits. Randy," Sarah mused. She picked up her papers and slipped them back in her bag.

"Sam, I'm going to get us something to eat. Any requests?"

"I'm not that hungry. Anything is fine. I imagine Mrs. Mitchell cooked for us again. We owe these people big time."

While Sarah was gone, Sam watched the window intently. Now that it was getting darker, he could tell the light was on over there again. Maybe it had been on all day. He was sure Mac was over there. It took all of his self-control not to rush over and storm the attic.

Five minutes later Sarah was back with a tray of sandwiches, soup and sweet tea. She divided the food in front of them on the table. Sam began on the soup. He didn't feel hungry, but it was something to do, while watching the window. They ate in silence for a few minutes.

"Sam," Sarah spoke, "Do you think he's the sniper?"

"Maybe," said Sam, "I know he has Mac, and I can't figure out why. If he was the sniper, does she know something that would give him away? She just doesn't know she knows."

"That's possible," Sarah agreed, "He's definitely crazy. Maybe he just took her, because she turned him down at the barn dance. If he is the sniper, how did he do the shooting at the barn? It seemed like he was inside the whole time."

"By his own admission, he went out to his car right before the shooting started. He said he went to get his camera, but when the shooting started, he came back. He could just as easily have been the one shooting from the parking area. He shot who he could, then came back in, made sure he was seen, in particular by me. Almost perfect alibi. We didn't search the cars of the people inside the barn. After we questioned them, they were allowed to leave. I'm sure he had the gun hidden. I don't know how, but…"

Suddenly Sam's head jerked up, and he muttered, "His camera case." Then he stared at Sarah.

"His camera case is huge. He could easily dismantle a rifle and hide it in there," he said.

"Yes, and he can take it anywhere around here without being questioned or searched," said Sarah.

"It was in the attic hallway, outside the darkroom that he wouldn't let me into. The rifle could have been right there."

"You didn't have a warrant, Sam," Sarah reminded him.

"And I still don't," he sighed, "I wish they could find the dealer who sold him that ATV."

They finished eating in silence, both of them watching the window most of the time. The light in the Bayard attic remained on, as it got darker outside. At about 9:30, Sam looked at Sarah and said, "You'd better get some rest, girl. You have to teach tomorrow."

"I know," she said, "I'll leave at 10:00. I won't sleep anyway."

Sam's phone rang. It was Jeff again.

"Hello," Sam answered, then listened, and after a few minutes, slapped his thigh, "That's great! Get to Stan Frohock right away. Bring the warrant as soon as you can. Yeah, bye."

"The ATV?" asked Sarah.

"Yep, we got him! Private seller outside Lexington. Word of mouth. Someone Gabe and Connor gave us knew someone who knew someone, etc. He lives out in the country north of Lexington, so it took awhile to find him, but he identified Randy. Very definite. Said he was paid extra to deliver the ATV down here. Not to Randy's house, so we have to check the property ownership, but he said it was a shed down here, outside Belleriver," Sam paused, " Sarah, you really should go home, while we do this."

"No way, Sam," Sarah said, "I'll leave the house if I have to, but I'll be in my car. Are you making the Mitchell's leave? I'll just stay here with them."

"All right," Sam shook his head, "I knew you'd say that. I don't know who is more stubborn, you or Mac. Jeff should be here within an hour. Please don't call Connor or Gabe, until we have her. Or Aunt Tina, or anyone else."

Sarah frowned, but nodded.

"I'm going downstairs for a minute to tell the Mitchell's and the other lookout what's going on," said Sam, "You're as good as I am at keeping a lookout."

When Sam reached the dining room, he was surprised to see the Sheriff sitting at the table, binoculars to his eyes.

"Sheriff Dade," he said, and stopped.

"Hi, Sam," said Parker Dade, "Thought I'd take a shift. Besides, Gabe Quinn is a friend of mine."

"Thanks, sir," answered Sam, "We've got a warrant coming."

"About damn time," said the Sheriff.

Sam continued to fill him in on the news from Jeff Parker.

"Could you tell the Mitchell's?" asked Sam, "I need to get upstairs…"

"What's up?" asked Dave Mitchell, as he and Vivian walked into the room, "Thought we heard our name. Actually, we could hear a lot in the living room."

"Especially when someone turns down the sound on the TV," Vivian looked sideways at her husband, "Sorry for eavesdropping, Sam."

"It's OK. You've been a huge help. Just please stay here, in the house, when we head over there. Sheriff, do you want to call for backup?"

Just then, they heard feet on the stairs, and Sarah ran into the room.

"Sam, come up now," she cried, "You have to see this."

Sam was running up the stairs before she could finish, Sarah in the lead, followed by the Sheriff and the Mitchell's. Sam was staring at the window. The Bayard's attic light was still on, but he didn't see anything different at first. Sarah handed him the binoculars, and pointed to the lower left hand corner of the sill.

"Look down there, Sam," she said, her voice shaking, "Do you see it? It's a brushstroke! Paint. Fresh brown paint."

Chapter 49

Sam didn't say a word. He turned and ran to the stairs.

"Sam!" called Sheriff Dade, "Wait."

Sam paused and looked over his shoulder.

"You need to think first. Tell me how a brushstroke gives us probable cause without the warrant. Besides you need backup."

"I can handle Randy," said Sam, then he sighed and turned around to face the Sheriff, "Mac is an artist. I have no idea why she has paint as a kidnap victim, but there is less reason for Randy to be painting, let alone on the window. She's over there, and that's a signal."

"OK. I'm going with you. Let me call Mary and get us more backup, no sirens. You call Jeff. Then we'll go."

Both men quickly made their calls, and headed down the stairs. Sarah was trembling, wanting to follow them, but she made herself sit down, and continue to watch the window.

Sam stopped again at the back door, when Sheriff Dade touched his arm.

"We need to decide the best way to do this," Dade said, "It would be easier and smarter to wait for backup."

"I'm going in, Parker," Sam said, "I'd suggest that you go to the front, sweet talk whoever answers. I'll be at the back door. If you don't come and get me in two minutes, I'm coming in, one way or another."

"OK. Just one question," answered the sheriff, "How are you getting over that fence?"

"I can do it," said Sam, and took off down the stairs Sheriff Dade right behind him.

Sam stuck his head out the back door and looked at the Bayard's eight-foot fence. On the Mitchell side, he saw a picnic table, which he dragged over to the fence. When he stood on it, he could easily reach the top of the fence, but it was much harder to pull himself up and over the top. Dropping on the other side sent a shock through his knees, but he reflexively bent them on landing, which helped some. He hurried up to the back steps that led to a screened-in porch. That door was unlocked, so Sam stepped inside. The inner door was half window and he could see into the kitchen. It looked like someone had been cooking, and didn't bother to clean up. A loaf of bread sat open on the counter, along side a blender. Sam could see the door that led to the attic, the "servants' stairs". Gently he tried the handle. Just then he heard footsteps behind him and turned back to the kitchen. Striding toward him was Sheriff Dade.

"I think Mrs. Bayard has lost it," said the sheriff in a low voice, "She told me it was about time I showed up, and to get that woman out of her attic. Then she sat down and stared, wouldn't talk anymore."

"I think you'd better go up the front stairs, all the way to the third floor," Sam said quietly, "I'll take the back stairs."

Sam pulled his weapon, as did the Sheriff, who left the kitchen, heading toward the front of the house. Sam gently opened the stairway door, and climbed as quickly and quietly as possible up the three flights. When he opened the door at the top, he saw three closed doors, and the sheriff's eyes peaking over the floor between the banisters. When Dade saw Sam, he nodded and climbed quickly up to the landing. Sam stood on one side of the door that led to the middle room, and motioned Sheriff Dade to stay on the other side. Just then Randy Bayard's voice called out from inside.

"The door is locked, Sam, and you're not invited. I need for you to go away, and let Mac finish her work."

Sam leaned back and side-kicked the door as hard as he could. It cracked and fell inward with a loud bang. About ten feet ahead of him Mac was sitting on a straight-backed wooden chair with an easel in front of her. In her hand was a paintbrush poised in front of a two feet by three feet portrait of a dark-haired man with piercing, dark brown eyes. Behind her stood Randy Bayard holding an x-acto knife to Mac's neck, and smiling furiously at Sam.

"Don't even think…" began Randy, when Sam's pistol exploded. Randy fell backward, dropped the knife, and grabbed his left shoulder. Blood spread down his shirt. Sam was on him in a second, rolling him over, pulling his arms behind his back, and locking on cuffs. Randy was screaming, and thrashing on the floor, so Sam sat on his legs, and held him down. Then Sam felt a hand on his shoulder, and Sheriff Dade said, "I've got him."

"Hold still, son," Dade spoke to Randy, "We'll get an ambulance on the way."

"He shot me, that son of a bitch," shrieked Randy, "I'll kill him! I'll kill him!"

Sam turned Mac, and grabbed her in his arms. She held him tightly; then he felt her talking into his shoulder, and pulling back.

"I'm getting paint all over you," she repeated, laughing.

"Oh my God, who cares?" Sam said, pulling her back into his chest.

"Sam, can you untie my legs?" Mac asked, "What day is it?"

Sam pulled out his pocketknife and slit the tape holding her legs. She rubbed her legs where the tape had been. After a few minutes Mac tried to stand, but fell back in the chair.

"It's ok, babe," said Sam, "Give yourself time."

Just then Jeff Parker and another cop appeared in the doorway.

"Are you OK, Mackenzie?" asked Jeff.

Mac nodded, and tried to stand again with Sam's help. This time she stayed up. Jeff and the other policeman slipped past her to help Sheriff Dade. Randy was sobbing and muttering unintelligibly.

"Let's get you out of here," said Sam.

"Just a minute," Mac answered, and then called, "Randy. Randy, stop crying. I'll finish it."

Bayard's sobs died down to deep, shuddering breaths and sniffling. Sheriff Dade and Jeff turned him over and up into a sitting position.

"You will?" Randy looked at Mac in disbelief.

"I will," she said.

Then she and Sam walked slowly out of the attic, arms around each other's waists.

Chapter 50

Sam finally drove Mac home around midnight. He insisted she go to the hospital to get checked out. First she and Sarah hugged, then Sarah called Connor and Gabe at the ranch. Mac talked to them both and convinced them not to come to the hospital. Sam would bring her home as soon as possible. Mac tried to tell Sam he could stay at the scene, but he just smiled and said, "I think they can handle it." It seemed like every officer and deputy in the county was somewhere on the Bayard property. Sam settled Mac in the passenger seat of his car and drove her to the Bluegrass Community Hospital. Sarah met them there with clean clothes for Mac, who hugged her hard, and teared up for the first time. Sarah headed back out to the ranch to begin answering questions. After a very short wait and a much longer examination, an emergency room physician pronounced Mac fit to go home, and resume normal activity, as she felt like it.

"Is it really OK, if I do my statement tomorrow?" Mac asked for about the fifth time, as they turned in the lane to the ranch.

"Yes," said Sam, "Call me first, although you'll probably give it to someone else. I think you'll be telling this story over and over for a long time."

"Starting now," she said, looking with love at the people standing on her front porch. As Sam braked, Gabe hurried down the front steps. Her father was opening her car door before Sam could get around to that side. He scooped her out of the seat and hugged her gently. Mac hugged him back hard.

"I'm OK, Dad. I won't break."

"Thank God," said Gabe.

"Pass her along, Gabe," said Aunt Tina, reaching in for her hug. Then Connor, then Sarah again.

"Let's get her inside," said Aunt Tina, brushing tears from her cheeks, "I'll bet you're exhausted, honey. Time for bed."

"Oh, no," said Mac, "I've had enough lying down to last me awhile. I need some real food and I can tell you what happened. I'm tired, but not ready for sleep yet."

They went into the living room. Mac sat on the couch with her Dad on one side and Aunt Tina on the other, but Tina jumped back up.

"I'll get you something to eat. How's a roast beef sandwich and lemonade sound? And Sam, you sit next to our girl, where I was. You saved her, after all."

Sam sat next to Mac, and reached for her hand. Her father held her other hand.

"You guys realize I'll need these when the food comes?" Mac said, squeezing their hands.

"OK, what happened?" asked Connor, "Do you even remember Randy taking you?"

He and Sarah were happily sharing a large, soft armchair that was usually Gabe's.

"I remember bending over Sarah, then nothing," said Mac, "Let's wait for Aunt Tina."

Just then, Tina returned, and handed a plate of roast beef sandwich and potato salad to Mac, putting a glass of lemonade on the coffee table.

"I can't talk and eat, so why don't you guys fill me in on what happened to Sarah, and what you all have been doing," Mac took a big bite of her sandwich, and closed her eyes briefly.

By the time everyone had contributed, Mac was finished eating. She put her plate down, and told them about her two days in the Bayard attic, leaving out nothing. She was embarrassed about the bathroom situation, but these were the people she loved most in the world, and telling them the truth was better than them imagining. As she finished that part, she realized what she had just thought: the people she loved most. Including Sam. She looked at him, flushed, and went on with her story.

"Last night was the worst. Once he saw that I would paint his brother's portrait, he wouldn't let me stop. Yesterday, sometime in the daylight, he tested me to see what I would do, if he left me unsupervised with my hands untied. Luckliy, I figured that was his idea, so I kept painting, and pretended to be totally engrossed. He just went in the bathroom, and after a minute or so, he peeked out. I pretended not to see him. I finally asked to eat and sleep, and that's when he talked to me about helping Marcus. Apparently his brother "told" him to kill the animals, which was supposed to give Marcus power and rejuvenate him. I lied to him about my purpose in watching him as a kid. I said I thought he was brave to kill. Anyway, I guess he believed that I was won over to his side, even after he told me that he was the sniper. Sometime yesterday evening, he actually left the room. I waited, but he didn't peek in, so I quickly stood up, shuffled over to the window, and swiped a brushstroke, then recovered the window with the curtains. I wasn't sure that you were watching over there, but thought you might be."

"Thanks to Sarah and Aunt Tina," interrupted Connor.

"Yes, " said Sam, "Have I thanked you ladies enough? We might've gotten in there eventually, but you got us moving, and we might not have been in time otherwise."

Sarah and Aunt Tina smiled. Mac smiled back at both of them.

"Randy was back ten minutes later with food. My hands were still shaking, but he didn't notice. We ate, and he insisted I keep working. He kept talking while I painted, telling me about how he shot all of those people, and Cat on Fire, without being caught. He was so proud, and thought he got away with it, because he had a righteous purpose: bringing Marcus to life. He believed Marcus's spirit was alive in the doll. He said Marcus told him to kidnap me for company and to be his witness. I don't think I believe that. I'm pretty sure he would have eventually killed me too. Anyway, suddenly he stopped talking, and went out of the room for a few seconds. I don't know what he heard, or how, since he said the room is soundproofed."

"It's not," said Sam, "His mother knew something was going on. She is terrified of her son, and pretty off balance herself. When Sheriff Dade came in, and said we had a warrant to search on the way, she broke immediately. She told him that Randy had company in the attic. The Sheriff told her to sit down and not move, and she did. Then he headed up the front stairs, while I came up the back."

"When Randy came back into the room, he hissed at me to keep painting, but that we had company coming. Instead of going back to his rocker, he sat right next to me, holding the x-acto knife. When Sam kicked in the door, Randy moved the knife up to my neck. Randy started to talk to him, but Sam didn't answer. He just shot. He hit Randy in the arm or shoulder holding the knife, which he dropped, and Sam dived on him. Then Sheriff Dade took over holding Randy. It was so fast. I'm just glad to be home."

Mac slumped back against Sam, who gently pulled her against him.

"Thank you, Sam," said Gabe hoarsely. "I can't thank you enough."

"Thank you, Sam," said Tina. Sarah and Connor nodded.

Sam blushed, head down, released Mac, and slowly stood up.

"I'd better be going," he said. "You should try to sleep."

"I'll walk you out," said Mac, standing, and taking his hand.

They walked out on the front porch, listening to the night sounds, and the quiet goodnights from inside the house. Mac slowly turned toward Sam, and slid her arm around his back. Suddenly he pulled her close, and buried his face in her hair. They stood that way for a long time.

"I can't lose you, Mac," Sam whispered next to her cheek.

"You won't," she said softly into his chest, "You won't."

Chapter 51

Mac and Sam walked hand-in-hand along the Keeneland track rail. They had come early for the race, so that Mac could show Sam around. John Blake had given Mac a seat in his box, and when she asked if she could bring Sam, Blake was delighted to give her seats for her whole family. She and Sam had even been allowed to visit Cat on Fire, and Mac thought he looked incredible. He was calm, letting Mac rub his neck and Sam stroke his nose. Mac could feel the power under the sleek dark coat.

It was about a month since Cat on Fire had been nicked by a sniper's bullet. You had to look hard to see the scar, and Blake said he'd been desensitizing Zeke to the sound of gunfire. "Didn't take much work," was his comment, "That horse is unflappable."

Mac had finished the painting of Cat on Fire, running not in fear, but with pure joy. Blake had been thrilled, and purchased two of her watercolor studies, and a pencil sketch, as well.

Countless reporters, and a true crime writer had approached Mac to tell her story, but she declined. She didn't plan on ever telling the story publicly, except in court. Some gossips in the area would buzz about the sniper for years, but most of Belleriver wanted to put the ordeal behind them. Mac and her family didn't talk about it much, and didn't badger Sam for information. Randy Bayard was being held without bail in the Woodford County Detention Center. His mother was in a mental health facility in Lexington. She sat in a chair and didn't speak. The family lawyer insisted she be kept on suicide watch. The Bayard home was off limits, still draped in yellow crime scene tape.

Mac and Sam stopped and leaned on the rail, looking out over the track.

"I finished the painting of Marcus," said Mac abruptly.

Sam was quiet for a minute, waiting for her. He knew there was more.

"I'm going to give it to him at some point," she said.

"OK," Sam responded, still waiting.

"I know what he did was evil," Mac went on, "I don't feel sorry for him. He killed innocent people, and caused so much pain. He'll be quite a case study for some psychiatrist, even if he gets the death penalty. He is insane, but that doesn't exonerate him. His parents are guilty too, hiding his brother like that. No wonder Randy's so messed up. I can't exactly explain it. Partly I did it for Marcus. He's the one innocent in this mess. I had to finish the painting, and I want to give it to Randy, even if it makes him happy."

"It's OK, Mac," said Sam, putting his arm around her shoulders, "You don't have to know why. Maybe it will make him more manageable for whoever has to take care of him for the rest of his life. Do you want to give it to him in person?"

"Not particularly. Could you find out what the jail allows? Or maybe I should wait until the trial is over, and we find out where he'll be."

"I'll look into it," Sam said, relieved that she didn't want to see Randy again.

Just then they heard their names being called. Looking back at the grandstands, they saw Sarah and Connor waving, and moving quickly through the benches on the ground level. Sarah was grinning, hanging on to Connor's arm, and he was beaming. Sarah let go of Connor's arm, and held up her left hand. A sparkling diamond ring glittered on her ring finger. Mac grabbed her, while Sam and Connor shook hands.

"Congratulations!" grinned Sam.

"This is so great!" crowed Mac, "Now you'll be my sister! Does Dad know?"

"Yep," said Connor, "We told him first, well, after we called Sarah's parents and sister. He and Aunt Tina are up in Mr. Blake's box. They're waiting on you two to open the champagne."

"Surely Mr. Blake wants to save that for Cat on Fire's win," said Mac.

"That's what we said, but he insisted," answered Sarah.

The two couples wove through the gathering crowd and climbed up to Blake's private seats. The relatively small group of about twenty was dressed to the nines, as Aunt Tina said. None of Mac's family dressed up often, but today was special, and more formal attire was required for the private box. Sam wore a grey suit, while Connor's was dark blue, and Mac and Sarah sparkled in knee-length dresses with fitted waists and swirly skirts. Sarah's was navy blue with tiny white polka dots and Mac's was dark green. Blake and Cat on Fire's colors were hunter green with a white cat's paw print on the back and sleeve of the silks, and Mac wanted to show her support. Robert Blake made sure Mac's family had their own table, and he introduced her as the artist who had painted Zeke. Luckily Blake's other guests were too polite to interrogate Mac, or had been told the story ahead of time, so she got to enjoy a fairly normal day at the races.

Mac, Sarah and Connor pored over the program and the tip sheets they'd bought. Sam was looking at a printed sheet with handwriting in the margins, and marking his program.

"Whatcha got there, hotshot?" asked Mac, grinning.

Sam looked back at her sheepishly.

"I did tell you about my dad, didn't I?" he said.

"Oh, yeah, he's a gambler, which you hate," she answered.

"Sort of," said Sam, "I sure hated it when I was growing up, but now he's a horseplayer, and he's damn good at it. He's been making a living at it for years now. He doesn't do any other gambling at all, which is good, because he always lost at anything else. My mom wouldn't even need to be a nurse anymore, but she likes it, and puts most of it in savings or investments, and spends it on her grandkids. I've been visiting them more, and talking with him about racing."

Mac was watching him, and trying not to smile too much.

"And?" she said.

"And he gave me some pointers on today's races. He actually showed me what he does to research every horse. He doesn't bet every race, only if the odds are good. "

"So, are you going to share?" Mac asked. By now, Connor and Sarah were listening too.

"Sure, if you want," said Sam, "but I can't make any guarantees."

"Well, in that case, what good are you?" laughed Connor.

"I want to wait and see how you do," said Sarah, "before we make this a syndicate. I'll probably use my tried and true prettiest horse method."

"Who did your dad pick in the Futurity?" asked Connor.

"Cat on Fire to win in a trifecta wheel, " said Sam, "Cat on Fire has to be first, then he picked two other horses to be second and third, interchangeably."

"Well, that's a good sign," said Mac, "Zeke's the second favorite as of now, but I'll bet him to win in an exacta or trifecta."

"Why not just bet him to win?" asked Sarah.

"He's at 2 to 1 now," said Sam, "If you bet $2.00, you'll get $4.00 back. But if you bet him with another horse or two that have longer odds, you'll win more money. If a longshot came in second, and you picked him, you'd win a lot."

"Well, I'm not betting more than $2.00 on any race," said Sarah, smiling, "Not on a teacher's pay."

"Oh, come on," said Connor, "Let's splurge a little on Zeke. It's our lucky day. We just got engaged. I might go up to $5.00!"

The joking continued throughout the races, and John Blake's guests bet on every race with varying results. Mac and her group did fairly well, partly because they considered Bill Kincaid's recommendations. There was a lot of yelling, laughing, and screaming as the horses came down the stretch. Sarah won $36 on a beautiful dark grey filly in the fifth race. She was stunned.

Finally it was 25 minutes until the 8th race, the Breeders' Futurity. Mac grabbed Sam's hand, led him out of the box, and called to Sarah and Connor.

"I want to watch the race on the rail," she said, "Let's place our bets and head down there."

They watched the horses file out onto the track ten minutes before race time. There were eleven horses in the Futurity, a one and one-sixteenth mile race. Cat on Fire was number seven. He walked calmly, head up, looking around, and Mac could have sworn that he looked right at her. She smiled at him and whispered, "You can do it, Zeke."

Time dragged as the horses trotted, loped and finally walked one-by-one into the starting gate. The bell clanged, and the announcer yelled, "And they're off!"

The horses spread out with the favorite, number four, taking the lead. Cat on Fire floated along near the rear of the pack, as if he didn't have a care in the world. He stayed behind as they loped down the backstretch.

"What is he doing?" cried Sarah.

"Don't worry," said Mac, "This is what he likes to do – come from behind."

The horses rounded the third corner, and immediately began to change places. The 8 horse passed the 4 to take the lead. Five horses were in a tight bunch at the front, the jockey's whips flying. Just as they flew around the fourth corner, Cat on Fire went into another gear. One by one, he passed horses on the outside, until finally, he was neck-in-neck with the leader. The crowd was in a frenzy. Sarah was screaming, and pounding on the rail. Mac smiled, seeing the same horse running for fun in the pasture, running for pure joy. Suddenly Cat on Fire leaped ahead, stretching his lead to four lengths as he crossed the finish line!

Mac jumped into Sam's arms, and Sarah into Connor's. Zeke trotted back to the winner's circle, like he'd just been let out of the barn, ready to go again. Mac and Sam grinned at each other, and Mac thought, "I'm ready to go again, too."

His Brother's Eyes, Travers 229

Made in the USA
Monee, IL
12 January 2022